An Encore!
Renée Gardner

And the Dog Took the Cat

A Sutton Place Mystery

Renée Gardner

Publish America

PublishAmerica
Baltimore

First printing

ISBN: 1-60703-369-0
PUBLISHED BY PUBLISHAMERICA, LLLP
www.publishamerica.com
Baltimore

Printed in the United States of America

For my parents, Rose and Sydney Wachs.
They would have loved to see themselves in print.

Acknowledgments

A hundred million thanks to my dear husband Frank, who encouraged me to write *The Tap Dancing Gorilla*, the first book in the *Sutton Place Mystery* series, and who continued to cheer me on as I wrote the second installment *And the Dog Took the Cat.*

A million thanks to my sister Doris, who read the comics to me every night until I learned to read. Why I couldn't read until I was in the third grade is another story.

Many thanks to the helpful people at the New York Public Library who provided me with the information I needed to add authenticity to the library scene.

A special thanks to Fran Gallo, my circus maven. Thanks also to Tim Zello, my computer guru, who came running every time I tried to do something that computers aren't meant to do.

A heartfelt thank you to my old friends in Manhattan and to my new friends in Southwest Florida for their friendship, encouragement and advice.

And finally, my deepest thanks and love to the City of New York for providing the inspiration for my stories.

Chapter 1

"Marvelous, isn't it? It will be your very own maisonnette. This is *the* apartment for you," real estate broker extraordinaire Aldyn Sheridan gushed.

"It's marvelous, if you like chocolate brown, which I don't. And it's dark. Carla Miller craned her neck to look beyond the chocolate brown dining foyer into the small chocolate brown living room, plucked clean of decorative ornaments. The gaping empty spots on the wall where pictures once hung reminded her of missing teeth in the middle of a grinning smile.

"Let's go." Carla dismissed the apartment with a wave of her hand.

Aldyn arched a finely plucked eyebrow. "Of course, it's dark. A man owned the apartment. He lived here during the summer and spent the rest of the year in Florida. Disregard the heavy dark furniture. Visualize how it will look after you've put your personal stamp on it." Her tight smile suggested a new face lift.

"I can't visualize anything." Carla spun around on her three-inch heels. She'd seen enough of the ugly one-bedroom apartment.

"Wait, don't go." Aldyn's blade thin fingers grabbed hold of Carla's arm. The realtor resembled a one hundred and five pound arsenal: razor sharp elbows, hip bones that jutted out like drawn revolvers, burgundy hair lacquered into lethal spikes and a voice sharp enough to cut steel. A shapeless jacket hung from her rapier-thin shoulders. Armani, Carla figured. Who else could make puce chic?

"Please, Ms. Miller, keep an open mind until you've seen the entire apartment." Aldyn pushed Carla into the small, spotless chocolate brown kitchen crowded with old, unused appliances. "Now isn't this marvelous space? Imagine the room refurbished with Euro style cabinets and a Sub-Zero fridge. It will be your dream kitchen."

Without warning three loud achoos drowned out Aldyn's voice.

"Oh, excuse me. Something in the air makes me sneeze." Carla dabbed a tissue to her nose. The culprit had to be Aldyn's musky Opium perfume. "Actually, I'm not interested in kitchens as I don't plan to do much cooking after I move to Manhattan." If Carla chose to tell the truth, she'd admit that her lack of cooking skills forced her children, Robbie and Nancy, to flee the Miller home. Robbie took off for Silicon Valley the day he graduated from college and Nancy skipped college to enroll in the Culinary Institute of America (which she affectionately dubbed the CIA) to learn to cook properly so she wouldn't copy her mother's cooking blunders, like using a barbequed chicken to make chicken soup.

Aldyn's sharp voice drilled into Carla's consciousness. "Well, if you don't cook, use the space as a walk-in closet. Let's look at the bedroom and bath." The realtor closed the kitchen discussion with a quick shrug of her shoulders and hurried down the short, narrow hall.

Carla sneezed again.

"You might want to keep the lovely molding, Ms. Miller." Ignoring her sneeze, Aldyn pointed out the woodwork that surrounded the built-in floor-to-ceiling mirror at the end of the hall. "Regency-style, you know."

"It is nice the way the foyer is reflected in it." Carla snuck a glance in the mirror to see if her short amber curls had wilted in the summer heat. They had.

The small bedroom proved to be as unfeminine as the rest of the apartment—chocolate brown walls and massive dark furniture. And, the same as in the living room, someone had made off with all the *tchotchkes*.

"Dee-vine, isn't it?" Aldyn looked at Carla for confirmation.

"Not really. Honestly, this apartment isn't for me."

The realtor's eyebrows shot up to her Botoxed forehead. "How can you say that about an apartment in a building of this caliber? A federal judge, four attorneys, three doctors and a top, top, super model live here. The co-op board allows only the *very* best people to buy in," she bragged.

"No crazies?" Carla's voice had a husky Kathleen Turner quality.

"Most definitely there are no crazies in this building or, for that matter, anywhere on Sutton Place." Aldyn referred to the exclusive six-block enclave between East 53rd Street and East 59th Street just steps off the East River, jammed packed with elegant high-rise apartment buildings and town houses that many of the city's most influential citizens call home.

"But this apartment building isn't *on* Sutton Place. It's on East 56th Street, a half block west of Sutton," Carla reminded the status-conscience broker. "And no matter what its address may be, it isn't for me and neither were any of the other apartments you showed me. I've seen enough for one day."

When Carla made an appointment to go apartment hunting with Aldyn Sheridan she never anticipated that she'd be dragged all over the Upper East Side to view a succession of over-priced, dark, mouse-hole size apartments. Now she had blisters on her feet and a vise like tension headache that was every bit as fierce as the one she got last December when her then-husband Larry the Louse announced his desire to trade her in for a 27-year old bosomy blonde, which made the home wrecker exactly 20 years younger than Carla. The minute the judge pronounced her a divorced woman, Carla became keenly aware of the wary looks she got from her married friends and the gapping holes in her social calendar. She didn't need a big "D" for divorced pinned to her designer jacket to know that she had become as welcome in Merrick, Long Island as crabgrass. That unpleasant epiphany convinced her to seek a new life in Manhattan. Too old to attract a second glance from Brad Pitt or Matthew McConaughey, Carla hoped to find someone in the age range of Pierce Brosnan.

"Please, Ms. Miller, you can't leave until you've seen the *pièce de résistance*. It's to die for," Aldyn shrieked. Then fast as a cockroach scurries across a counter top, she dragged Carla back to the living room, and triumphantly flung open a chocolate brown curtain. "Look!" She pointed a finger beyond the French doors.

"Oh, my!" Carla stepped outdoors to drink in the dazzling panoramic view from the large terrace—a brilliant cobalt sky, the gray Queensboro Bridge, the murky East River and the glistening windows of surrounding apartment buildings.

"Admit it, Ms. Miller, the view is to die for. And look there," Aldyn's forefinger waggled far below them at a formal garden dotted with white benches, "a shining jewel in Sutton Place's crown, reserved exclusively for the residents of this building and its twin around the corner. A locked door in the lobby of each building is the only access to the secret garden."

"That should keep it secure." Carla said. "And speaking of security, how safe is this building?" Her friend Mimi Berk told her to ask about building security. On the plus side, Mimi, the wife of Mervin Berk, Carla's divorce attorney, didn't back away from her after the divorce. On the minus side, it was Mimi who sicced Aldyn on her.

Another tight smile flashed across the broker's face. "A fortress couldn't be more secure. Of course, the resident manager lives on-site, there is 24/7 doorman and concierge service and every building entrance plus the laundry room, the exercise room and the playroom are under constant video camera surveillance."

"How safe is this terrace?" Carla asked, still unconvinced that the building's security was as tight as the proverbial drum. "Could someone climb up over the terrace wall or down from above?"

"Not a chance of that happening unless he's Spiderman." Aldyn's annoying laugh mimicked the sharp sound of the car horns that floated up from the street. "This terrace isn't connected to any others on the floor. And need I point out that not only is the apartment twenty floors above the ground, but it's also five floors below the roof-top garden? Believe me, Ms. Miller, the building is safer than your house in Merrick."

"You may be right, but what's that?" Carla's eyes focused on a small puddle in the middle of the terrace.

"Nothing to be concerned about," Aldyn sneered. "It's just a clogged drain. The maintenance man can clean it out in two minutes." If Aldyn had a hot buyer for the Liberty Bell, she'd swear on a stack of Bibles that a dab of Crazy Glue would make it good as new in ten seconds.

"Bonkers would love to sit out here and catch flies," Carla confided.

"Who or what is Bonkers?"

"My dog. He's a West Highland Terrier. That is he was. He died two years ago, but if he were still alive, he'd love the terrace."

Aldyn nodded sympathetically. "One of those little white dogs with short legs? Of course, he would love it. Now that's an omen, and I always say one should never ignore an omen. Shall we chat inside?" Aldyn smoothly maneuvered Carla back into the living room.

"Let me share something with you, Ms. Miller." Aldyn folded her scrawny body onto the leather couch to sit beside Carla. Her small pointed teeth gnashed into a shark leer and her steely grays locked on Carla's trusting ambers. She resumed her unrelenting sales pitch, "I have been in the real estate business for 20 years and never have I seen an apartment in such an elegant location with such a marvelous terrace, such classic high ceilings, marvelous soffits and well-proportioned rooms. Grand, isn't it?" Her twig-thin arm made a wide sweeping circle.

"Well, I do love the terrace and the private garden, but I don't feel good about this apartment. I sensed something wrong here the moment you unlocked the door."

"What did you sense, Ms. Miller?" The solemn tone of the realtor's voice reminded Carla of the undertaker who had arranged her grandmother's funeral.

"I sensed that something terrible happened in the apartment." Carla paused before she verbalized the question that gnawed at her the entire time she wandered through the apartment. "Did someone die here?"

Aldyn's thick lashes fluttered like bat wings. "To be perfectly honest, and heaven knows I'm always honest with my clients, Victor Reynolds, the former owner, died here last December."

"December? But a little while ago you said he wintered in Florida."

"That's what I was given to understand…" The muffled chirp of her cell phone broke into their conversation. "Excuse me a sec." She snatched the phone from her black Prada bag to stare at the number displayed on the tiny Caller ID screen before she hit the "Yes" button. "I'll call you later" she whispered into the tiny flip. "So what's the problem, Ms. Miller?" She picked up the thread of the conversation as though there had been no interruption.

"The problem is why did Mr. Reynolds come back in December."

"I don't understand the relevance of your question, but if it's that important to you, I'll try to get the answer." Aldyn spoke very slowly and clearly, like she was fighting hard to hold onto her composure.

"No, don't go to all that trouble." Carla backed down.

"Good." She cracked a thin smile. "But if it makes you feel any better, Mr. Reynolds died as the result of an unfortunate accident. He slipped on a small rug in the foyer and fractured his skull on the edge of the console table." Aldyn pointed back at the bare floor and marble topped table. "If he had wall-to-wall carpeting, that man would be alive today. Make note of it, Ms. Miller, wall-to-wall is the way to go. Accidents happen all the time, and given the fact that this building is 34 years old, I'm sure many residents have died here."

"You're probably right." Carla's eyes wandered back to the terrace.

"I'm glad you see it that way. And I'll let you in on a little secret." Aldyn cupped her hand to the side of her mouth to whisper, "Mr. Reynolds's daughter, the executor of his estate and sole heir, is *tres* anxious to sell, so I know you can snap up this place for a fish cake."

"Exactly how much is a fish cake?"

"A real steal."

"How much is a real steal in dollars?"

Aldyn named a figure.

Carla gasped.

The small one-bedroom apartment cost ten times more than the price she and Larry the Louse paid for their first house twenty years ago.

"Forget it, I can't afford that," Carla stammered.

"But that's only the asking price. We'll negotiate."

Chapter 2

Carla stifled a sneeze as the three-man team from Gentle Movers ambled off to the service elevator, like gorillas disappearing into the mist. A series of sneezes punctuated her tour through the redecorated apartment crammed with bubble wrapped furniture, cardboard wardrobes and dozens of cartons. For better or worse, her new life had begun.

Mindful of her mother's advice, "The sooner you start a job, the sooner you'll be done," Carla retrieved her portable radio from the box labeled "Entertainment," tuned in her favorite soft rock station and began the tedious job of putting the apartment in order. She subliminally heard the same news repeated every fifteen minutes: the presidential family arrived in California for a late-summer vacation, brave rescuers pulled a dog from the Harlem River, the East Side Cat Burglar struck again and the temperature reached a sweltering ninety-five muggy degrees.

Carla bravely fought back tears each time she heard the rescued dog story. But when she caught sight of her dog's leash and toys inside the small carton labeled "Bonkers' Stuff," her composure flew out the window and a flood of tears rolled down her dirt smudged cheeks. She recalled the scene at the vet's office two years earlier when she held Bonkers gently in her arms until he peacefully slipped away. Carla knew she should get rid of his things, but she never could bring herself to do it. *What better time than now?* she asked herself. With the box clutched to her chest, she strode across the room determined to shove it into the dark recesses of the coat closet, but a better idea struck her. Bonkers loved to sit outdoors and sniff the fresh air, so why not leave some of his things on the terrace as a fresh air tribute to him?

Carla walked around the terrace three times before she found a spot under the wall-mounted lantern that offered the ideal spot for her tableau. She made a circle of his tartan plaid collar inside his water bowl, then she piled the metal links of his leash on top of the collar and finally crowned her work with his metal I.D. tag. As she stepped back to admire her work, a warm breeze, gentle as a caress, touched her face—a sign, she hoped, that happiness would come her way.

Cheered by that encouraging thought, Carla's eyes traveled to the tiara of lights that crowned the famous Queensboro Bridge. Her gaze shifted to the lighted windows in the apartment building across the street. She convinced herself that she wasn't spying, but merely observing her neighbors as they stared at their television sets or ate their take-out dinners, or walked from room to room chatting on their cell phones.

Her eyes wandered to a bedroom window level with her line of vision. Pale lavender walls complimented the gold trimmed antique white furniture. A woman lay face down on the bed. A long, shiny flamingo pink robe covered her body. Her unkempt long blonde curls fanned over the white pillow like a brassy yellow mat. A small black and tan dog frolicked beside her. Carla's idle gaze turned to serious scrutiny when she realized that the woman didn't move a muscle when the dog repeatedly pawed at her head.

"I want to report a dead body," Carla shrieked at a 911 dispatcher.

Minutes after she placed her Good Samaritan call, the doorman announced, "Two police officers are on their way up, Miz Miller."

"You reported a body, Ma'am?" A black name badge with white block letters identified the cop as Officer Ramirez. An anemic black moustache decorated his upper lip.

"Yes, Officer, it's out there." Carla pointed toward the open French doors.

"There's a body on your terrace?" Officer Murkowski's thick brown pony tail twitched when she spun her head around toward the terrace. Though barely a couple of inches taller than Carla, she looked like someone you wouldn't mess with. Carla wondered if the Kevlar bulletproof vest that she wore under her blue shirt made her look so solid, or if she really did have a thick-as-a tree-trunk torso.

Carla guessed that Officers Ramirez and Murkowski were about as old, or as young, depending on your point of reference, as Robbie and Nancy, which didn't make her feel too terrific. Cops, whose job it is to protect you, shouldn't be the same age as your children.

"The body isn't on my terrace. That's where I saw it."

Office Murkowski shot her a questioning look. "The body isn't on your terrace, yet you saw it there? You better explain, but first let's have your name. Pete, take this down." Carla detected the same condescending tone in her voice that Nancy used whenever she described a complicated recipe to her.

"I'm Mrs. Carla Miller, C-A-R-L-A Miller. I moved into this apartment today. I went out on the terrace a few minutes ago to get some air, and glanced across the way. That's when I saw the body. It's in an apartment across the street." As the words tumbled out of her mouth, Carla realized that she sounded like a damn peeping tom. Now, wouldn't it be a nice turn of events if she reported a murder and wound up being arrested for looking into someone's window?

"We better have a look on the terrace." Officer Ramirez glanced up from his notebook.

Carla followed the cops to the terrace.

"Do you see what I see?" Ramirez asked his partner. He glanced across the low brick wall into the window where Carla claimed to see the body.

"Sure do." Murkowski smiled.

"Ma'am, would you like to take a look at this?" Officer Ramirez motioned for Carla to approach the wall.

The scene in the room appeared totally different from the way it had been when she spotted the "dead" body. A sapphire blue satin comforter covered the bed. A young man with a full head of curly dark hair sat in front of the dressing table engrossed in brushing a long matted blonde wig. He wore red bikini shorts. The damn dog romped at his feet. The robe had disappeared.

"I mistook the body for the rumpled robe and the wig for a head, didn't I? I'm so sorry I bothered you, but I'm glad she, he's not dead." Carla looked from Officer Ramirez to Officer Murkowski.

"The 'she' you thought you saw is a he, Mrs. Miller. That's your neighbor, Donna Delicious. He dances in some of the West Village clubs. He's a transvestite," Officer Murkowski said.

"Oh, I feel like a fool."

Officer Ramirez closed his black plastic notebook. "No problem, Mrs. Miller. It happens. People sometime see things that aren't there. Officer Murkowski and I'll be leaving now, Ma'am, but if you ever see anything else suspicious give us a holler. That's what we're here for. Maybe you should get a cup of coffee or a slice of pizza. You look tired."

"Thanks for the advice, Officer, but I'll pass. I still have a ton of unpacking to do."

In the weeks that followed her bid being accepted for Victor Reynolds' apartment, Carla's life became a series of passes. Her mortgage application passed, she passed the scrutiny of the six busybodies collectively known as "The Co-op Board," the estimator from Gentle Touch made a pass at her and she nearly passed out when she saw her dwindling bank balance. If she had gallstones, she would have passed them, too.

Carla sat down on her bubble wrapped couch.

Hate the smell of fresh paint.

She sniffed back a tear.

I need a cigarette.

Her hand pawed her pockets.

What am I doing? I quit fifteen years ago.

Then I wish I had a drink.

She substituted one vice for another.

I finished the wine last night.

Oh, screw it!

Sure, who?

Chapter 3

What's a person to do if she doesn't know how to do anything except be a wife and a mother? From the moment Carla accepted the death of her marriage, she knew that if she wanted to keep her sanity and continue to live in the style to which she had become accustomed she would eventually need to find a job. By the beginning of September it became obvious that unless she gave up eating, that day had arrived.

Carla slammed shut the five-inch thick Manhattan Yellow Pages. She'd spent the better part of an hour devouring the employment agency ads without finding one agency that welcomed applicants with no skills. Desperate to begin her job search immediately, she scrunched her eyes tight shut, ran her pen across a page filled with display ads and randomly marked a big X. When she opened her eyes, she discovered that her scientific selection process had come up with a Madison Avenue agency within walking distance of her apartment, if she wore sensible shoes—which she rarely did.

Carla pushed open the glass door to Career Steps—The Agency with a Heart and stepped into a deserted reception room, crowded with half a dozen empty royal blue molded plastic chairs. A large desk held a pile of unopened mail. Not a light blinked on the telephone console.

"Hello, anybody here?" she called out. A faint sound from behind the closed door marked "Private" attracted her attention.

"Hello, anybody here?" Carla repeated her greeting. She cautiously opened the door, and found herself in a room reminiscent of a cozy Victorian parlor, right down to a wrought iron coat rack, an Oriental rug, gold-framed paintings and an inviting couch. A very large woman sat behind a mahogany desk. A very small champagne and white Shih Tzu sat at her feet.

"Who the heck are you?" The woman's thick false eyelashes fluttered like a pair of caterpillars in heat.

"I'm Carla Miller…that is I was Carla Miller until… I don't know who I am. I need a job…" Carla's awkward introduction ended when the little dog trotted up to her and wagged his tail at her as though she was an old friend.

"Well, you've come to the right place to find a job. I'm Kitty Larsen, the owner of Career Steps, and that little guy who's taken an instant liking to you is Tootie. Take a load off your feet, kiddo." Half a dozen jeweled bracelets clanked together when Kitty waved her hand toward the big rattan peacock guest chair opposite her desk.

"What brings you out looking for a job today?"

Kitty peered at Carla over the top of her rhinestone frame granny glasses. Her big blue eyes took in the tiny tension lines around her eyes and the tell-tale indentation on the naked third finger of her left hand. Up close, she judged Carla to be older than she looked when she stood in the doorway—maybe mid to late forties. Kitty estimated that her simple silk dress, handbag and shoes easily cost a lot more than an administrative assistant's monthly salary.

"What's so special about today, Mrs. Larsen?"

Kitty patted her lopsided platinum updo and rolled her eyes toward the ceiling. "Call me Kitty, and in case you don't have a calendar, today is the beginning of the Labor Day weekend. Nobody is interviewing or looking for a job today. Only reason I'm in the office is to catch up on the paper work that piled up while I recovered from an accident." Kitty tapped her right shoulder.

Carla slapped her hand to her forehead. If she hadn't been so wrapped up in her own problems, she would have recognized Kitty Larsen from her newspaper photographs as the feisty senior citizen who brought down the tap dancing killa' gorilla. "I feel so stupid not to have connected you with the pictures in the paper," she stammered.

"That's okay, kiddo. Most of my friends didn't recognize me in those unflattering pictures. Now, like I said, what brings you out job hunting on the day before the start of the Labor Day Weekend?"

It took three false starts before Carla spat out the short version of her life story including her two kids, the trauma of being dumped by her ex, the discovery of a not so dead body and the need to find a job now that she'd spent most of her divorce settlement on the purchase of her creepy apartment, which it turned out was just around the corner from Kitty's Sutton Place co-op.

"So what kind of experience do you have?" Kitty led off with the basic question that she asked all her apps—industry shorthand for "applicants." The cornered rabbit look that darted across Carla's face gave Kitty her first clue that she wouldn't be an easy placement.

Carla flinched. "None, unless you count my job as a camp counselor and the volunteer work I did at the school library."

"Can you use a computer?" Kitty asked expectantly. On the surface, Carla didn't appear to be employable, but Kitty hoped that if she probed deep enough, she'd find a marketable skill buried in her background.

Perhaps it was her gumption to look for a job at the start of a holiday weekend, or perhaps it was the way she nervously tugged on an amber curl at the nape of her neck, but Kitty immediately liked her.

"Sure, of course, I can use a computer. My kids taught me," Carla said.

"Are you good on the telephone?"

"I love to talk on the phone."

"Do you enjoy working with young people?"

"I told you, I have two kids in their twenties." Carla didn't exactly answer the question, but she hoped that Kitty would take it as a "yes."

"So how would you like to work for me?"

Carla dabbed her forehead with a linen handkerchief that smelled faintly of tuberose and jasmine. "Me work for you? I don't understand. I thought you'd send me on interviews to advertising agencies or television networks or something like that."

Now it became Kitty's turn to fidget. She needed to play her hand just right and not appear too eager to hire Carla as a replacement for her last assistant, who left a month ago to join a road company of *The Mouse Trap*. "It's like this, kiddo. You need a job, but you don't have any skills or a résumé, which means that if I send you out on interviews you'll embarrass yourself and Career Steps, but I feel sorry for you because you seem like a good person with a bad problem. So here's the deal. I'll hire you as a combo receptionist and employment counselor-in-training, same as the last gal who had the job. I'll pay you a weekly salary until you've made four job placements, then you'll start to earn commissions. The more placements you make the higher you're commission will be, though your base salary will drop. You'll have to work your tail off, but I'm giving you the opportunity of a lifetime. So, what do you think, kiddo?"

Kitty fingered the strand of nine millimeter pearls that encircled her thick neck while she considered if she should tell Carla that her former assistant also helped her solve a couple of murders. She decided to use the "don't ask, don't tell" approach—if Carla didn't ask about Phyllis' involvement, Kitty wouldn't tell her.

Carla squirmed around in her chair till the old rattan squawked like its peacock namesake. "I know you're offering me a great opportunity, but I'm not qualified to be an employment counselor. I did tell you that I never had a paying job, didn't I?"

Kitty nodded. "I know all about that, but what have you got to lose, kiddo? Try it. You may like it."

Chapter 4

Carla fast stepped across the marble lobby of the office building that housed Career Steps—The Agency with a Heart. Exactly two weeks ago she either bluffed her way into a receptionist/counselor-in-training job at the employment agency, or Kitty Larsen talked her into the job. Carla didn't know exactly which way it happened and she didn't much care, for she loved her new job. And the whipped cream on her cake was the job placement that she'd made her first week as a receptionist/employment counselor-in-training. She fast talked NYU graduate Betsy Rider into believing that typing letters and answering the phones for Aldyn Sheridan would be the best way for her to learn the real estate business. Only three more placements and Carla would begin to earn the promised commissions.

"This one's got room, Miz." Cromwell the elevator starter motioned toward an elevator packed tight as a jar full of cocktail olives.

"No, thanks." Carla walked into an empty one. The elevators to the right and to the left filled up with people, their doors shut and they began their ascent, while Carla's elevator remained on the ground like a missile waiting on a launch pad. "Hold it," a man's deep voice boomed across the lobby. Carla stabbed the OPEN button just as the doors started to close.

"Thanks. I'm late for an appointment." The man hit the button for the twenty-eighth floor and the elevator took off.

Carla offered a quick nod of acknowledgment then turned her head and stared straight ahead. She had a firm rule against exchanging pleasantries with fellow elevator passengers. Her rationale being that these strangers are in and out of your life too fast to make conversation worth the effort.

"Doesn't feel like we're moving, does it?" A friendly smile flashed across his face.

Carla felt trapped. He had broken the No Speaking to Fellow Elevator Travelers Rule and now she must respond or pretend to be deaf. "Of course, we're moving," she said. "The elevator is just slow. Believe me, it's always like this."

"If you say so."

A couple seconds of immobility passed in awkward silence while Carla stared at the molding on the door and he adjusted the knot in his red regimental stripe silk tie. Finally, her shrill laugh betrayed her embarrassment. "You're right, you know, the elevator should have stopped at my floor by now. I guess we're stuck."

"I thought so." He nodded in agreement.

"I hope the lights don't go out. I hate to be alone in the dark," Carla said.

"Not likely to happen unless there's a power failure in the building. Anyway, you're not alone. I'm here." The stranger's eyes crinkled like a cowboy squinting in the hot sun.

"Oh, yes, you're here, aren't you? Then I'm not alone." Carla's heart pounded wildly at the thought of being trapped in the elevator with a man who might harbor less than noble thoughts, though a side glance at the stranger reassured her that he looked more like a friendly teddy bear than a sex fiend. He was a little thick in the middle, but not fat, and was probably on the lean side of fifty. Curly dark hair flecked with gray set off a more than a pleasant face. He was taller than Carla, but not so tall that she had to strain to see his warm brown eyes.

"Hey, is anybody down there? Get us out," he bellowed into the speaker box.

"Nothing I can do, folks. But don't worry; 'cause the service company is on its way." Cromwell's nasal voice filled the cab.

Ever the optimist, Carla smiled at her fellow prisoner. "Now that's encouraging, isn't it?"

The man shook his head "I'm not waiting for the service company to rescue us. Hold these while I investigate." He thrust his briefcase and jacket at Carla. Then without breaking a sweat, he forced open the elevator doors. A brick wall faced them. "Great, we're between floors," he said, and pushed the doors shut.

"That's good? No, it's terrible. We're trapped." Though Carla's tremulous voice betrayed her panic, she refused to admit to him that she suffered from mild claustrophobia brought on after she accidentally locked herself in a closet when she was a child.

"It's good. Trust me. The top of the cab is probably level with the door on the next floor, so we have a way out. All we need is a ladder." His dark eyes surveyed their prison. "We'll use our briefcases." His was the extra thick type used by accountants and lawyers; hers was the ultra-slim career girl special. "Do you always carry the Yellow Pages with you?" He pointed to the familiar thick book that Carla clutched in her hand.

"I, no, that is I took it home last night to research prospective companies..."

"Lucky break," he interrupted. "Our briefcases plus your phone book should give me enough height to reach the escape panel up there." He pointed to the top of the elevator.

"I think we should wait for the repairmen. They'll be here any minute."

"Look, I'd stay if I thought those bozos would show up before Halloween, but I've got an important meeting upstairs, then I have to see a man about…" he hesitated, "a job, so hold everything steady while I investigate."

Before Carla could answer, he'd balanced himself on top of the makeshift ladder, banged his knuckles on the panel till it slid back and hoisted himself through the opening.

"Wait. Don't go. Don't leave me alone." Carla tugged on his legs as they disappeared into the darkness above her. Alone in the elevator, she slowly began to count backwards from one hundred. This was a trick she used to steady her nerves whenever she felt overwhelmed with problems. She reached eighty-seven before he shouted, "I've got the door open on the floor above. Now I'm going to lie down on top of the cab, grab your arms and pull you through the opening."

"You're going to do what to me and I'm going where?"

"You heard me. Stand on the briefcases and phone book like I did. Trust me. I've done this dozens of times. When I say 'reach' grab my arms and hang on tight. Got it? Ready? Let's do it!"

Carla hesitated a moment to debate with herself whether or not she should trust her life to a stranger who minutes ago she thought might be a rapist. "Wait a minute. Do I…"

"Reach!"

Carla obediently reached up and a pair of rock hard hands pulled her through the top of the elevator onto the filthy roof of the elevator cab.

"Not the cleanest place in town, but we're free. Give me a minute to open the doors and we're out of here." The stranger exerted all of his amazing strength on the doors that blocked their way to freedom until they slowly parted.

"I can't believe it," Carla gasped. "We're on my floor." She pointed to the plaque on the opposite wall inscribed with a large number 10. "You're wonderful. We would have been trapped for hours if you hadn't...hey, what's happening?"

Carla and the stranger watched in stunned silence as the elevator doors slowly closed then reopened to reveal the elevator cab. They held each other is a silent gaze for a second and then dashed into the cab to retrieve their belongings that lay scattered on the floor like abandoned toys.

"I told you that we'd get you out safe and sound. See, you just had to be patient," Cromwell twanged through the speaker box.

"So I should have waited." The stranger flashed Carla a sheepish grin while he vainly attempted to brush the dirt off his trousers. "Sorry to have been so rough on you. Let me buy you dinner tonight to make up for it."

"Dinner? Dinner tonight, oh..." Carla stammered.

"Say 'yes.' I don't bite. What's your name?"

"I'm, my name is Carla, Carla Weinstein. No, that was my name before, now I'm Carla Miller." Her face tingled like she had a very bad sunburn.

"Glad to know you. I'm Tony Vitale. Where can I call you?" He flashed a warm smile that showed his thick, sexy lower lip.

"Career Steps. Call me there. It's in the phone book." Carla clutched her briefcase to her chest and waved the Yellow Pages on high for emphasis. "I'm there till five-thirty." She looked like the Statue of Liberty shilling for Verizon.

"Career Steps, right. I'll call." He stepped back into the elevator, the doors closed and he was gone.

Carla offered the half dozen apps in the waiting room a quick wave on her way into Kitty's office. If she hadn't been in such a rush to explain to her boss what had made her late for work, she would have noticed the questioning looks that the young women exchanged.

"It's really a pickup, Kitty. I don't know a thing about him. Do you think I should go?" she asked at the conclusion of her blow-by-blow reenactment of her adventure in the elevator.

"Are you nuts?" Kitty croaked in her raspy voice. "You told me that since your divorce you've gone out with exactly three men, and by their descriptions, I'd call them all losers. Now this hunk comes along and you're worried because you weren't formally introduced."

"They weren't losers. They just weren't for me."

"Carla, baby, wise up. Losers I know from way back. A fifty-three year old never been married librarian and a forty-two year old three times divorced salesman at Radio Shack are not exactly competition for George Clooney. They're doggie dogs. If Tootie were a she, he wouldn't date them." The mop haired Shih Tzu stood close to Kitty's chair patiently waiting for whatever treats she might hand him. He'd snap up a dog biscuit or an M&M with equal zeal.

"How bad could they have been? They both got engaged right after I went out with them. And what about Jack Demmer, the furrier? Carla asked hopefully. Remember him, the son of my mother's friend?"

"You mean 'Monsieur Jacques'? The fake Frenchman who models his own coats on television? Get real, kiddo." Kitty raised her eyebrows—the only part of her body that could be accurately described as thin.

"Maybe you're right. I only went out with him to be polite."

"You know damn well I'm right. And listen, don't stand up to greet any apps today. The grease stain on your skirt looks awful."

Chapter 5

At seven thirty that evening Carla flung open her apartment door. "Hello!" She flashed a nervous smile.

"Hello!" Tony smiled back. Beyond the foyer he could see the living room bathed in a warm glow of soft pink lights.

Carla's smile widened. "Hello, again." She stood in the doorway still as a sentry guarding Buckingham Palace.

Tony smiled again and motioned toward the living room. "Can we go inside?"

"Oh, yes, of course, come in." She slammed the door shut behind her.

The sound of the buzzer surprised her. She flung open the door.

"Hello again." Tony's smile had faded by twenty degrees.

"What are you doing out there? Never mind, come in. Would you like a drink?

"Wine would be fine."

"Great, that's what I'm having. I hope you like red." Carla stammered. She tapped a button on the remote control for her new fifteen-foot long built-in wall unit. A panel slid up to belch out a 47-inch flat screen television set.

"Sorry, I don't have the hang of this yet," she stammered.

"No problem. Just moved in, did you?" His eyes swept over the obviously new furniture, the carefully placed accessories and the freshly painted walls.

"Last month." Carla successfully tapped the right button and the panel swallowed the TV set. Another tap raised the opposite panel. This time a mirrored bar appeared stocked with premium liquor and a variety of crystal glasses. An open bottle of red wine stood on a silver wine coaster.

"I'll pour." Carla turned her back to Tony so he couldn't see how badly her hand trembled as she filled two wine goblets. *First dates suck*, she thought.

"Well, here's to your new apartment." Tony saluted Carla with his raised glass. "Who's that guy?" He nodded toward the framed photo of Bonkers on a shelf in the monster wall unit. "Is he here?"

Carla wistfully smiled at the photo of the little Westie whose midnight black eyes stared down at her. "No, Bonkers died of old age a couple of years ago, but I still miss the crazy little dog. He'd nip your ankle if he didn't like you and my friend's husband has the scars to prove it." She stifled a laugh at the thought of Bonkers' unprovoked attacks.

Tony arched an eyebrow mischievously. "So much for man's best friend."

"But he was *my* best friend." Carla's voice rose with indignation, then softened. "I feel as though he's here watching over me. There's something strange about the apartment, but I'm not sure what it is."

"What's wrong?"

Carla motioned Tony to join her on the couch. Without stopping to think whether or not she should share her concerns about the apartment with a stranger, she answered honestly, "Nothing is exactly wrong. There are just little things that don't sit right with me, like the previous owner, Victor Reynolds, died here. Right over there, I was told."

Tony took a sip of his wine before he looked back to the spot where she pointed. "How did he die?" he asked softly.

"I'm not sure. I think he fractured his skull. My real estate broker called it an accident. She got the story from his daughter, who's the executor of the estate, but I don't think she told me the truth. You know how real estate brokers are..." Carla nervously popped a snack into her mouth. Too late she realized that her hand had gone into the wrong bowl, so instead of munching on unsalted cashews, she found herself chewing on Floris Oriental Bouquet potpourri. Faced with the choice of swallowing the fragrant mixture or discreetly getting rid of it, she coughed it into her cocktail napkin. "...they'll say anything to make a sale," she continued as though nothing odd had occurred.

And Tony, who had observed her plight, also chose to ignore it. "If you're so curious about Reynolds' death, why not ask his daughter what really happened? She's got nothing to lose now by telling the truth."

"I'm not that curious. He's dead and that's it, but there's something else strange here." Carla nervously clasped her hands together.

"Like what?" A glint of more than casual interest flickered in Tony's eyes.

"Sometimes I sneeze when I'm in the hall or in the kitchen. It's like I've sniffed pepper but since I don't cook, I don't know what it can be..." Carla stopped short when she realized that for the second time today she had babbled nonsense to Tony Vitale. And damn if she hadn't finished her wine in one gulp.

"Describe the smell."

"It's hard to explain. I don't exactly smell anything. There's just the suggestion that I smelled it once before, but I'm not sure where."

"Interesting. Maybe you should stay out of the kitchen." Tony finished the last of his wine. "Shall we go?"

They cabbed it over to Villagio, a chic restaurant on East 58th Street off Third Avenue where the Northern Italian food is wonderful and the male clientele are rich and their female companions are beautiful. Sometimes it's the other way around.

Carla nibbled focaccia drizzled with olive oil while Tony discussed the food and wine with the captain and sommelier. An occasional nod to a suggestion was the only part she took in the selection process. While they shared an appetizer of buckwheat pasta with mixed vegetables, Tony filled in some of the blanks about himself—he's a business insurance broker and his agency places insurance policies for large businesses; his son Dom is a partner in an ad agency and his daughter, Constance Ricci, acts in soap operas. "She took her mother's maiden name as her stage name," he explained.

Carla washed down a forkful of veal piccata with a sip of Pinot Grigio Pighin before she asked, "Do you live in Manhattan?"

"No. I have a house in Nyack. I kept it after my wife… Oh, hell why don't you shut me up? I'm doing all the talking, now it's your turn." Tony motioned for another bottle of wine.

"I was born in Queens but my family moved to Westchester when I was two…" Carla's dessert and divorce arrived at the same time.

Chapter 6

Carla peered intently into the bathroom mirror. Her thoughts were not on applying Lancôme High Definition black mascara to her long eyelashes or the sneezing attack she had in the hall last evening or the caterer Mr. Everett and his crew who were setting up for her housewarming party. Her thoughts were on Tony.

After more than two weeks of dating, he still hadn't told her if he was divorced, widowed or married and until he did their relationship would remain chaste—which was not what Carla wanted. She'd circled around the burning question several times, but he always managed to squirm out of giving a direct answer. But tonight would be different. After the other guests left, Carla would play "Twenty Questions" with Tony and if he didn't give her the right answers, their romance would be kaput before it ever got started.

"What am I to do with the person who just arrived? It is barely three o'clock and we're not prepared to receive guests until five." Mr. Everett, a quivering mass of disapproval, stood in the hall outside the bathroom. In back of him stood Aldyn Sheridan, resplendent in a midnight blue Donna Karan pantsuit, a thick strand of pearls and four-inch high Jimmy Choo stilettos.

"Carla, darling, you don't mind that I'm a teench early, do you?" Aldyn's shrill voice screeched before Carla could answer the miffed caterer. "I came directly from showing Caitlin Oliver's fab-u-lous penthouse apartment. Of course, you know her. She's your neighbor. She's on the cover of *Vogue* or *Harper's Bazaar* every other month. She's on a fashion shoot in Brazil for a couple of weeks, but I have the key to her place. I have an exclusive on her apartment. She has this absolutely dee-vine collection of jewels—diamonds, sapphires, rubies, the works. Lord, she sat in the front row furiously waving her paddle like a crazy woman the last time some of Jackie Kennedy Onassis' jewelry collection came on the auction block. And don't remind me that it's Sunday, darling. If a buyer wants to see an apartment, I'm there no matter what day or hour it may be." One of Aldyn's explosive shrieks threatened to crack Carla's makeup mirror.

Carla bobbed her head up in down in mock interest while Aldyn rambled on. "I knew you would just kill me if you discovered that I went home instead of popping in here to freshen up. I'm so happy you invited me to your party."

"After all you've done for me, I wouldn't think of giving a party without you." Carla forced a weak smile at her lie. Actually, it was the guilt she felt after Aldyn sent her an obviously expensive housewarming gift—an ugly crystal vase tucked inside a blue Tiffany box—that forced Carla to send the realtor a party invitation. What Carla didn't know was that realtors often send buyers gifts so when they eventually sell the property, they'll list it with that broker, as it's the seller who pays the broker's six percent commission. Reputable brokers buy the gifts from high end stores. Chinzy brokers, Aldyn included, put cheap gifts in boxes from fancy shops.

"That's not what you're wearing, is it?" If ever a voice could sneer, Aldyn's voice sneered.

"Yes, I thought..." Carla defended her choice of a flattering bottle green silk jumpsuit, but Aldyn had already changed the subject.

"Darling, could I use the bathroom for a sec? I have to tinkle something fierce but there's no way in heaven that I would use Caitlin's bathroom. You won't believe it, but the T.P. she buys is as hard as a shingle. Of course, she's not my only client who has plenty in the bank, but lives like a miser. The stories I could tell. The apartments I have seen." Aldyn rolled her eyes to the ceiling in mock horror. "Jewels scattered in ashtrays and store brands in the cupboard. Not that I'm nosey, heaven forbid, but when one is showing an apartment one must show everything.

"Oh my, what's this?" She pointed to the hall floor.

"What is it?" Carla thought she saw a glint of gold before Aldyn swooped the object up in her talons.

"For heavens sakes, it's my earring. How lucky that I found it. It has great sentimental value." Aldyn's infuriating laugh grated in Carla's ears. "Now do be a darling and get me a fresh towel. I'll fix my face then I'll sit quietly in the living room and enjoy a lovely Bloody Mary that I know one of those gorgeous waiters will adore fixing for me." Aldyn slithered out of her suit jacket to reveal a form-fitting white camisole.

The door shut, leaving Carla outside the bathroom and Aldyn inside the bathroom.

Carla had instructed the concierge to send her guests up without being announced, and when buzzer rang at exactly five o'clock she knew that Mimi and Mervin Berk stood on the other side of the door. The Berks took it as a moral obligation to be the first to arrive and the last to leave every party they attended.

They were a perfectly matched couple. Tall and willowy, Mimi always looked picture perfect, with every mahogany hair in place, perfectly applied makeup and the perfect outfit for every occasion. And Carla knew for certain that Mimi's beige pants and white and beige intarsia tissue cashmere sweater would remain wrinkle-free throughout the evening. Tall, slim as a straw, bald as a basketball and forever tan, Mervin wore cocoa gabardine trousers and a coral silk shirt. The high shine on his brown Gucci loafers drew attention to his unsocked feet.

"I promised to do the most awful things to make Mervin agree to come to your party."

Carla wondered what Mimi had promised that would entice Mervin to give up a sunny autumn day in the Hamptons. He spent every weekend from May through November at their beach house working on George Hamilton tan. Mimi, on the other hand, treasured her unblemished skin and rarely joined him unless the weatherman guaranteed foul weather.

A non-committal flash of Chiclet white teeth substituted for Mervin's response to his wife's confession. His steel gray eyes surveyed the foyer and living room before he passed judgment. "What a charming apartment. When Mimi told me about it, I questioned your judgment but now I know it will work out fine. Congratulations." Carla turned her head away from him, yet he still managed to plant a dead fish kiss on her cheek. She didn't dislike Mervin; she just didn't have any great affection for him.

"Thanks for your stamp of approval, Mervin." A glint of humor flickered in Carla's amber eyes. "Now come say hello to Aldyn Sheridan. I have her to thank for this apartment." Carla turned toward the empty chair where she'd last seen Aldyn.

Soon a jumble of friends and relatives crowded the apartment—all dressed in assorted Sunday house party outfits that ranged from Upper East Side chic to Tribeca *avant garde*. In deference to the unseasonably warm October day, Tony wore a short sleeve silk black mock turtle neck shirt paired with beige trousers. Carla observed his amused smile as he endured Mimi's scrutiny. A murmur of surprise rippled across the living room when Kitty Larsen and her husband Charlie Blumenfaux, the world-famous Seer to the Stars, made their jaw-dropping entrance decked out in their everyday costumes. She wore a flame red custom-made tent dress accessorized with dyed to match Reeboks, a lot of makeup, thick false eyelashes and her usual assortment of gem-encrusted jewelry. Charlie wore black from the neck down. His black outfit topped by his smoke white Lyle Lovett hairdo, made him look like a giant, flickering black candle.

A warm glow of motherly pride radiated from Carla's eyes when Nancy walked into the apartment. She had substituted her usual torn jeans for a royal blue spandex mini dress that hugged her slim body and complimented her translucent skin. Instead of wearing her shoulder-length chestnut hair frizzed out like a mop in the throws of an electric shock, she had pulled it back into a loose French braid, the better to show off her delicate heart shaped face.

"You look beautiful, darling. Now get something to eat," Carla gushed. "And you too, Willpeterbob," she said to Nancy's companion. Carla refused to take the time to remember the names of Nancy's ever changing line-up of male friends. Her philosophy being here today, gone tomorrow, so why bother.

"This one seems nice..."

A whispered voice interrupted Carla's exchange with Nancy, "There is a mouse in the house, Madame."

"I beg your pardon."

"I'm sorry to be the bearer of unpleasant news, but a rather small gray rodent has been observed scampering across the kitchen floor." Mr.

Everett sneered his most distasteful sneer. "I thought I should warn you about the creature and, if I may suggest, don't eat the white food."

"Why? Did the mouse jump into the food?" Carla gathered her pant legs close to her and silently prayed that her guests were too engrossed in conversation to overhear talk of rodents.

"Of course not, Madame." The two carat diamond in the caterer's left ear sparkled when he shook his head. "You see the cap on James' front tooth popped off. James is our very best waiter. The accident occurred just as he placed a bowl of white food on the buffet. Unfortunately, at the moment he lost his cap, the other waiters switched all the bowls around, and consequently he doesn't know which bowl holds his tooth. It could be in the paella, the potato salad or the chicken salad. We dug around in each bowl, but we couldn't find the cap." Mr. Everett paused, and then added, "I would also avoid the whipped cream."

"Well, thank you for your concern. I'll look out for the mouse and the cap." Carla closed her eyes then opened them wide. She looked like one of those windup dolls that winks and blinks before it takes a couple of stiff steps and falls over.

"Yes, Madame, and if you find it, please give it to James."

"The cap or the mouse?"

"Madame?"

Carla turned her attention back to her guests. She spotted Aldyn and Jack Demmer, sharing a platter of hors d'oeuvres. But from the pained look on the furrier's handsome face, Carla suspected that he wouldn't be sharing anything else with Aldyn in the near future.

"Please don't pinch the chocolates," Carla said sweetly to Eleanor Callahan, who she not so fondly referred to as "My Next-Door Neighbor from Hell."

"But I only eat the truffles." Mrs. Callahan snorted out a stream of gin breath that threatened to asphyxiate Carla. "I always left the nuts for Mamma—Wilbur's mother, you know, not mine. The bitch tried to nosey around, but I found a way to keep her out of my hair. You know what I..." Mrs. Callahan suddenly staggered toward the bathroom.

Before Carla could recover from her encounter with Mrs. Callahan, a voice hissed at her, "For god's sake, take off that damn tape." Though a cloud of cigar smoke obliterated his face, there was no mistaking the demanding voice of Harold Weinstein. Sole ownership of 100 Shoe Heaven stores that sold hideous manmade footwear had earned Carla's brother the dubious title of the "King of Manmade Shoes," as well as a bundle of money. He had property in four states, a diversified stock portfolio and hemorrhoids. He also had a thing for Bunnies. Not bunny rabbits, but women bunnies. Every five years he traded in his current wife named "Bunny" for a new "Bunny" who was exactly the same age the first "Bunny" had been when he married her. The Bunnies were all interchangeable—tall, thin bimbos with big breasts and long blond hair. Bunny IV stood in a corner looking very tentative.

"What are you talking about, Harold?" Luciano Pavarotti's golden voice floated through the stereo system. But as Carla listened closer to the familiar strains of *Vesti la guibba*, she heard a distorted echo that reminded her of a gargling walrus.

"Oh god, Harold, it's Dad's 'Sing Along with Pavarotti' disc. He sent it to me for my birthday. It got mixed in with the other CDs." Carla gave her brother a helpless shrug.

"Well, for chrissake take it off. He sounds like a cat in heat. The man's got no class." Harold flicked his cigar ashes into a bowl of beluga caviar.

Carla turned away in disgust from her brother only to be grabbed by

Mrs. Callahan. "That man over there, the one with the sexy mouth, I've seen him before," she said. And to make sure that Carla knew exactly who she meant, Mrs. Callahan pointed her rheumatoid misshapen finger directly at Tony, who had thoughtfully replaced the offending disc with a new Nora Jones release.

"You probably have seen him before. He's been here several times. Now sit down and I'll fix you a platter." Aldyn's piercing loud voice, relating over and over again her story about Caitlin Oliver's apartment and her jewel collection, kept Carla from hearing what the old woman mumbled about Tony.

The party wasn't turning out to be the fun evening Carla had planned. The combined aggravation from Aldyn, Mrs. Callahan and Harold made her feel as though a gallon of hot digestive acid had burst into flames in her stomach. Just as she considered how nice it would be to exchange the chaos of the living room for the quietude of her bedroom, she saw Nellie Cooper glide graceful as a swan across the living room. The blonde member of the Carla/Mimi/ Nellie triumvirate appeared fragile as a gardenia, and reminded Carla of a woodland sprite. The Victorian style dresses she favored suited her delicate features. Today she wore a lavender ankle-length voile dress accessorized with a large brimmed hat trimmed with faded silk flowers. One dainty hand held a plate piled high with paella and Caesar salad, the other clutched silverware and a glass of white wine.

Nellie appeared to be headed toward her husband, Eddie the Obstetrician, who sat alone in a corner staring into space. Being alone suited Eddie just fine, as he rarely spoke to anyone who wasn't dilated at least seven centimeters. But for no apparent reason, Nellie suddenly veered toward Mervin just as his boomerang eyebrows shot up to his vanished hairline in response to something Aldyn said to him.

"Oh, oh," Nellie cried. Every eye in the room turned toward her in time to see her trip over Mervin's bare ankle. Fortunately, Mervin's lap broke her fall and she came to no harm.

But Aldyn wasn't so fortunate. Red lobster meat, black mussels, white chicken and red pimento strips spattered her white camisole. Brown and white gummy rice grains clung to her spiky hair; rivulets of golden wine dripped from her flushed chin. She looked like a Jackson Pollock canvas. Carla and Nancy rushed to Aldyn's aid. While Nancy pressed crumpled napkins to the realtor's dripping face, Carla picked rice out of her hair. Carla's act of kindness gave her an excellent view of Aldyn's bare ear lobes.

The accident marked the official end of the party. Directly after Mimi and Mervin walked out the door, Carla grabbed two Champagne flutes from the bar while Tony put a bottle of Champagne into a wine cooler, then hand-in-hand they strolled out to the terrace for their private party. They stretched out on matching lounge chairs to silently gaze up at the stars etched against the night sky like hundreds of sparkling diamonds tossed haphazardly on a black velvet cloth.

At last Carla decided that the time had arrived for her to ask her questions. "Tony, remember our first date," she began.

"How can I forget it?"

"Well, you mentioned your wife, but you didn't say if..."

"Mrs. Miller," Mr. Everett interrupted.

"Are you finished?" Carla dug her fingernails into her hands. *Damn him. He has no sense of timing.*

"Yes, we're leaving, but I found something."

"The mouse or the cap?"

"Neither, Mrs. Miller. It's this." A diamond and ruby earring sparkled in his hand.

"It's not mine. Where did you find it?"

"It was tilted on its side in the corner of the kitchen counter, which explains why no one noticed it until we began to clean up."

"Thank you, Mr. Everett. I'll find its owner."

Anxious to pick up the threads of her conversation with Tony, Carla barely looked at the earring. "It looks like a good imitation of the real thing. Probably belongs to Kitty. She adores fake jewelry."

"Let me see it." Tony examined the earring carefully under the light. "As far as I know, Cartier doesn't make imitations. Look here." He pointed to the world famous jeweler's name engraved on the mounting. "It's the real thing. Do you recall seeing any of your guests in the kitchen?"

Carla shook her head. "Mr. Everett put the kitchen off limits to guests. He even stationed a waiter at the entrance to keep anyone from wandering in and getting in the way." As if on cue, Carla heard the door close behind Mr. Everett and his crew.

"Then who besides the catering staff was last in the kitchen?"

"Only me on Thursday. I had another sneezing attack when I came home, so I've pretty much stayed out of the kitchen since then. I'm sure whoever lost the earring will call." Carla slipped it into her pocket. "Now, Tony, remember what I was saying before Mr. Everett interrupted us?"

"Will you look at the time." He pointedly glanced down at his Rolex. "Sorry, Carla, got to catch an early plane." He kissed her gently on the cheek and was out the door before she could say a word.

Chapter 7

"Career Steps—The Agency with a Heart. Good afternoon." Carla's husky greeting rippled through the phone lines. Besides being an employment counselor-in-training, she also answered the telephones, opened the mail and performed all the other receptionist duties that her predecessor had performed. During these stints, Kitty insisted that she use a Voice Changer that adjusted her voice ten pitches to fool clients into believing that the agency had a large staff. Carla forgot to turn on the gadget today—an oversight she would dearly regret.

"That you, Carla?" a metal sharp voice demanded, then barreled on like an avalanche speeding down a hill knocking down everything in its path. "You're harder to reach than the president. I called several times this week, but someone with a horrid high pitched voice always told me you were out or with an app, whatever the hell that is. Listen, we have to talk. I'm previewing an apartment in the building around the corner from you at four. It shouldn't take more than ten minutes to look at the place, then I'll whiz through the garden to you. The key to that apartment opens the door into your building."

"Aldyn, how are you?" Carla feigned surprise when the realtor finally screeched to a halt. "Love to see you, but I don't get home till after six o'clock. What a shame. We'll have to talk another time." Carla didn't want to talk to Aldyn. In the months since they'd met, Carla had formed a strong opinion about her: she was obnoxious, nosey and rude. Talking to Aldyn reminded Carla of a lemon concoction that she adored in her childhood. You slice off the top of a lemon, carve out the core, then suck out the juice with a lemon flavored candy straw. Carla identified with the lemon—sucked dry of all its juices.

"I won't take 'no' for an answer," Aldyn replied. "I'm leaving tomorrow for a two-week vacation. One of my fab-u-lous clients said, 'Aldyn, dear,' they all call me dear, 'you look so pale, take the key to my place in Hilton Head. Make yourself at home and be sure to check out the new tennis pro at the club. He's got a bod to die for.' So I'm off. I'm driving down all by my lonesome, but I must see you today. I know what's going on. Tell you what I'll do, there are a couple of apartments for sale in a building on Beekman Place. I can preview them to kill time, and I'll see you at a little after six." A click told Carla that Aldyn had hung up.

Carla dashed into her apartment at five fifty-five. She placed a vase filled with roses from a "Roses Only" shop in the center of the coffee table, then she raced from room to room to stash clutter into drawers and toss every bit of rubbish from the wastebaskets into a large black plastic trash bag. Nothing personal could be left out for Aldyn's prying eyes, for Carla knew without a doubt that Aldyn would find an excuse to inspect every room in the small apartment.

Her housekeeping chores finished, Carla lugged her trash bag down the hall to the large tiled trash room. She shouldered the metal door to make it open, same as she always did, but this time it wouldn't budge. It took two hard shoulder bumps before the door grudgingly opened halfway. Through the narrow opening, Carla saw the neat recycling bins, the door to the service elevator, the trash chute large enough to accommodate a rhinoceros. She also saw what blocked her path to the trash chute—a large bolt of gray cloth that had become jammed between the chute and the door.

Carla glared at the obstacle. If she wanted to get close enough to the chute to dump her garbage, she had to walk over it. A sneeze caught her by surprise when she placed one delicate foot on the discarded fabric.

It's too soft to be a roll of cloth, she told herself. Carla gingerly stepped back on firm footing while she debated her next course of action. Her eyes were fixed on what blocked her path. The small room began to spin. Her mouth went dry. Her knees buckled.

It wasn't a bolt of gray fabric. It was the body of a woman! She wore a gray pants suit. She was turned toward the wall, her face was hidden and only the back of her jacket and long trousers were visible.

Nervous sobs caught in Carla's throat as she knelt down and gently pushed aside the clump of burgundy hair that had fallen across the woman's forehead. She forced herself to look at the distorted blue face, the bulging eyes, the protruding tongue and the swollen lips covered with bloody froth—the terrible face of Aldyn Sheridan.

Chapter 8

Carla didn't remember running from the trash room to her apartment. Nor did she remember dialing 911. But she must have done that too, or why else would Officers Ramirez and Murkowski be back in her apartment?

"I thought I recognized the apartment when the call came in. How are you, Mrs. Miller?" Officer Ramirez slipped his black plastic notebook out of his back pocket, ready to take Carla's statement.

"Terrible. She's…it's my real estate broker, Aldyn Sheridan. Her face is purple. She's dressed in gray. Her body is still warm, so I must have been in my apartment when it happened," Carla spat out short, distorted sentences.

"Take it easy, Mrs. Miller. Where is the body?" Officer Ramirez asked.

"In the trash room. Down the hall. I'll show you." Carla took a step toward the door.

"No, please wait here. We'll go alone." Officer Murkowski's request sounded friendly enough, but the steely glint in her eyes warned Carla not to join them. Twenty minutes later the officers returned.

"She looks terrible, doesn't she? I've never seen anyone look so terrible. Do you want to use my phone to call someone, or will you use your cell phones?"

"There's no one to call, Mrs. Miller," Officer Ramirez replied, "because there's no body in the trash room. We even searched the basement. No body down there, either. We spoke to the super, Mr. O'Grady? He didn't see or hear anything suspicious and neither did the doormen or porters, so we'll be going." The officer gave Carla a sympathetic smile, but his partner didn't go along with his white glove treatment.

Officer Murkowski glared at Carla. "Now look here, lady. This is the second time you called 911 for no reason. We're gonna write up an information report this time, but if you do it again, we'll charge you with filing a false police report, which could get you jail time." Her face came so close to Carla that she could see the cop's contact lenses floating on her irises.

"But I saw her; I touched her, and what about me? Suppose the killer comes back? Aren't you going to protect me?" Carla pleaded.

"Remember what I said," Officer Murkowski warned sternly.

Sympathetic Officer Ramirez answered her questions with questions of his own. "Are you on medication? That'll do it. Or maybe you saw a bolt of fabric, like you said, or a pile of rags on the floor and thought it was a body. Do you have someone who can stay with you for a while?" He closed his notebook and joined his partner at the door.

"I saw her. I'm not crazy and I'm not on drugs. Please look again," Carla begged the officers. "And suppose I did see a pile of rags. What happened to it? Where is it now? Why did I sneeze?" Carla continued to talk to the closed door, a habit she acquired during her marriage. She waited in the foyer and hoped that the officers would return, yet as the minutes passed she knew they'd long since left the building.

Carla suddenly craved a tuna melt, her favorite comfort food. But when she opened the cabinet, she discovered that her stock of tuna fish had gone missing. *Then how about a blueberry muffin? That would be good,"* she told herself.

While she waited for the toaster oven to do its job on the muffin, Carla held a nervous conversation with herself. *The cop said I should forget about it, but I can't. How can I forget about Aldyn? Maybe someone killed her because of what she wanted to tell me, or...* The shrill whine of the kitchen smoke detector interrupted her thoughts. Orange tongues of flames shot out of the little oven. Carla disconnected the toaster, doused the flames with salt then tossed the charred remains of the muffin into the garbage can. She had a lot of experience with burnt food.

But ridding the kitchen of the thick cloud of smoke turned out to be more of a problem than the fire itself. Carla futilely swatted a linen towel upward toward the air vent above the cabinets. She reasoned that a clogged air vent had caused the problem, so how difficult could that be to fix? She had the equipment to do the job—a chrome kitchen ladder from Gracious Home to climb up to the vent and the housewarming screwdriver that Mimi bought at her father-in-law's hardware store to remove the vent.

Carla undid the four screws that held the grate in place and peered into the vent. She expected to see a sooty, greasy opening in the wall that allowed air to circulate up the shaft. That's not what she found. Someone nailed green quilted fabric to the back and two sides of the shaft and bolted a piece of plywood covered with the same fabric to the walls to form a bottom. It was the wooden bottom that cut off the flow of air and prevented the smoke from dissipating. For the second time in less than an hour Carla expected to see one thing, only to discover something entirely different.

The makeshift storage box was enough of a shock, but it was the dozens of velvet jewelers' boxes and suede drawstring pouches neatly stacked in the seven-inch-by-ten-inch space that nearly sent Carla flying off her perch. Without giving a thought to the consequences of her actions, Carla tore open the boxes and pouches to discover a breathtaking assortment of jeweled rings, bracelets, necklaces, broaches and earrings. Chills of excitement rippled up and down her spine as she slid a large solitaire diamond ring on her finger, then she caressed a choker of unbelievably sensuous gun metal gray pearls. Finally she wrapped a wide Art Deco emerald bracelet around her wrist. Carla gasped when she saw a single diamond and ruby earring nestled in a burgundy velvet sack. The piece looked suspiciously like the mate to the one Mr. Everett found the night of her party. It now rested in her sweater drawer waiting to be claimed by its owner.

Carla wondered if Victor Reynolds put the jewels in the air vent, then forgot about them. If that were true, how could the mate to that earring turn up on her kitchen counter months after his death? No, it didn't seem likely that the jewels belonged to Reynolds. Carla wondered if they could be connected to Aldyn's death.

No matter who put them in her kitchen air vent or why, Carla's gut feeling told her that she better stop playing dress up with the baubles and put them back in their hiding place. As she returned the velvet box that held the pearl choker, she spotted a piece of ivory paper stuck to the bottom of the box—and received her third surprise of the day.

It was the back flap of an envelope for her housewarming party invitation—the part with her return address—that had become affixed to the box. From the haphazard angle at which a strip of tape held it to the box, it may have become attached by accident. Either someone she invited to her party meant to save her address, or whoever hid the jewels in the air vent wanted it. She put her money on the person who stashed the jewels.

Carla's heart thump, thumped, her stomach tied itself into a giant knot, beads of sweat glistened on her face; the apartment walls marched forward pushing her back and back into a tiny cell-like space. She had to leave. But where could she go? She took a deep breath to open the blood vessels and speed an idea to her brain. In seconds, she had a plan, yet she didn't flee. An urgent task cried out for her attention.

After Carla closed the grate, she grabbed the squat crock pot that sat atop the kitchen cabinets beside the air vent. She held it protectively to her chest as she climbed down the ladder, then she shoved it into the foyer coat closet beside the half-filled box marked "Bonker's Stuff." At last, she fled the apartment and rang for the elevator. The doorman and the concierge were too engrossed in studying the *Racing Form* to notice Carla as she snuck down the hall and ran through the door marked "Garden."

Her thoughts still fixed on murder, Carla ran down the winding flagstone garden path oblivious to the beautiful little oasis abloom with green shrubs and brilliant orange and yellow autumn flowers. Steps from her destination, she tripped. A thick Filofax diary with the initials A.S. stamped in gold in the middle of the cover blocked her path—proof to Carla that Aldyn Sheridan used this route to get to her apartment building. She tossed the diary into her bag, unlocked the garden door and ran through the other lobby onto East 55th Street.

Chapter 9

Everything will be all right once I get there, Carla repeated her mantra over and over as swiftly beating wings of fear carried her toward her sanctuary. Faster and faster she walked—north on First Avenue, west on 57th Street and finally north again on Lexington Avenue. Carla accelerated her pace to a graceful gallop the moment she saw the ugly gray building that squatted on a full square city block between Lexington and Third Avenues. Bounded by East Sixtieth Street to the north and East Fifty-Ninth Street to the south, it occupied one of the most expensive pieces of real estate in Manhattan.

Carla shoved her way past a pair of giggling tourists in her frenzy to fling open the Art Deco doors and hurl herself into the mad, mad world of Bloomingdale's. Once inside the world famous emporium, nothing could distract her from reaching her destination—not the fifty percent off sale of designer handbags, not the promise of a free makeup application, not even the pitiful wails of a lost child. Arms pumping, eyes straight ahead, Carla rode the escalator to the second floor and scurried down the wide avenue of boutique-style Generation X fashion departments to the moderately priced shoe salon, a haven for undisturbed quiet contemplation, that is, if you know how to play the game—and Carla was a Grand Master of the game.

She used a simple ruse. She selected the cheapest shoe on display, clutched it tightly in one hand, then plunked herself on a turquoise cotton banquette and assumed an expression of bovine patience, confident that she would be left alone to ponder her problems. Carla knew that sales associates stake out their customers as carefully as guys look over the ladies at a singles bar. Nine times out of ten they approach a customer who has selected half a dozen shoes to try on and avoid the poor wallflower who wants just one pair of cheap shoes. If a sales associate offered to bring Carla her lone choice, she would ask for a size five quadruple A shoe, an odd ball size that few stores stock. The associate would invariably say, "I'll be right back," never to return.

Carla didn't try her game in the fourth floor designer shoe salon. Up there in the rarified air of shoes priced in the triple and quadruple digits, a whole new set of rules came into play. If she rested her derriere on one of the soft beige leather settees with a seven hundred and fifty dollar Chanel black silk shoe or a two thousand dollar Gucci purple lizard boot clutched in her hand, it would take only a couple of seconds for the curtain to drop on quiet contemplation. She learned that sad lesson last year when she came into the city to get away from her battle with Larry the Louse over the distribution of their joint assets. No sooner had she stepped into the salon than an eager sales associate scurried toward her, magically discovered her true shoe size and immediately brought out a dozen boxes of shoes. Carla didn't solve any of her problems that day, but she left the store with three lovely pairs of designer shoes.

While Carla pretended to examine the seventy-two dollar sample shoe, her mind sorted through the afternoon's horrifying events: the discovery of Aldyn Sheridan's body, its subsequent disappearance, the jewels in the air vent and the return address portion of an invitation envelope to her party. The shoe fell out of her hand when she realized that the party guest list included most of her friends and relatives. Could the burglar be one of them? Who could she trust? What should she do? She couldn't go to the police again, that's for sure. Unexpected tears glistened in Carla's amber eyes.

"May I help you?"

"Oh, if only you could," she responded to the eager, bright face that peered quizzically at her.

"What size do you want?" The face flashed a dazzling smile that displayed a mouthful of very white straight teeth.

"Size?" She blinked.

"Yes, the shoe, what size do you want?" The smiley face pointed to the shoe in her hand.

"Five quadruple A, please." Carla tucked her size six and a half B feet out of sight.

"No problem. I'll be right back. Just sit there," the face ordered.

"You have that size?"

She shook her head up and down. "Absolutely. Just yesterday a customer asked for a four double A, but all I found was your size, so you see, today is your lucky day." The face treated Carla to another view of her perfect teeth.

"Some luck," Carla muttered as the face trotted off to the stockroom.

The moment the eager sales associate disappeared into the stockroom, Carla ran onto an UP escalator with the unwanted shoe clutched in her hand. She stepped off the escalator at the fourth floor, hurried down the marble corridor lined with high priced designer boutiques and entered the serene beige shoe salon. Then she marched up to the center niche against the wall, the one with the pinpoint light that illuminated one clear Lucite block, the place reserved for the finest shoe in all the Kingdom of

Bloomingdale's. On this hallowed spot she gently placed the humble seventy-two dollar shoe and hurried away without a backward glance.

Her brave smile evaporated when her eyes strayed from the marble corridor to a mannequin dressed in a gray Donna Karan pantsuit. A flashback to the moment she saw Aldyn's horribly distorted face sent her stumbling through the lingerie department to the ladies lounge. A pink banquette opposite the makeup tables invited Carla to sit down while she placed a call. She stabbed a speed dial number on her cell phone and listened to the far away ring of the phone while she silently prayed, *Mimi, please answer. I need you.*

"Hello," Mimi's crisp voice responded on the fourth ring.

Mimi, is that you? Oh, of course, it's you. It's Carla. I'm glad I got you."

"Carla, what's the matter? Are you crying? What's wrong?"

"Something terrible is going on in my apartment. I'm in Bloomingdale's…it closes in forty-five minutes and I can't go home because somebody… I'm so scared that…"

"Stop babbling and tell me what's wrong. Begin at the beginning."

"Aldyn called this afternoon and…"

Mimi stopped Carla's monologue when she got to the shoe salon episode. "Could the police be right? Maybe you did imagine seeing Aldyn's body. You're under a lot of strain—the divorce, the move, a new job, a new man. All that can take a lot out of a person." Mimi had slipped into her soothing psychiatrist voice.

"I don't care what the police said. I saw Aldyn's body and I know someone strangled her." The panicked expression on the face of the woman to her left forced Carla to lower her voice. "I can't stay on the phone any longer," she whispered.

"Don't hang up!" Mimi's sharp retort stopped her from ending the conversation. "I'm on the train headed into the city to cat sit for my cousin Audrey. Stay there with me the weekend and we'll talk out your problems without being disturbed.

"Where's Mervin?"

"In the Hamptons, of course. The weather forecast is for an unseasonably hot and sunny weekend, so he's going to the beach house directly from the office to work on his tan. Whatever you do, don't go back to your apartment. Buy everything you need in Bloomies or at Duane Reed. You know Audrey's address, don't you?"

"She's on East 65th Street off Second Avenue, isn't she?"

"Right. I'll call her doorman to tell him that I'm expecting you. I should be there no later than eight o'clock. Don't worry about anything. I'll help you."

"Oh, would you? Mimi, I love you. You and Mervin have helped me so much. I'll never be able to repay you." A wave of relief engulfed Carla.

"Yes, I know, Carla. And remember what I told you—don't go back to your apartment. Do you hear me?" Mimi barked orders the same way she did when she coached her college soccer team, and she got the same response from friends and family as she did from her teams—instant obedience.

In a half hour of frenzied shopping, Carla filled three Bloomingdale's big brown shopping bags with clothes and lingerie for the weekend, including a pair of very expensive gold sandals. She had no choice but to buy them in the designer shoe salon, for she couldn't risk going back to the second floor where she might be recognized as the stupid thief who made off with one inexpensive shoe.

Carla ran toward the Third Avenue exit seconds before a store closing announcement sent buyers scrambling to make last minute purchases.

She had just scooted passed the Swatch wristwatch display in the Men's Department when three fast rat tat tat sneezes brought her to a dead stop. *Oh lord, whoever or whatever made me sneeze in the apartment has followed me to Bloomingdale's.*

Carla fled the store.

Chapter 10

Carla ran down Third Avenue to 63rd Street, then hung a right onto Second Avenue and whizzed into a Duane Reade store, one of those ubiquitous no frills cosmetics/pharmacy/mini-supermarket stores that have spread all over Manhattan like mushrooms after a rainstorm. She jogged up and down the aisles, filling her basket with everything she needed to keep herself clean, sweet smelling and looking pretty all weekend. She even bought a sewing kit. She liked to be prepared for any contingency.

Mimi's cousin, Audrey Castleman, lived in a thirty-six floor high spiffy white co-op building that had a curved driveway, a health club in the basement and a doorman with an attitude. "Whom do you wish to see?" The doorman's porcine eyes squinted half shut, as though he preferred not to see Carla.

"Mrs. Castleman's cousin, Mimi Berk. She's watching Mrs. Castleman's cat this weekend because the cat sitter got sick and I'm staying with her, but maybe she's not here yet because I am a few minutes early." Carla nervously blurted out more of an explanation than necessary.

"I don't know Miz Berk and Missus Castleman is away for the weekend." A nasty Jack Nicholson leer oozed across his face.

"I know Mrs. Castleman is away," Carla snapped. "But my friend Mrs. Berk is staying in her apartment for the weekend, and I'd be ever so grateful if you would tell me if she has arrived."

"Oh, her. Why didn't you say so? She's not here yet. You can wait over there." He waved his hand toward a large white leather couch that would be more appropriate in a movie star's living room than an apartment building lobby.

"Thank you so much." Instead of losing her temper and ripping out the nasty doorman's throat, Carla offered him a sweet smile that paid tribute to one of Kitty's homilies: "Sometimes a woman's gotta do what a woman's gotta do to get what she wants."

Carla sashayed across the mirrored lobby as confidentially as model on a cat walk—until she glanced at her reflection. Then she stopped dead in her tracks. *Oh, my god, no wonder the doorman treated me like dead meat. I look like a bag lady.* And she did. Her makeup had slipped off her face, her thick curls had morphed into a tangled mass of tight little squiggles, her linen dress had acquired more wrinkles than Fortuny had pleats and thanks to a network of runs in her pantyhose, her legs looked like an interstate on a Rand McNally road map.

With her confidence deflated flat as a punctured tire, Carla collapsed onto the couch. She needed to fix herself up before perfectly groomed Mimi arrived. Her hand searched deep within the dark recesses of her satchel for a tube of lipstick, but instead she found the business card that Tony gave her that first night at Villagio. No fancy logo or company slogan adorned the beige engraved card. The words "Vitale Associates—Business Insurance" and a New Jersey address appeared dead center. A telephone and fax number occupied the left hand corner of the card. The words "Anthony J. Vitale, President" appeared in the lower right hand corner. Tony had scrawled his home phone number on the back of the card.

Tony told Carla to call him anytime at either number. Yet she never could reach him at the office, and always had to leave a message for him. She decided against calling the home number with the Rockland County, New York area code. Carla tossed the card back in her bag with the promise that the next time she saw Tony, she would learn the truth about Mrs. Vitale's death and her current status—divorcee, dead or had she taken off for parts unknown. Carla routed around again in her bag like an anteater digging for a tasty bug. Just as she retrieved her wayward lipstick, Mimi's greeting exploded across the marble lobby. "I'm here!" Carla would have to face her best friend looking like what she was—a frazzled, distraught woman who had recently stumbled across a dead body and had dipped her hands into a fortune of jewels.

"Hi, Mimi."

"Hi, Sweetie." Mimi punctuated her greeting with a smack-the-air cocktail party kiss. "Grab your stuff and let's go upstairs. You must be wilted." Mimi, who wore an unwrinkled navy blue pantsuit and perfectly applied makeup, tactfully chose not to comment on Carla's less than perfect appearance.

"Thanks for inviting me to stay with you this weekend. I don't know what I'd do if I had to go back to my apartment," Carla blurted as the express elevator sped them up to the thirty-fifth floor.

"It's the least I can do. Mervin and I will always help you. Now give me a couple of your shopping bags. They look heavy."

Mimi deftly swung her Fendi weekend tote onto her shoulder and waggled her free hands at Carla, who handed over her bags without protest. From the moment she found Aldyn's body until she sat down in the lobby, those twin spurs—fear and determination—kept her going. But now that Mimi had arrived to help her, all of Carla's strength ebbed away.

The two friends walked in silence to the last door in the half-block long corridor. "We're here." Mimi inserted a key into a highly polished brass lock.

Carla had been in the apartment only once before and when she entered it today, she felt the same sense of awe she had experienced on her first visit. Everything was white, black, glass or chrome, except for the abstract art that covered every wall. A widow, Audrey owned a fair sized investment firm that provided her with enough money to indulge herself in her passion for art and anything else that she craved.

"I'll take the pullout couch in the library and you can have Audrey's room." Mimi quickly stowed Carla's shopping bags in the master bedroom before she could protest.

"Where's the cat?"

"Ginger? She stays in the closet. She'll come out to eat and use the litter box when we're not around. And, speaking of her litter box, whatever you do, don't touch the mirrored column in the entrance. Her litter box is hidden behind it."

"I promise to restrain myself if I get the urge to use it." Carla forced a smile.

"Just so you remember. How about some coffee?" Once again, Mimi took charge of the situation and marched into the large eat-in kitchen, dumped the right combination of gourmet coffee and spring water into the Cuisinart coffee maker, and emptied a bag of Audrey's supermarket chocolate chip cookies onto an expensive Limoges porcelain plate. As they sat across from each other at the glass breakfast table waiting for their steaming hot coffee to cool, Mimi's dark eyes narrowed. "So, let's talk about murder. What happened?"

"I told you everything I know on the phone and I don't care what the police did or didn't find—I saw Aldyn's body as clear as I see you right now." Carla's firm voice didn't leave an ounce of doubt that she saw a body, not a discarded bolt of fabric or a rug.

"I can't describe how horrible she looked. She'd turned a ghastly shade of purple. Her tongue stuck out. I'll never forget her face as long as I live." Carla shuddered violently, as though she'd ventured onto a glacier without a heavy coat.

"I know how you feel," Mimi sympathized. "I felt awful when I found Mitzi all stiff and cold. Of course, she was sixteen and that's old for a cat. Such an obnoxious bitch. Aldyn not Mitzi," Mimi added in response to Carla's questioning look. "But why would someone kill her? Maybe a mugging gone bad?" she said with little enthusiasm.

Carla shook her head. "A mugger doesn't come back for the body. I'm positive her death is connected with the jewels that I found."

"Where are they now?"

"I put everything back in the air vent exactly as I found them except for the piece of paper with my return address. It looked like it had become accidentally attached to the box, so I took it. But now I'm not sure that I did the right thing. I'll put it back as soon as I go home. You know what that scrap of paper means, don't you?" Carla stared at Mimi over the top of her coffee mug and waited for her to confirm her fears.

"Sure. A guest at your party is either a thief and possible murderer or is missing a choker. Do you know anyone who owns a piece similar to that one?" Mimi rummaged around in a cabinet until she found another bag of cookies and dumped them on the plate. This could be a long koffee klatch.

"No. My friends and relatives have jewelry, not JEWELRY." Mimi and Carla knew the difference between lower and upper case jewelry. Lower case jewelry meant costume stuff or non-precious gemstones that a woman bought for herself at Bloomies or Saks or at one of the funky boutiques in SoHo. JEWELRY meant the diamond, ruby, emerald or sapphire necklace, ring or earrings purchased by a husband or lover at Cartier, Tiffany, Van Cleef & Arpels or Harry Winston.

"Then everyone you invited to the party is a suspect—except Mervin and me. We didn't get an invitation."

"Right. You said you would crown me if I sent you one." Carla wanted her party to be perfect down to the last detail, including hand addressed invitations. But when Mimi learned how much it cost for a calligrapher to address each envelope, she insisted that she and Mervin didn't need a formal invitation.

"You know who else didn't get one?" Carla grinned, happy as a cat with a tuna fish sandwich. "Tony! He also said he could remember the date without an invitation." Carla's heart felt lighter now that Tony was off the list of suspects.

"Anyone else?"

"No, that's it, but I didn't mail Mrs. Callahan an invitation. In fact, I didn't plan to invite her until I realized that if I didn't, she would complain about the noise, so at the last minute I handed her the one meant for Tony."

"Did you put it in an envelope?" Mimi asked the logical question.

Carla nodded. "The calligrapher had already done the return address when I told her to hold up on the rest."

"Then she could be the thief."

"Don't be ridiculous. She's too frail and she's bombed out of her head most of the time. And come to think of it, we should take Kitty and Charlie Blumenfaux off the list of suspects. I'd trust Kitty with my life, and Charlie is too frail to strangle a hot dog, let alone a person. Can you picture him climbing up a ladder to hide his loot?"

"Listen, Carla, those thin, wiry types can be strong as an ox, and he could have an accomplice. Maybe Kitty did the climbing. So I say Charlie and Kitty stay on the list."

"Kitty climb a ladder? I doubt it."

Carla's eyes fixed on Mimi's hands as she shredded the corner of her paper napkin. Her messy nervous habit signaled that Mimi had something unpleasant to say. "You must tell the police what's going on," Mimi said firmly after she'd reduced the napkin to a neat pile of shredded paper. "If you don't, something terrible may happen to you. You may get killed or charged with withholding evidence or even murder."

"I told you before," Carla snapped, "the police and I aren't on good terms because I reported a body that wasn't a body and Aldyn's body disappeared before they arrived. They even threatened to send me to jail if I report another body. As far as the Seventeenth Precinct is concerned, I'm the neighborhood nut. So forget it, I won't call the cops again." Carla's response stunned Mimi into silence. The two friends stared at each other until Carla shattered the cloud of tension that hung over them. "How well did you know Aldyn?" she asked.

"Well enough not to like her," Mimi mumbled in a voice barely loud enough for Carla to hear. "I met her when Mervin and I lived on the West Side. Back then she was plain Alma Solomon, married to a music student at Julliard. I think he played the cello. Can you imagine a musician listening to that voice day and night?" Mimi giggled, then stopped. "Sorry,

I shouldn't speak ill of the dead, but we didn't keep in touch after Mervin and I moved to Merrick. A couple of years ago I ran into her at Nail Mania.

"I don't remember her." Carla's mind drew a blank when she tried to recall meeting Aldyn in Merrick.

"You wouldn't. At that time you went to Salon Sylvan for your manicures. Anyway, we saw each other every Friday—we both had standing ten o'clockers. Afterward we'd have lunch or go shopping or both. By then she had divorced her second husband, changed her name, got her real estate brokers license and, as usual, had a couple of lovers. Did I mention that she always had someone on the side? For while she stopped gossiping and became very secretive, so I assumed she had a local married man on the string. The affair must have fizzled because a couple of months later she announced that she bought a co-op in Manhattan. When you dropped the bombshell that you wanted to move to the city, I put the two of you in touch." Mimi spooned more sugar into her coffee. Sugar was her only vice, except for the one Cosmopolitan martini that she sipped every night before dinner.

"Thanks a lot. Sending Aldyn to me was like sending Attila the Hun to baby sit Bambi."

"Look, she didn't hurt you and I only wanted to help, so let's forget it. But there is someone who worries me."

"Who?" Carla whispered.

"Tony. Something isn't right about him." Carla opened her mouth to speak but Mimi raised her hand to signal that she still had the floor. "Don't jump on me, just listen. Do you think Tony could be at the bottom of all this?"

"No!" Carla shot back then shifted gears and said softly, "That is, I don't think so. You met him. You know he is too good to be mixed up in a murder."

"Too good is right. The whole business with him is too good and too pat. You and he are the only people in an elevator when it gets stuck. He takes you out and right away he's nuts about you. He's handsome and rich. But on the other hand, you're not sure about his marital status and you don't exactly know what he does for a living."

"I know exactly what he does. When we met in the elevator, I thought he was an accountant because of his big briefcase, but actually, he's a business insurance broker."

"Which could be a euphemism for the protections racket," Mimi snapped.

"You have a wild imagination. He's nothing of the sort." Though Carla sprang to Tony's defense, she knew that Mimi's imagination might not be all that wild.

"Even if I'm wrong about the rackets, you must admit that he's out of town a lot. And, don't forget that you didn't find the jewels until after you met him. Think about it."

"Stop, stop it. I don't want to think about it." Carla pressed her hands against her ears to block out the wild accusations. "Why can't a man care about me? Isn't there life after Larry?" Carla slammed her mug down hard on the table, sending a mini tsunami wave of coffee over the rim.

"Come on Carla, calm down. I only want to help." Mimi put a comforting arm around her friend's shoulder. "You may be in real trouble. Suppose Tony is a spy and is using you as his beard."

"Don't be ridiculous. It's nothing like that. I'm sorry I snapped at you, but let's leave Tony out of it. Let's look through Aldyn's Filofax." Carla pulled the book out of her satchel and laid it on the table between them.

"What's on her calendar for today?" Mimi asked.

"Only 'Look' at three o'clock with two red dots, nothing else listed for today and she drew a line through the next two weeks. Not a clue to where she's staying. She said she had the use of a friend's place in Hilton Head. Maybe we could track her down there."

"Forget it," Mimi answered. "In case you didn't know, Hilton Head Island is a barrier island in South Carolina that's wall-to-wall hotels, condos and timeshares, so unless we know her friend's name, we'll never find her. Do you think her secretary would know where she's staying?"

"Maybe," Carla replied. "I'll call her on Monday. I got her the job with Aldyn, so I'm sure she'll tell me but that doesn't help us now. Her calendar is of no use." Carla sighed. "It looks like she wrote it in code. Probably as protection in case another broker got hold of it."

"You're right," Mimi agreed. "She told me that real estate brokers are a sneaky bunch...just like her."

Carla looked up from Aldyn's diary to exclaim, "The words 'Show' and 'Look' appear over and over followed by different colored dots and initials, must be her damn code again. She wrote 'Show CM' with three green dots the day we first met. I wonder what the dots mean. And look what she wrote every day since my party in the 'Things to Do' section." Carla waved the book under Mimi's nose, her finger pointed to the red initials "CM" followed by exclamation points. "'CM' is me, but why?"

"Never mind that. Look at these. They fell out of her diary." Mimi gathered up a fistful of bank deposit slips. "The bitch cried to me all the time that the real estate market stunk, yet last Tuesday she deposited three thousand dollars in the bank and on Thursday another five thousand. Two weeks ago she put in ten thousand. And they were all cash deposits.

The deposit slips total more than fifty thousand dollars. What the hell is going on?"

"Look at the checks she wrote." Carla's manicured finger ran down the check register as she rattled off the names of expensive specialty shops like Bergdorf Goodman, Henri Bendel, St. John and Escada. Didn't that lady know from Macy's? Her combined monthly mortgage and maintenance payments on her apartment ran sixty-two hundred dollars and she paid nearly four hundred and fifty dollars a month for a garage and car wash."

"Maybe someone is keeping her."

"Get real, Mimi. Who would pay to sleep with her? But I think I know how she made her money." Carla quickly compared the dates on Aldyn's deposit slips with the dates in her calendar. "Bingo! Look at this. She made a big cash deposit every day there is a single initial notation. I bet you a hundred dollars that your old friend was a blackmailer." She flashed a triumphant smile.

"Oh, for heaven's sake, Carla, you read too many mystery novels. Those weird plots have softened your brain."

"Then how do you explain the money?"

"I don't know. I'll think about it. In the meantime let's look in her phone directory."

Carla and Mimi turned the dog eared alphabetical pages, and lingered now and then over a familiar name. "You gotta hand it to her. She knew a lot of famous people," Carla said. "She has phone numbers for celebrities like Tom Cruise, Steven Spielberg and George Clooney. Do you suppose that really is George's number?" An impish smile lit Carla's face as she tapped in the California telephone number.

"Hang up. You're acting like a twelve year-old."

Carla waved her hang back and forth to silence Mimi. "Oh, excuse me. I have the wrong number."

"Not George's number, right? Aldyn probably put those names in her book to impress people." Mimi sniffed indignantly.

"Is that so? Then why did a man answer, 'Clooney residence'?"

Mimi gave a non-committal shrug and snatched the book from Carla. "This is unbelievable. Look, she even has the phone numbers for Kitty, Monsieur Jacques, your brother Harold, you, me, Mervin's office number. Most of the people who came to your party are in her phone book. Only Tony's name is missing, but she could have memorized his number. Aldyn had an amazing memory. If she looked at something once, she remembered every detail forever.

"Well, even if Aldyn is alive, she can't go very far without these." Mimi pointed to Aldyn's driver's license and platinum credit cards, all tucked into the appropriate slots in the Filofax.

Carla grabbed the phone. "Aldyn, this is Carla. I found your Filofax. I know you must be desperate for it. I'm not at home this weekend, so call me at 212-7…"

"You got her voice mail, right?"

"Yes. I didn't think she'd be home but it was worth a call." Carla gulped down the last of her cold coffee. "I've got a terrible headache. Would you mind if I skipped dinner? I'd like to take a bath and go to bed."

Chapter 11

"Strangers in the dah dee dah dee dah..." Carla's off-key voice repeated the old Sinatra song over and over as she took full advantage of Cousin Audrey's drop dead black Roman tub. Her firm, pink nipples poked through a blanket of jasmine scented bubbles; her amber eyes stared at the images reflected in mirrored walls and ceiling—the flickering scented candles, the glass of chilled Chardonnay on the edge of the tub, the sleek Italian telephone on a stool beside the tub, the chrome étagère...the telephone...the telephone... Her hand rose out of the water, snatched up the phone and dialed the number she knew by heart. Though well past normal office hours, after only two rings a female voice responded, "Good evening, Vitale Associates." Carla sunk deeper under the foamy bubbles. "Is this the answering service?"

"No. This is the receptionist. May I help you?" The voice reflected annoyance that Carla presumed an outside service would be entrusted to take messages for Anthony J. Vitale and his associates.

"This is Mrs. Miller. I know Mr. Vitale is out of town, but if he should call, would you please tell him that I'm away and won't be home until Sunday night?"

"Of course, Mrs. Miller. Would you care to leave a number where Mr. Vitale may reach you?"

"No. He doesn't have to return my call. Thank you. Good night."

Carla hung up. She wondered why she called and why she didn't leave her cell phone. She didn't learn anything that she didn't already know. After her divorce, her daughter Nancy took her aside and explained how the rules of dating had changed in the quarter century she'd been out of circulation. "Men are people, too, Mom. Don't play silly games with them." And that's what she'd just done. She wasn't pleased with herself.

She sank back in the tub to study the upside down reflections. This time her eyes locked on the corner chrome étagère filled with Audrey's heady perfumes: Fendi, Coco and Coriandre. Mimi also wore Fendi. Carla's preference ran to classic floral scents like Fracas and Joy

The sparkling perfume bottles brought back memories of other scents. Carla recalled a faint woodsy masculine aroma. She thought she smelled it whenever she sneezed in the apartment and most recently in Bloomingdale's. The more she thought about it, the more certain she became that she had also smelled it on someone a long time ago.

A half-hidden flacon of Opium channeled Carla's thoughts to the unanswered questions that surrounded Aldyn's death, like why she demanded to see Carla that afternoon, did she know her killer and was blackmail the motive for her murder. Still pondering her list of troubling questions, Carla sipped the last of her wine, returned the glass to its safe perch on the edge of the tub, took a deep breath and disappeared under the bubbles. Seconds later she rose out of the water. Foam clung to her body and a broad smile brightened her face. "I've got it," she exclaimed to her multiple reflections.

"I'll tell all the men who were at the party that I'm writing a book on the psychology of men's cologne and I need to know the name of their favorite scents." Carla explained her plan to Mimi.

"Your idea is full of holes. Like, if the murderer came to the party, why didn't you sneeze then?" Mimi said.

"There's an explanation for that. The killer didn't wear that cologne to the party. I don't wear the same perfume all the time, so why should he?" Carla replied defensively. She and Mimi were in Audrey's white bedroom. Mimi sat in a white leather chair, while Carla reclined on the bed with her back propped up against the white quilted leather headboard.

"Who will believe that you're writing a psychology book? You didn't graduate from college. You left in your junior year to marry Larry." Mimi cast aside Carla's plan.

"But I majored in psychology and maybe someday I'll write a…no?" Carla fidgeted with the bath sheet she had wrapped around herself sarong style.

"No. You need a better excuse than that to smell the men. How does this sound? When you go to their offices, like your brother Harold…"

"Wait a minute. Do you think Harold is the killer?" Carla broke in.

"You put him on the list, not me and I'm only using him as an example." Mimi pointed to the list of men who came to the party. "Tell him that you dropped in to get some shoes, or ask if he's heard from your parents, or anything, but if you sneeze, he's it and you get out fast and call the police."

"Police? I can't call the police. They won't believe me. We already went through that scenario."

"All right, no police. Let me think." Mimi got up from her chair to pace the room while she reconsidered her friend's problem. "I've got it."

"What? What have you got?" Carla's eyes widened as though she was waiting for the oracle to speak.

"When you find the man who makes you sneeze leave fast and call me."

As if on cue, the phone rang. Mimi answered. "Hi, darling." Mimi mouthed "Mervin" to Carla. "Guess who's here? Carla. No, nothing is wrong. Tony is away, so she's staying with Ginger and me for the weekend. Yes, that's a good idea. We'll have brunch before I take the train back to Merrick. I'll give her a kiss for you. See you Sunday night. Good night."

"Mervin always calls when he gets to the beach house to let me know he's safe," she said. "He sends you a big kiss. And even though he isn't a suspect, you might as well know that he wears Égoïste. I didn't tell him about Aldyn or the jewels," Mimi added as though Carla hadn't heard the one-sided conversation.

"I appreciate that, Mimi. I'd like to keep it between us for the time being. Before Mervin called you said that if I find a man who makes me sneeze, I should call you. Why? What can you do? You're way out in Merrick, while the murderer is in New York."

"I know, but I'll call Mervin. He'll know what to do. He's a lawyer. This is right up his alley." Mimi had stopped pacing and had stretched out on the white leather chair with her feet propped up on a blood red silk floor cushion that exactly matched her silk pajamas.

"Well, if this is right up his alley and his alley is New York City, why don't I call him and ask him what to do?"

"Because he thinks you're nuts," Mimi mumbled.

"What?" Carla sat up straight in bed, her hands locked on her slender hips.

"Calm down. Don't get hostile. You know that Mervin has absolutely no sense of humor or patience with feminine problems. That's why it would be better if you are sure about your facts before we go to him."

Carla hunched her shoulders. "Are you implying that I'm menopausal and I imagined all of this?"

"Me, think that's what's causing your nutty behavior? Of course, not." Mimi scoffed. "It's Mervin who has problems with hysterical women. That's why it would be better if I talk to him first. Remember how much he helped you during the divorce. Trust me, honey, it will be okay."

"Maybe you're right. Okay, I'll call you," Carla agreed. *Unless I think of a better plan*, she assured herself.

Early the next morning, the sensation of sandpaper being rubbed against her cheek roused Carla to wakefulness. A heavy weight sat on her chest. She opened one eye. A pair of unblinking turquoise eyes stared at her. "Mimi," she screamed. "Get it off me!"

Poor, frightened Ginger scurried out of the bedroom as Mimi dashed in. "Oh, for heaven's sake, Carla, the cat only wanted to be friendly. You should feel honored that she came out of the closet to visit you. And breakfast is ready."

Carla staggered into the kitchen five minutes after her encounter with Ginger. She'd washed her face, brushed her teeth and improved her humor. "I'm sorry for the way I behaved. My nerves are shot."

"Forget it. Grab a bagel. We'll eat while we decide what to do this weekend." Mimi pointed to a wicker basked piled high with bagels and a platter of artfully arranged nova, smoked fish, cucumbers and tomatoes.

"I'll do anything you want today, except talk about Aldyn and the jewelry."

"Agreed. While you slept, I made a schedule for us. First we'll go shopping, then catch that new French film at the Paris, eat dinner at a

Chinese restaurant and if you want, rent some DVDs for later. How's that sound, or do you have some other suggestions?"

Carla nodded. "Whatever you want to do is fine with me."

"And on Sunday," Mimi continued, "we'll sleep in, leisurely read the *Times*, have a late brunch at Tavern on the Green, then I'll catch the train home."

"Let's get started." Carla bit into her bagel.

"Larry the Louse!"

Carla shouted her ex-husband's name just as she and Mimi enjoyed their first sips of the famous Central Park restaurant's delicious Mimosas.

"What are you talking about and lower your voice. People are staring." Mimi nodded her head toward the couple seated at the table beside them.

"He should be on the list of suspects." Carla broke their agreement not to talk about her problems.

"Why? You didn't invite him to the party."

"Of course not, but he always bought any men's cologne that came with a free umbrella. The last time I counted, he had twenty-three umbrellas, all with stupid duck handles. And no matter how bad the scent might be, he refused to throw it away. I think he wore the foul smelling ones to spite me"

"But he doesn't wear cologne anymore," Mimi confided.

"You're kidding." Carla leaned back in her upholstered chair, a look of disbelief plastered on her face.

"No, I'm not kidding. Cybil is allergic to scents. She forced him to get rid of his entire collection of cologne along with all the dumb umbrellas."

Incredible. In less than twelve months Cybil accomplished what I couldn't do in twenty-six years. Carla remained silent until after they settled the bill. "I'll go with you to Penn Station," she announced.

"That's crazy. On the way to the station my cab can drop you at your apartment."

"I WANT to see you off." Carla's voice turned shrill.

"Okay, but you're only delaying the inevitable. You have to go home sometime. Do you want me to go with you into the apartment?"

"No. I'm fine. By the way, I've been meaning to ask—how's Nellie? Carla abruptly changed the subject. "I haven't heard from her since the party."

"Beats me. She's out of town a lot. First she's visiting her sister in Philadelphia, then she's off to Chicago to see an old college friend, next it's a weekend at a spa in Massachusetts. Very strange." Mimi shrugged.

"Doesn't Eddie mind?"

"Don't be silly. He's so busy delivering babies that he wouldn't notice if she stayed away for a year."

"Maybe she's got a boyfriend."

"Are you kidding? She hasn't looked at another man since she met Eddie in high school."

"Forget what I said. Nellie isn't the type to have an affair. A few years ago we spent the afternoon shopping for lingerie at Saks. I bought a couple of Le Perla lace bra and panty outfits while she selected Hanro cotton panties and bras and a batch of white long sleeve ruffle neck nightgowns. She must look like the Ghost of Christmas Past when she goes to bed."

"That's not nice, Carla, but it is funny." Mimi shrieked with laughter. "Okay, you can see me off at Penn Station. You'll make me feel like a tourist."

While they waited for Mimi's train to arrive, Carla shifted uneasily from one gold sandaled foot to the other. They chatted about the weather, their children and the state of the economy—everything but Aldyn or the jewels. When a small silver dot appeared far down the dark track, Mimi gushed, "Don't worry about a thing. Aldyn will turn up alive and well. It's really too bizarre that anyone would murder her. Dreadful things don't happen to people we know."

"I'd like to believe you, but I don't and now that you're leaving, I'll tell you the truth. I'm scared to death to go home. I'll faint if anything is wrong in the apartment." Carla twisted her face into a nervous grimace. Her sense of dread increased in direct proportion with the growing size of the dot lumbering down the track.

"Why, that's it!" Mimi clapped her hands and did an uncharacteristic Rumpelstiltskin hop, hop dance. "We should have thought of it before. Aldyn fainted in the trash room and came to after you went back to your apartment to call the police. She became confused, forgot about her appointment with you and went home. It's very logical."

The dot became a very large electric train.

"You're right." Carla shouted to be heard above a loud rumbling noise that could be either the train or her heart. "I'll call you," she said. The forced smile that clung to Carla's face as she gave Mimi a farewell hug, faded as soon as the train pulled out of the station.

Chapter 12

"You can come in now, Miz Miller. Not a mouse in sight." Carla used a variation on the caterer's mouse in the house story to explain her unusual request that the super Timmy Shannon escort her into the apartment. "I'll have the exterminator stop by first thing tomorrow morning." He waited for Carla to step into the foyer before he added, "I hear the police came to see you again the other day. Anything wrong?"

"No, just a mistake."

Carla knew from the smirk on Timmy's face when she handed him a large tip that he judged her to be a kook. And why shouldn't he? In the short time that she'd lived in the building, the police had called on her twice and she had just told him a cockamamie mouse story that only a fool would believe. But no way would Carla confess that the "mouse" might be a hidden jewel thief/murderer. Better she should over tip him and let him believe that she's nuts.

Carla dashed into the kitchen a nanosecond after the door closed behind her skeptical super—and sneezed. The terror she felt when she discovered Aldyn's body flooded back over her. She forced herself to climb her step stool and unscrew the air vent grate. She carefully laid the grate on top of a cabinet before she stuck her head in the hole and saw exactly nothing—no velvet boxes, no velvet sacks, no jewels, nothing. Nada. Zilch. Zippo. The hiding place looked as bare as Old Mother Hubbard's cupboard!

Someone—a friend or relative—had entered the apartment over the weekend and made off with the jewels. The thought of what might have happened if she had been home when the visitor came calling propelled Carla from her stark kitchen into her cozy English country-style bedroom. She had decorated the room in shades of coral and green, right down to the green digital light that flashed on her phone, indicating there were voice mails waiting for her. Carla's trembling finger pressed the "PLAY" button.

"Hello, Mrs. Miller." A hesitant voice came out of the speaker. "This is Myrna Verde. Hope I'm not bothering you, but I'm so excited. I got the job. I start on Monday. Thank you for helping me. Bye."

A weak smile lit Carla's pale face, but quickly faded when she heard the beep, beep, click that signaled a hang up call. The call disturbed her. Did the caller have a legitimate reason for not leaving a message or did he, or she, just want to annoy her?

Another message started. "Hi, Carla, I'm still away" She moved closer to the machine to savor Tony's words. "Called to say hello. Miss you. Oh, yeah, it's Friday night. Hope you're having fun." His warm voice boomed from the phone.

Beep, beep, click.

A tingle of apprehension caught in the back of Carla's throat at the second hang-up call. Could the killer be keeping tabs on her?

The last call brought another smile to her face. "It's me again. It's Saturday morning. I got the message you left at my office. I'm glad you're not waiting for me, though I'd love to talk to you. I won't be back till Tuesday. See you then. Goodbye."

Carla frowned at the answering machine when the message came to an end. Did Tony mean that she shouldn't waste her time on him or she shouldn't stay home when he's away? She couldn't figure it out.

She hit the delete button and automatically glanced at the telephone. Phones enticed her. On Friday it was Audrey Castleman's Italian phone, while today her own ivory telephone drew her hand to it as strongly as steel shavings are pulled toward a magnet. She tapped a the number. On the second ring, the recorded message began: "Hello. This is Aldyn Sheridan. Obviously, I'm not at home, or why would a stupid machine answer? Puhl-eez leave a detailed message and your phone number after the beep and I will return your call the second I return. Tah, tah and have a nice day."

A morbid sense of curiosity compelled Carla to redial the number. Aldyn's grating voice sounded so alive, yet she could clearly visualize her lifeless body in the trash room.

She wandered aimlessly through the apartment. It felt eerie, as though haunted by an unwelcome presence. She tested windows and the locked terrace door. The sight of her tribute to Bonkers on the terrace comforted her. After Carla rattled the door a second time she raced back to the bedroom to retrieve the fat Yellow Pages directory. She kept it in a deep drawer in her night table along with a jumble of things she had no other place for including a flashlight and a selection of new batteries.

"Sutton 24-Hour Locksmith? I need to have my locks changed right now. It's an emergency."

Chapter 13

A sharp sound woke Carla from a troubled dream about Aldyn. It didn't sound like the loud thunder and torrential rain that woke her at two a.m. This noise resembled shrill squeaks. She raised her head high enough to focus a blurry eye on her green enamel bedside clock. Delighted to discover that she had thirty more minutes before the alarm went off, Carla pulled the covers over her head to muffle the squeaks and snuggled back down for a nap.

"Damn it," she shouted when the noise continued. She flung back the sheet, wrapped her shapely naked body in a white terry robe and marched to the window to discover the cause of the commotion on her terrace.

"Be quiet. How's a person supposed to sleep through that racket?" she demanded of the quartette of boisterous sparrows that flapped their wings happily in a large puddle near the clogged drain. The birds fell silent. Two seconds later the chirpers resumed their song. Carla knew there would be no sleep until they finished their early morning ablutions. Rather than get back into bed and stare at the ceiling until the alarm went off, she filled her tub with water, tossed in some jasmine scented bubble bath granules and took another long, leisurely bath.

Feeling fit and relaxed, Carla gave the super a warm smile in response to his "Good morning," when she breezed through the lobby at 8:15 a.m. "Is everything hunky-dory in your apartment, Miz Miller?" Carla's smiled sagged. Should she give him her new key so he could fix the clogged drain or should she co-exist with the rowdy birds? "Yes, Timmy, everything is fine, thank you." The chirping sparrows would stay.

"Aren't you the early bird?" Kitty glanced up from the pile of unopened mail when Carla arrived at the office loaded down with their coffee and muffin breakfast.

"Don't mention birds to me," Carla snapped.

It took Kitty just one look at the deep frown on Carla's face to know that her assistant had a problem. "You look as glum as a hypochondriac who passed her physical. What's happened? Is Tony giving you a hard time?" she asked.

"No, it's not that. Robbie and I had a hassle about his infrequent phone calls." Carla lied.

"Well, I'm here if you ever want to talk about your problems." Kitty's wry look indicated she took Carla's lame explanation to be a crock, same as Timmy's smirk meant he doubted her cockamamie mouse story.

Carla's face brightened. "Actually, I do have a problem. My father's birthday is next week and I want to send him a bottle of cologne, but I don't know what's good. My ex bought any cologne that came with a free give-away, so sometimes he smelled good and sometimes he smelled like a dead skunk. What does Charlie wear?" She hoped Kitty believed her thin story, for that's the best she could think of to get the conversation around to men's scents.

"Charlie doesn't wear cologne. He says smells get in the way of thought transmissions from his clients. First thing he does when he arrives at his office is take another shower and change his clothes. He does it to get rid of the smell of anything he may have picked up on his way from our apartment to his town house where he has his office." Kitty's answer knocked Charlie off the list of suspects.

"But if you want something good, get your father a bottle of Russian Leather," Kitty continued. "That's what my dear late husband Julius Silverberg wore. It's so elegant. When Charlie was in the circus, he wore Old Spice. It covered up the smell of sweat real good. It's a classic, you know. Old guys like the stuff."

"Charlie, in the circus? Did he impersonate a thin man?" Carla broke in.

Kitty's hand flew to her hefty bosom in a pose of wounded pride. "That's not kind, Carla. Circusing is in his blood. He comes from an old circus family. Did you ever hear of The Flying Fergusons?" Carla shook her head from side to side. "Well, that's them. The rest of the Ferguson family called his father the black sheep of the family, because he left the life to become a doctor. But he allowed Charlie to perform with them every summer till he went to college. They made him a catcher."

"They had a baseball act?"

Kitty took a sip of coffee before she replied. "Jeez, Carla, no, the Flying Fergusons had a trapeze act. They were real famous in their day. Charlie swung out to catch the other guy when he came flying high across the ring. He had wrists of steel and was nimble as cat. And he hasn't lost much of his old ways," Kitty added proudly.

So, thin fragile Charlie Blumenfaux has strong wrists, but where they strong enough to strangle Aldyn? Carla mentally put his name back on her list of suspects. "Then why is Charlie's last name Blumenfaux, instead of Ferguson?" she asked logically.

A gravely laugh rumbled in Kitty's chest. "That's Charlie's joke on his father. You see, after his papa became rich, he looked down his nose at his relatives. Nearly busted a gut when Charlie said he wanted to give up medical school to go into the family business. They had a terrible row and Charlie accused his father of being a bloomin' fake. Then he set out on his own and changed his last name to Blumenfaux. Don't you get it? The joke? Blumenfaux, bloomin' fake."

"I get it. But how did Charlie become the Seer to the Stars?" Carla had been curious about Charlie's unique talent, but until now she hadn't found the appropriate time to question Kitty about the subject.

"You have to hand it to my Charlie. He's a real hustler." Kitty leaned back in her chair, ready to take Carla down the winding road that carried her husband from a circus "catcher" to be the world-famous Seer to the Stars. "Charlie only joined the circus to get out of medical school. See, he hated sick people, especially the ones who died on him. He took it real personal. You know what I mean?" Kitty stared at Carla over the top of her Sixty is Sexy coffee mug.

"He stayed with the circus maybe a year, then shoved off for a string of odd ball jobs. He sold vitamins door-to-door, next he became a non-denominational minister then he got a job as a masseur. And man, oh man, can he give a good back rub."

"But how did he get to be a seer?" Carla prodded her back to her story.

Kitty swallowed a piece of apple muffin before she continued. "Let me see if I remember the whole story. One day just for fun he went to a psychic convention up on Cape Cod, think it was in Provincetown, and right then and there he decided to give the seer game a try."

"But he didn't have any experience." Carla pointed out the obvious.

"Not exactly true, kiddo. He inherited the gift of gab from his Grandpa Ferguson and second sight from his mother. Born in New Orleans, you know," Kitty added as though her birthplace explained her talent.

"And how did he become so famous?" Carla loved stories about people who became rich and famous through an odd talent or quirky invention. It renewed her faith in the little man's ability to rise above corporate America.

As Kitty screwed up her face to consider the question, Carla saw the startling resemblance to between her and her faithful little Shih Tzu, who sat by her feet waiting for a crumb to fall into his open mouth. They each had a turned up button nose set in the middle of a tiny face, large soulful eyes—blue for Kitty, black for Tootie—and a large mop of light colored hair pulled up into an unruly topknot.

"Remember Joley Barker?" Kitty said.

"You mean the famous comedian who died from food poisoning?" Carla played straight man for Kitty.

"You got it. He came to Charlie for a reading, but when Charlie told him not to eat meat loaf, Joley laughed in his face. The next day, just for spite, he had meat loaf for dinner. Twelve hours later he was dead. Thanks to a couple of anonymous phone calls to the local papers and TV news programs, the story spread like a fire storm and zip everybody wanted a reading from Charlie. So you might say that the end of Joley Barker marked the beginning of Charlie's career as Seer to the Star. Now it's time to go to work." Kitty and Carla finished the last of their breakfast seconds before the first app opened the office door.

After the influx of lunch hour apps thinned to a trickle, Carla announced, "Be back in an hour. I'm going to see my friend Jack Demmer—you know, Monsieur Jacques, the furrier. He's having a summer sale, and I thought I might pick up a cheap shearling jacket." Monsieur Jacques' pre-winter sale ended a month ago, and even if he had kept the sale going, Carla had no need for a shearling jacket. She'd concocted the story to explain her absence while she interviewed Jack.

Kitty slowly scratched Tootie's ears as she considered Carla's story. "He's the jerk on television, the guy at your party, right? Why did you go out with him?"

"Come on, Kitty. I told you that our mothers are best friends. He's been divorced for years. I ran into him right after my divorce, and he asked me out. We had a couple of dates, but we didn't click." Carla lowered her eyes. She didn't want to talk about their dinner at Le Zen Auberge, a grungy Chelsea bistro that served food high in fiber, low in fat and very low in taste. She also preferred to forget his hour-long sermon on the dietary importance of fiber.

Chapter 14

Carla eyed the gold "Monsieur Jacques" signature scrawled across the thick glass double doors that opened into Jackie Demmer's Fifth Avenue fur salon. *Crass and tasteless, same as the real Jackie,* she decided. A light tap on the pressure sensitive brass door handle and the doors swooshed open.

"Hi, Jack!" Carla waved her hand at the tall, handsome Richard Gere clone surrounded by a bevy of adoring female customers.

Jack Demmer's good looks didn't come easy or cheap. A daily personal trainer and strict vegan diet kept him slim and trim. All his teeth had Hollywood caps—far superior to New York caps—he had explained to Carla, although she couldn't see the difference. Lasik surgery gave him 20-20 vision and tinted non-corrective contact lenses transformed his watery hazel eyes into piercing black orbs. A famous plastic surgeon held his sags and wrinkles at bay, while an equally famous unisex hair salon dyed and straightened his curly salt and pepper hair.

What a shame he's such a jerk, Carla thought as Mr. Wonderful rushed toward her with a fake smile plastered on his Clarins self-tanned face.

"Car, *mon cherie, mon amie*, how are you?" Monsieur Jacques discreetly untangled a customer's caressing fingers from his Brioni black cashmere blazer.

"I'm fine Jacques, Jack, I'm just fine." Swept up into Jack's Gallic performance, Carla automatically raised her right hand when he bent forward to kiss it. *I can't believe I did that. I'm as loony as he.* She pulled back her hand but not before she allowed him to kiss it.

"I'm zo 'appy to zee you zo zoon. A *tres charmont fete* you gave. Let me zhow you haround. You haven't been here zinze we redecorated." The Fur Baron's compound fractured French accent was known and loved by millions of viewers of a home shopping channel.

Jack propelled Carla through an ankle-deep sea of dove gray carpeting into the semi-circular main showroom where he twirled her around to give her a swirling view of an undulating wall of coats that would send shivers down the spine of the entire PETRA membership. The furs blended gradually from pure white through the spectrum of beiges, grays, browns, inky black, and finally exploded into a rainbow of bright colors.

"*C'est merveilleux, n'est ce pas?*" Jack's high school French equaled his fake accent. "A ribbon of *fourre*! Let me zow you what I have *por toi.* Louise, *por madame.*" He pointed to a spot in the furry wall. "Try it on." Jack wrapped Carla in a sensuously silky fox coat. His arms reached around her to allow him to gently stroke the front of the coat. Each time he caressed the sensuous skins, his hands slithered farther down her body. "It's *Le Cristal Renard*, crystal fox. Zee ze pale apricot underhairs, *c'est toi,*" he whispered in her ear.

"Oh, I don't think so. No!" Carla stripped off the coat. "I don't need another fur coat." *And I certainly don't need his grubby hands all over me.*

Jack shook the coat till it shimmered like water sparkling in a pristine stream.

"Well, maybe just for a second." Carla succumbed to the temptation and allowed him to drape the coat on her shoulders. Carla swore the coat called out "CARR-LAH, OH, CARR-LAH". She resisted. "It's gorgeous, but I can't afford it." She sighed wistfully when she caught her reflection in the triple mirror. "I've got bills to pay and a mortgage on my co-op and..."

"*Pour toi, ma amie*, I give it to you."

"No, Jack, I can't accept it. I absolutely refuse to let you give me the coat."

"Car, don't be a lulu, not 'give' like in 'give it away'." Jacques' French accent disappeared. "If you walked in off the street, the coat would cost you a fast fourteen thousand bucks, plus sales tax, but for you, my childhood friend, the daughter of my mother's best friend, it's a steal—eight thou nine ninety-nine and it's yours, no tax. How's that for a deal? I gave your friend Aldyn Sheridan the same deal."

Carla spun around. The coat fell to the floor. "You knew Aldyn before my party?"

"Of course, Aldyn plays the field, I play the field. It's a small world. We've shared more than one bottle of vino. Though, I gotta tell you I got the surprise of my life when I saw her at your party. Didn't think she'd be your type. A little too common, if you get my drift. Now would you take your nails out of my arm. You're drawing blood."

"Oh, I'm sorry, Jack. Aldyn sold me my apartment and..."

"That bitch sold me my place two years ago," Jack interrupted. "That's when our sometimes relationship turned nasty. The winter that year was real bad—frigid temperature, lots of snow and sleet—every lady and half the men in New York wanted a fur coat. I had more business than I could handle, so like a fool, I made the mistake of taking her up on her oh so friendly offer to deliver my financials to the mortgage broker. How could I know that she'd memorize the whole kit and caboodle? She's better than the IRS when it comes to sniffing out phony figures. Not that I'm a thief.

Hell, everybody cheats a little on their taxes. Anyway, she's been…" Sparks of anger glowed behind Jack's coal black lenses.

Jack's confession of his less than loving relationship with Aldyn laid two bombshells in Carla's lap. On the one hand, it backed up her theory that Aldyn's shady activities could have earned her a lot of enemies. On the other hand, it gave Jack Demmer, the son of her mother's best friend and the creep who tried to play doctor with eight-year old Carla, an excellent motive to kill Aldyn.

"So how about the coat, Car?" he pleaded. "Come on, you can afford it. I heard you got one hell of a settlement from your ex. Be a sport, buy the coat." Jack snatched the fox from the floor and tenderly cradled it in his arms like a baby.

"I don't want the damn coat. This is what you've done since we were kids." Carla's voice raised a couple of decibels above a normal conversational level.

"Done what? What have I done, and please lower you voice. I don't want my customers to think that I made a pass at you." Jack's handsome face crumpled into the pout he used to melt the resistance of his toughest customers.

"Come on, Jack, admit it. You just want to manipulate me into doing something I don't want to do."

"And what's wrong if I give you a good deal on a coat?"

"I didn't come here to buy a coat," Carla snapped.

"So you don't want the coat? Okay, no big deal. How about a jacket? I could give you a great buy on a tanuki jacket."

"No, Jack. Listen to me. I don't have much time. I've got to get back to the office, but I need your advice. What I want to know is…"

Jackie's eyebrows knotted together into one black dash on his forehead. "Just a sec, Car." He beckoned to his assistant. "Louise, return this *magnifique manteau de fourrure* to its place. Obviously, Madame is not the woman of quality I believed her to be. His eyes followed the coat until Louise hung it safely back in its proper spot. "So what is it you want to know?" What the hell, if Jackie couldn't sell her a coat, he'd listen to her problem. Maybe she'd ask him to dinner.

Carla sniffed the air. She couldn't pick up the scent of cologne or any other odor coming from Jack's direction. "What cologne do you wear?" She had decided to tell all her suspects basically the same crazy cologne story that she used with Kitty.

"Cologne? You came here to ask me about cologne?"

"Well, sort of, you see Bunny, my sister-in-law…" Carla neglected to specify which Roman numeral Bunny she meant "…invited me to Harold's birthday party. I thought I'd buy him an 'in' cologne and since you're so trendy, I came to you for a suggestion." Carla cringed at her words. What if he didn't believe her story? She'd die rather than have him think she came here to inveigle him, heaven forbid, into asking her out again.

"Boy, you really do have your head in the clouds, Car. Didn't you ever notice that I don't wear cologne? I hate it. It's not, you know, masculine. Sorry, can't help you." Jack adjusted the knot in his one hundred and ninety dollar Hermes tie.

"You don't wear cologne? Not even a little spray of something now and then?"

"Nothing. And I mean it, nothing. Now, come on, how about trying on the coat one more time. Believe me, you put it on again, you're sold."

Carla ran out of the store. She continued to run up Fifth Avenue to 48th Street, then around the corner to Madison Avenue and into the welcoming arms of Career Steps—The Agency with a Heart. She kept half a dozen apps waiting while she called Ellswood & Daugherty, the real estate firm where Aldyn worked. "Miss Sheridan's line," perky Betsy Rider answered.

"Betsy, it's Carla Miller. Can I speak with Aldyn?" she panted, still out of breath from her sprint.

"Oh, hi, Mrs. Miller. Don't you know she's on vacation for two weeks?"

"Oh, I forgot. Did she leave a number where she can be reached?"

"No, but she keeps in touch whenever she's away. I'll tell her to call you the minute I hear from her, and I sure hope she calls soon because she's in trouble."

Carla knocked a file off her desk. "What's wrong? What did she do?"

"Well, Mr. Daugherty is very strict about clients' apartment keys. They have to be returned to the office no matter how late in the day the agent finishes showing the apartment. Some agents, and especially Miss Sheridan, are pissed about the rule. They hate to come back to the office just to return a set of keys, but they dare not do it because Mr. Daugherty checks the key box at odd hours. I heard he came in last Christmas Eve to make sure all the keys had been returned."

"You mean Aldyn didn't return a set of keys?"

"You got it. She left on vacation on Friday without returning the keys for the apartment in your building and for 15E at 653 East 55th Street. The owner of the 55th Street apartment is in Europe for six months and Aldyn took the only key we have. Mr. Daugherty is so mad he can hardly talk. He says he'll kill her the minute he finds her."

Chapter 15

Life was good. Tony had returned to New York a day early and would be at her apartment in less than an hour.

Carla hummed a happy tune as she brushed her teeth. She used a fast circular motion that ringed her mouth with toothpaste foam—she called it her rabid animal look. Brush, brush, hum, hum, brush, brush, hum… She stopped in mid-brush. *Did the front door just close?* She cocked her head to the side to catch another sound, but only heard silence. *It must have been my neighbor opening her door*, she reassured herself and resumed her brush, brush, hum, hum routine. A moment later she stopped again. She positively heard a floorboard creak in the uncarpeted hall between the bedroom and the bathroom.

Carla jabbed her toothbrush back into its holder. She slid open the medicine cabinet and wrapped her hand around a long, sharp metal nail file. She raised her weapon overhead and lunged through the doorway. Strong arms grabbed her. A warm mouth urgently sought hers. A husky voice whispered, "Hi, gorgeous."

Carla battled her way out of the tight grip. "Never mind the compliments. How did you get in? I thought you were a burglar. I could have killed you," she shrieked.

"I know, but you look great." Tony's appraising gaze took in her glowing makeup-free face and the hint of cleavage revealed under her white terry robe.

"Don't try to change the subject. How did you get into my apartment?"

He flashed the lopsided smile that never failed to make Carla feel weak in the knees. "I rang the bell a couple of times, but you didn't answer so I opened the door." He lowered his head to kiss a dollop of toothpaste foam from the corner of her mouth.

"Opened the door? How could you? You don't have a key." Carla firmly knotted the belt on her robe. "And why didn't the doorman announce you?"

"What doorman? I didn't see a doorman in the lobby." He shrugged. "You know, for a first class building, the security stinks."

"Don't change the subject. How did you open the door?" Once more doubts about her relationship with Tony buzzed about in Carla's head. Should she be happy to see him, or be angry with him because he broke into her apartment? How could she be so strongly attracted to such a secretive man? Did she take up with a murderer because she was a lonely single woman, just as Mimi suggested?

"I did it with a credit card."

"With a what?" Carla glared at him. "Where did you learn that trick?"

All the while Carla and Tony bickered back and forth Carla slowly nudged him away from the temptation of her bedroom and toward the safety of the living room.

"It's no big deal. My cousin Louie the Burglar showed me how to do it as a thirteenth birthday present." Tony's dark eyes sparkled with humor.

"You're teasing me. I remember now. I left the door unlocked when I threw out the garbage." Carla did not explain that ever since she discovered Aldyn's body in the trash room on her floor, she took her garbage to the floor below her.

"Garbage? What garbage do you have? You don't cook." Tony's laughter firmly closed the question of the open door. "How about if I make dinner and you do what you do best—make me one of your great vodka martinis."

"You're a male chauvinist," Carla snarled, then switched to her throaty voice. "Don't go away. I'll be right back."

When she returned to the living room she wore tight stone washed jeans, a white shirt and denim suede ballet slippers. A light dusting of blush accented her high cheekbones. She headed straight to the bar to mix her famous classic vodka martini. She learned her martini making skills from Harold around the same time he taught her how to smoke a cigar. She never put her cigar smoking knowledge to use, but from time to time she did mix a mean martini. First she tossed a handful of ice cubes into a martini shaker then she added a generous splash of Ketel One vodka with just the tiniest smidge of vermouth. Next she shook the shaker until the ice cubes made a bing sound instead of a ting, which meant that they were round and the time had come to pour the delicious mixture into chilled Waterford martini glasses. She decorated one glass with a lemon twist, the other with three olives on a spear.

The martini with the lemon twist remained in the living room; the three-olive drink went to Tony in the kitchen. Carla kept out of his way when he cooked. He enjoyed cooking on the nights when they stayed home; at least he said he did. Carla guessed that a sense of survival would be closer to the truth, since he didn't like her dry fish or overdone steak or watery stew.

"Where's the flour?" Tony called.

"The what? What do you want?" Carla lowered the volume on the television set before she rushed toward the kitchen.

"Don't put a foot in this kitchen. I mean it, Carla, stay out of the kitchen. You could get into trouble." Tony swatted a linen towel around to keep her away.

Carla's eyes flashed. That word "trouble" popped up again. First Mimi told her that she could get into trouble and now Tony said it. Why did everyone warn her about getting into trouble?

"It's a disaster whenever you come in here, so stay out." Tony blocked her path like a quarterback defending his territory; that is if a quarterback would be caught dead wearing a black and white striped chef's apron.

"Don't be silly, Tony, let me in. I want to help."

"Are you crazy? The last time you tried to help, you upset an open box of rice and when you turned around to mop it up, you knocked over the olive oil. So stay out of my kitchen, lady. But before you go, tell me what happened to the sack of flour I put in the refrigerator."

"Nothing happened to it. I needed more space on the shelf, so I combined the little bit left in the bag with the flour in the plastic container. That's why you can't find the flour. It's all mixed together." Carla's smile suggested pride in her domestic ingenuity.

"No, you didn't! But, yes, you did." Tony sputtered like a dying firecracker while Carla's head bobbed up and down in affirmation of her deed. His hand landed on his furrowed brow with a loud thwack sound. "How can such a beautiful woman be such a klutz in the kitchen?"

"What did I do? What's so terrible?" Carla hunched her shoulders. She wondered why Tony didn't show any appreciation for her help. "I only wanted to make room in the refrigerator. You know, Tony, you keep too many leftovers. They clutter up the shelves. Throw out what we don't eat."

"That's wasteful!" he shouted.

Tony believed, with what Carla termed "religious fervor", that God decreed every morsel of uneaten food must be embalmed in a grubby old scrap of recycled aluminum foil and stored in the refrigerator until it grew a healthy green mold before it could be deep sixed in the garbage can.

"Did you look in the plastic container? Did you smell it with your cute nose? Did you notice that it didn't look or smell like flour?" Tony asked.

"The flour did look odd, kind of yellowish. I thought it changed color as it aged. No, they weren't both flour?" The strange gurgling sound, halfway between a sigh and a groan that came from Tony's throat told Carla she had erred.

"They weren't both flour." He definitely groaned. "You mixed forty-five cent a pound flour with hand-grated Locatelli Romano cheese that costs thirteen dollars a pound. So now, my sweet, the whole mess goes in the garbage, and I think I will kill you." He kept his voice under control, yet as he slowly came toward her he looked like the King of the Jungle stalking a defenseless gnu.

"I am sorry about the cheese, really I am, but you have to admit that finely grated cheese and flour do look a little alike."

In an attempt to distract Tony from the damn flour and cheese fiasco, Carla pulled his head close to her and kissed his soft lower lip, nuzzled his neck and sniffed his collar. "Mmm, you smell wonderful. What cologne are you wearing tonight?" she asked, switching back into her detective role. "I may get some for myself."

"Eau de Chinese Laundry Starch. I don't wear cologne. Now, get out of here," Tony ordered. "Go back in the living room. Watch the news, call a friend, do anything but stay out of the kitchen."

"I don't want to talk to anyone and the local news is boring."

Carla stalked off to the living room. To prove her assessment of the evening news, she clicked on the television set in time to hear Cliff Stamford, the platinum blond local newscaster whose electric blue eyes seduced thousands of women nightly, report, "*A Police Department spokesperson announced that the robbery is attributed to the daring East Side Cat Burglar, who has plagued the posh Sutton Place area for the past two years. No signs of forcible entry have been found and the burglar appears to be an expert safe cracker. All the victims discovered their losses after returning home from extended trips, making it difficult for the police to fix the exact date of each crime. An eight-carat Harry Winston diamond ring is part of the latest haul.*"

"Oh, my." Carla ran up to the TV screen to get a closer look at the photo of the diamond ring that flashed on the screen. It looked exactly like the ring she found in her kitchen air vent.

"What did you say?" Tony asked. He stood so close to her that his warm breath tickled her neck, yet she had not heard him walk into the room.

"The ring, it's gorgeous, isn't it?" she replied to cover her excitement. "Why did Cliff call the burglar a 'cat burglar'?" Carla noticed that Tony intently watched the television screen.

"Because a cat burglar has a precise way of operating. He usually enters the premises through a window or a terrace, sometimes he leaps down from a high place like a cat, which explains his name. He's a whiz at opening locks and safes and bypassing security systems. The guy is only interested in light stuff like jewels and cash—nothing heavy that could hamper his escape. And he doesn't use violence, that's why he prefers empty houses and apartments. He's a class act. You might call him the Rolls Royce of the burglary profession."

"Why do you say 'he'? Can't a cat burglar be a woman?"

"Guess so, though I never heard of a woman cat burglar. Shoplifting, drug related crimes, or murder is more their line." Tony gave Carla a devilish wink.

"And did your cousin Louie the Burglar also teach you everything you know about cat burglars?"

"Sure."

"Come on, Tony, I'm serious and you're teasing. If you know so much about the subject, then tell me how a cat burglar gets rid of his loot?"

"Through a fence, of course, who pays him about ten cents on the dollar. He sure as hell doesn't sell the stuff on a street corner." Tony sipped his martini all the while he explained the M.O. of a cat burglar.

"Would he store the things somewhere before he sells them to the fence?" Carla asked. An idea formed in her mind.

"Maybe, but why the sudden interest in cat burglars?"

"Nothing, I'm just curious. Really, how do you know so much about them?" Carla threw the ball back into Tony's court.

"Okay. I confess. Cousin Louie didn't know squat about cat burglars. I helped my son write his college psych research paper on specialty criminals and some of the facts stuck in my head. My wife used to say that I never forgot anything," he added with a shrug.

There it was, at last—the opening Carla had been waiting for.

"Your wife, is she…"

The shrill ring of the telephone announced the time more accurately than a digital clock, precisely six twenty-five p.m. Carla put down her drink and ran into the kitchen to answer the phone.

"Hello, Mother. Hold it a second." She turned to Tony, who had followed her from the living room. "It's my mother." Her hand covered the phone's mouthpiece. "She calls every Friday at this time from West

Palm Beach. I'll call her back."

"No, talk to her. I'll watch the news." Tony retraced his steps to the living room.

"Mother, I'm back. How are you and Dad?" Carla held her cordless phone to her ear and paced around her tiny kitchen.

"Well *tut* dear, I got it." Mrs. Weinstein assumed that the world understood her fragmented manner of speaking. Maybe the whole world didn't understand her, but her family did. They also understood why she had become a Norma Day Cosmetic and Jewelry Consultant—Rose Weinstein coveted the Inferno Red PT Cruiser that the company awards to the saleswomen who top their sales quotas for four consecutive years.

"Oh, Mother that's wonderful. You've worked so hard for the car. You'll love it." Actually, Carla doubted that Mrs. Weinstein sold enough make-up and jewelry at house parties in her over 55-community to qualify for the car. She suspected that her seventy-eight year old mother bought the stuff herself.

"It's nice," her mother said without enthusiasm.

"Nice? It's more than nice." At that moment it occurred to Carla that you can't trust your parents. Just when you think you know what will make them happy, they change the rules on you. "I'd love to win a red PT Cruiser, but you don't sound happy with yours. Are you sick? Is Dad's arthritis worse? What's the matter?"

"It's not red." Another *tut* punctuated Mrs. Weinstein's response.

"Not red?"

"No, the car isn't red. The model I won doesn't come in red anymore and you know how much I wanted a red car. It goes so well with my coloring."

"Well, what color is it, Mother?"

"Gold. I know that I can't have everything I want, but I was so looking forward to red." Mrs. Weinstein's voice faded farther and farther away with each sad word.

"Snap out of it, Mother. It's not the end of world. There must be a million ladies in Florida who would love a free gold car."

"And speaking of free, dear," Mrs. Weinstein's voice miraculously became strong as a basso's. "I just had a phone call from Jessie Demmer. She told me that you refused the absolutely free beautiful fur coat Jackie offered you. Now dear, it isn't nice to refuse a present from my best friend's son." Carla heard a loud *tut*.

"He didn't give me a present, Mother," she snapped. "He offered to sell me a fourteen thousand dollar coat for eight thousand nine hundred and ninety-nine dollars. Jackie may have told Mrs. Demmer that he offered to give it to me free, but you know that with him, nothing is free." Carla lowered her voice so Tony couldn't hear her conversation with her mother. Talk of cars and fur coats might give him the wrong idea about her family's values.

"He's trying to be nice, dear. He feels so bad about your divorce."

"That's ridiculous. Why should he feel anything about my divorce?"

"Because he's a nice person. Now, you call Jackie and tell him that you'd love the coat but could he make it a little cheaper. I'm sure he'll do that and then you'll be happy and he'll be happy because he gave you the coat."

"I'll think about it, Mother." Those five non-committal words were Carla's way of avoiding squabbles with her mother. She hadn't said "yes," yet her mother would believe that she had won her point and would never bring up the subject again.

"Good, you'll love the coat." A definite triumphal tone filled Mrs. Weinstein's voice. "It's so nice talking to you. I feel much better about the car. And, you know, I'll have to buy some gold jewelry because my silver jewelry just won't do with that car. Isn't that nice? Bye, dear."

Click.

"Now, where were we?" Carla hurried back into the living room, ready to resume her conversation with Tony about his wife. But it wasn't to be. Tony lay fast asleep on the couch.

When Carla woke him from his peaceful nap, he'd lost his desire to cook. Twenty minutes later they sat side-by-side at Bo Lee, the beautiful Lexington Avenue restaurant reputed to serve the best Chinese food in all Manhattan. Except for praising the food, Carla and Tony abstained from conversation while they devoured platters of spring rolls, dumplings, sesame chicken, crispy hot beef and fried rice.

"You first." Tony pointed to the fortune cookies that appeared with their second pot of tea.

You will have many children. Carla giggled at the far fetched message. Instead of tossing the tiny paper onto the white linen tablecloth, she slipped it into her pocket. "Now it's your turn."

Tony put on a pair of half glasses to read, *You will live for one hundred years.* "And we should leave," he said in the same breath. "I have a seven a.m. appointment tomorrow.

"On Saturday?"

"I know, but this is a big client and I'm available whenever he wants to see me, no matter the time or the day." The similarity between his work ethic and Aldyn's did not escape Carla.

She gave Tony a chaste good night kiss outside her apartment building. After she'd double locked her door, she took the paper from her pocket and reread her fortune—*Remain silent and answers will come to you.*

Chapter 16

Saturday dawned a beautiful early autumn day—temperature in the low seventies, non-existent humidity, and huge fluffy white clouds punctuated the bright cobalt blue sky. After a hasty breakfast, Carla set out to attend to the chores that she didn't have time to do during the week. She got a manicure and a pedicure, had her hair cut, picked up some grocery staples plus a Greek salad at Food Emporium and browsed through Bed Bath and Beyond. Mid-afternoon found her on her terrace devouring the *New York Post* and the salad. Suddenly, she dropped the newspaper. *Holy cow, what a dope I am. The answer is in the newspapers.* Seconds later she dashed out of the apartment.

The 42nd Street cross-town bus left Carla off across the street from the two-block square New York Public Library, or more specifically the Humanities and Social Sciences Library. She bounded up the broad-terraced steps that lead to the magnificent Beaux Arts building without so much as a glance at the famous marble lions that guard the entrance to the library. Christened "Patience" and "Fortitude" during the 1930s by Mayor Fiorello LaGuardia, the lions are beloved by all New Yorkers. And, like most Big Apple residents, they have an extensive wardrobe—holly wreaths for the Christmas season, floral wreaths in springtime, graduation caps in May and the appropriate baseball caps whenever a New York team wins a world series.

This should be a snap, Carla thought after she explained her mission to the security guard who directed her to the Microforms Reading Room. But the young woman at the In-Desk became the bearer of bad news after Carla again explained that she wanted to read all the *Post* and *Daily News* accounts of the East Side Cat Burglar's exploits. Carla had decided against scanning the *Times* because the gossipy tabloids were sure to give more space to the daring burglar's adventures than the august Gray Lady.

"If you don't know the dates of the robberies, you've got yourself a problem. You're gonna need to scan all the microfilm copies of the papers." The librarian's weak smile indicated that Carla had a long job ahead of her.

Carla cut her search time considerably by following the librarian's suggestion that she read only the papers for the past two years and skip the sports, entertainment and classified sections. By the time she'd absorbed every fact reported about the East Side Cat Burglar, she became convinced that she knew more than the police. They knew that all the victims were on extended trips when the burglar struck, that the burglar entered their apartments through terraces or fire escapes, that the burglar bypassed alarms and only took jewels or cash. What they didn't know was that every robbery occurred within a tight three-block radius of Carla's apartment!

Lucky those people were out of town, she thought. *It would be awful to return home after an evening out and discover a cat burglar in your apartment.* The chilling vision of coming face-to-face with a burglar set off an alarm bell in Carla's head. She called back up on the screen a clipping dated December twenty-ninth of last year, and reread a key sentence: *"Mrs. Edward Dollard discovered her loss last night when she returned from a four-week Mediterranean cruise."*

A hurried request to the librarian brought her the *New York Times* reel of microfilm that included the entire month of December. The *Post* and *Daily News* went after the sensational news, but the *Times* had the most thorough obituary column. Carla scanned the daily death notices until she found the one she sought.

Victor Reynolds, 66, Law Partner

Victor Reynolds, partner in the New York City law firm Melrose Cavendish Reynolds & Lee, has died. He resided in Manhattan as well as in Naples, Florida. At the time of his death at 66 years, Mr. Reynolds held the position of the managing partner of the firm's Naples office.

According to a family spokesperson, he died of head injuries sustained in his Manhattan apartment. It is believed that he died approximately a week prior to the discovery of his body on Decembery 16th.

There it was—the connection she sought. Victor Reynolds died on or about December ninth, smack in the middle of Mrs. Dollard's cruise. Carla felt in her bones that his death wasn't an accident. She believed he returned to his apartment ahead of schedule and discovered the cat burglar stashing Mrs. Dollard's jewels in the kitchen air vent. Maybe Reynolds recognized him, maybe not, but in either case the burglar killed him. She puzzled over how the burglar knew his victims' travel schedules.

Carla wrote her deductions in a small note pad before she continued reading the obituary: *"Born in Manhattan as Vitorio Ricci, Mr. Reynolds later changed his name."*

The name "Vitorio Ricci" jumped out at her. Tony told her that his daughter used his wife's maiden name, Ricci, as her professional last name. Carla wondered if he and Reynolds were related, but quickly dismissed the theory. *Ricci is a fairly common surname,* she reassured herself, although the only Ricci she could think of was fashion designer Nina Ricci, who created L'Air du Temps perfume. That damn perfume connection again! The remainder of Reynolds' obituary detailed the dry facts about his education, failed marriages and survivors—Mrs. Henderson, who sold her the apartment plus three grandchildren.

Carla massaged the back of her neck to work out the kinks before she left the library. When she'd run up the broad steps of the building, shoppers and tourists crowded sunlit Fifth Avenue. Now in the gathering dusk, a thinning crowd scurried along the shadowed avenue that to Carla appeared like a menacing canyon of towering buildings where feral cats lurked in every deserted doorway.

Chapter 17

"Taxi!" Carla waved her hand frantically in front of a battered yellow sedan. Never mind that it was speeding downtown and she lived uptown. She had to get away from the menacing scene as fast as possible and she didn't much care in which direction she traveled.

"650 East 56th Street," she said. "No, take me to the corner of 54th and First."

An empty refrigerator propelled Carla to a neighborhood Italian restaurant that Kitty had heartily recommended for making the thinnest and best pizzas in the world. She would order a take-out mushroom pizza; eat half tonight and freeze the rest for later. Throughout her married life Carla fantasized about going to restaurants alone where she'd order her favorite dishes without compromising her selections for what Larry the Louse, Robbie or Nancy wanted to eat. Now that she could do it, the fantasy had lost its appeal. She'd rather make do at home than face a maitre d' alone.

"Near or far corner, lady?"

"What?" Carla asked.

"West or east side of the street?"

Carla frowned. Near corner, far corner, west or east side of the street, it all puzzled her. To overcome her directional deficiency she wore a thin gold bracelet on her left wrist, so at least she always knew which way was left. Points on the compass remained a mystery.

"This is fine." Indicating the west side of 54th Street, she tossed some bills into the drop-down basket hinged to the plexiglass partition that separated her from the driver. These dividers, smudged with fingerprint and who knows what else, were installed in New York City cabs to protect cab drivers from robbers. They rarely worked. As far as Carla could determine, the dividers only made it difficult for drivers and passengers to communicate—which sometimes could be a good thing.

"Over here, honey," a familiar voice trumpeted across Rocco's Family Restaurant & Pizzeria.

Carla heard the clank of bracelets before she spotted Kitty. Although the restaurant had a large comfortable back dining room, the crowded area around the front bar where Kitty and Charlie sat was the desired spot for people watching. You never knew who might stop in, as evidenced by the collection of autographed celebrity pictures that hung over the bar, all inscribed "To my friend Rocco. Best wishes and thanks for a great dinner."

"Look who's here." Kitty leaned across the booth to poke Charlie in the chest with a blood red fingernail. "Join us for a couple of pizzas. We just arrived. We got up very early, so we're having an early dinner," Kitty said to explain why they were dining at the unfashionable hour of six p.m. In Manhattan, only theater tickets for an eight o'clock curtain justified setting foot in a restaurant before seven thirty.

"We didn't get the menu yet, only a basket of bread. Shove over Charlie and let Carla sit next to you," Kitty ordered. Her command seemed redundant, for no way could Carla squeeze in beside her. "I'd love to, if I'm not intruding." Carla tried not to sound too eager to join them, when, in fact, she wanted nothing more than to have their company for dinner.

"I'm delighted to be surrounded by such lovely companions. This reminds me of my days aboard ship." Charlie popped a bit of crusty Italian bread dipped in flavored olive oil into his mouth and chewed methodically before he continued, "Did I ever tell you of my experiences as a tarot card reader aboard cruise ships?"

"Yeah, yeah, Charlie, we all know where you've been. What I want to know is what Carla's been up to on this beautiful day. Something interesting, honey?" Kitty's lashes fluttered at Carla like a centipede waving hello.

"I went to Lord & Taylor to get a couple of outfits for the office." And to explain why she didn't have at least one of the store's trademark white shopping bag with the red lettering, she added, "But they didn't have what I wanted so I ran down there for nothing."

"Yeah, I hear running is great exercise. I must try it some day—only joking." Kitty chuckled. "Boy this sure has been a day for jokes, wasn't it, Charlie?" Charlie nodded between chews.

"What are you talking about?" Carla asked.

"Ever hear of the East Side Cat Burglar?"

"The who?" Carla choked on a piece of bread stick. "You know, the burglar who's been stealing everyone's jewels on Sutton Place. Well, Charlie and I think the little squirrel got into our apartment. Opened the safe easy as pie like he knew the combination, but I had the last laugh on him." Kitty whacked the edge of the table, catapulting knives and forks to the floor. "He must have been mad as hell when he found nothing in the safe, because he left the door wide open and the Matisse on the floor. You would have thought he'd put the picture back. It's a nice painting with lots of flowers and pretty colors and it hides the safe real well."

"Why do you have a safe, if nothing is in it?" Carla ignored Kitty's naïve description of her masterpiece. As she grew to know her better, Carla learned to take Kitty's quirks in stride.

"It's like this, after Julius had his big H.A…"

"What is a H.A.?" Carla interrupted.

"A fatal heart attack. Julius Silverberg, Kitty's third husband, suffered a fatal heart"—a 'big H.A.' as Kitty so picturesquely describes it," Charlie explained.

Kitty tapped the Seer to the Star's arm. "Let me tell my own story, dear. When darling Julius passed away, I inherited the Sutton Place apartment, his jewelry store on West 47th Street in the Diamond District plus the entire inventory. Since I didn't know anything about the jewelry business, his lawyer, he's my lawyer now, told me to sell the store and put whatever jewelry I wanted to keep in the wall safe that Julius installed in the apartment. I didn't tell him that I'm a little dyslexic. Get numbers screwed up or can't remember them at all, especially safe combinations…

"If the jewelry isn't in the safe, where…" Carla paused in mid-sentence to stare at the amazing collection of jewelry that adorned Kitty's neck, ears, fingers and wrists and the pair of diamond panther pins perched on her right shoulder. "Oh, my, all that stuff that you wear every day is real," Carla stuttered. One of Kitty's quirks finally got a reaction from Carla.

"You bet it's real." Kitty beamed at Carla to show her pleasure with the joke she played on the world. "Since I can't remember the combination to the safe, I made myself the safe. I wear most of the pieces all the time, and what's not out in the open is tucked away in a little bag that rests comfy cozy right between these babies." Kitty patted her cabbage-size boobs.

"But somebody could snatch everything from you," Carla said.

"No way. You and Charlie are the only people who know that my junk is real and even if a thief suspects the truth he'd never mess with a big broad like me, who has a voice louder than a bull horn." Kitty laughed till tears streaked her rouged cheeks.

Charlie remained silent during the exchange between the women, but finally blustered, "Kitty refused to report the incident to the police because nothing is missing and there is no evidence of forced entry. I think she made the wrong choice. It is her civic duty to apprise the police of what is going on in the neighborhood and request that they keep an eye on our apartment. It's empty from early in the morning until evening except, of course, when Kitty leaves Tootie at home, but he couldn't guard a mosquito."

Charlie snapped his menu shut in a flurry of righteous indignation, and Carla noticed the tremors in the hands that Kitty claimed to be rock solid.

"Two pizzas, please. One with mushrooms and extra cheese, the other with pepperoni and we'll have a carafe of red house wine." Charlie gave the order to the silent waitress who hovered beside the table.

Carla waited until the waitress disappeared into the kitchen before she replied, "Sorry, Charlie, but I agree with Kitty that without evidence of a break-in, the police won't take you seriously." Though she spoke from experience, Carla chose not to tell them about her encounters with Officers Ramirez and Murkowski.

"You're right, kiddo. I told Charlie that if we called the cops, we'd be stuck in the apartment for hours waiting for them to show up, then they'd search the place and dust for fingerprints and in the end, they'd find nothing. So instead, I had a locksmith install a fancy four hundred dollar French lock. That should be the end of it, don't you think?" Kitty stared quizzically at Carla.

"Let's hope so. I don't think burglars return to the scene of their crimes." Carla knew her statement wasn't true, but she doubted that the cat burglar would make another no profit visit to Kitty's apartment.

"Dee-li-cious! A feast fit for the gods," Charlie changed the subject from the burglary to the bubbling hot pizzas placed before them. "I am extremely pleased to see you again, Carla. Kitty and I enjoyed ourselves immensely at your lovely party. I was hesitant at first to attend—I am very shy, though I cover it quite well." Charlie's precise way of speaking amused Carla. She suspected he put it on for his fancy clients to make him appear very ethereal.

"Charlie shy? No way." Kitty winked at Carla.

"I am, my dear, with strangers, but, happily, that day I found myself surrounded by familiar faces."

"We have friends in common?" Carla asked between chomps.

"Not exactly friends. But two of your illustrious friends are my clients." Charlie neatly cut a slice of pizza into small pieces and proceeded to eat them with a knife and fork.

"Who?" Carla couldn't imagine her friends using Charlie's services, famous though he may be.

"My lips are sealed. The Seers' Code of Ethics, you know," he said emphatically. In response to her quizzical look, he added, "Oh yes, we seers do have a code of ethics, the same as doctors and lawyers, which forbids us from bandying about the names of our clients."

The longer Carla observed Charlie, the more convinced she became that she should trust her instincts and disregard Mimi's warning. Charlie Blumenfaux might be weird, but he didn't kill Aldyn.

"Please, Charlie, tell me who you know. It's very important." Carla drained her wine glass then added softly, "My life could depend on it."

"What?" Kitty and Charlie asked in one voice.

Carla shifted her body a quarter turn to face them. "What would you say if I told you that I found Aldyn Sheridan's body in my trash room and jewels in my air vent and then they disappeared and I think there's a ghost in the apartment that makes me sneeze?" She willed herself to keep her voice under control.

Kitty laid aside her crust of pizza. "You drinking or doing drugs? There's no such thing as ghosts and no one dumps bodies in buildings on the Upper East Side, especially on Sutton Place. Sure, maybe up in the Bronx or down in the Bowery, but not in our neighborhood. Maybe you better explain."

"...and I think someone wanted to keep Aldyn from telling me..." Carla related her suspicions about the cat burglar, but stopped short of revealing her plan to find him. Smelling men could be too outlandish even for these two eccentrics.

"If you want my advice, the first thing you should do is figure out what is going on in your apartment. Too bad I didn't keep up with my mob connections. They could help," Kitty said casually.

"You in the mob?" Carla asked.

"She did..." A glare from Kitty silenced Charlie.

"Not IN the mob. I used to know some of the boys when I danced in their joints in Chicago."

Another surprise for Carla. Kitty never mentioned her dancing career before.

"I haven't danced in fifty years or more, so I guess they're all either dead, in jail or retired back in Sicily." Kitty's face sagged.

"It would be hard to track them down after such a long time, but thanks for the offer. Anyway, I think Charlie can be more helpful than your friends." Carla turned toward him. "Won't you at least tell me if you ever did a reading for Aldyn?" she pleaded.

"No, my dear, I cannot."

Carla pushed aside the slice of pizza that Kitty had plopped on her plate. Her appetite had evaporated.

"Come on, honey, tell Carla what you know. This is a matter of life and death," the seer's beloved commanded.

Charlie's rheumy eyes darted nervously around the crowded restaurant. "Swear on your word of honor that this will go no further," he demanded.

Carla took the most solmen oath she could think of. "I swear on Bonkers' grave that I won't tell a living soul."

"Who is Bonkers?"

"For cripes sake Charlie, it's her dead dog—a West Highland Terrier. Now tell her, already."

"Well, since Kitty is so fond of you, I will admit that I did see Aldyn Sheridan on a professional basis. A rather a strange lady." Charlie's mass of white hair bobbed from side to side in disapproval. "She visited me three or four times a year for nearly five years, then she vanished like a puff of smoke. I last saw her directly after her then liaison broke up, which I sensed ended badly. I laid eyes on her again for the first time in two years at your party.

Carla bit her lip to force herself to keep quiet. Two years ago appeared to be a crucial time. Mimi also thought Aldyn broke up with someone two years ago, and the East Side cat burglar robberies started two years ago. There had to be a connection between the events. Carla recalled that none of the men Aldyn spoke to appeared pleased to see her. Could it be that one of them was her former lover and the cat burglar?

"Who else did you know at my party?" she asked.

"My lips are sealed. I only told you about Aldyn Sheridan because it appears that a terrible tragedy has befallen her. To name my other client would be wrong as that person is not a suspected criminal. But if it will help, I will be honored to give you a reading. Perhaps I will be able to unlock clues to your future. Beyond that, my dear, I can do nothing further for you. It's been a trying day for Kitty and me and bed beckons. We'll get a cab and drop you at your apartment. Check, please." Charlie signaled the waitress.

Chapter 18

Kitty offered Carla a valuable piece of advice within the first hour of her employment at Career Steps—The Agency with a Heart: "Timing is crucial when you need to make an important telephone call. If you want information, call after ten o'clock. Early calls make you appear to be over-anxious. If you have good news, anytime is a good time to call, and if you have bad news, anytime is a bad time to call."

Carla recited Kitty's advice over and over in her head while she pondered the correct time to Myrna Verde. If she called too early, her former app might correctly suspect that Carla made the call for a reason more urgent than her desire to know how she liked her job at the Perfume Council. Somewhere in the neighborhood of ten twenty-three seemed to be an innocuous enough time not to arouse suspicion.

She wrote a nice "hello, how are you" intro, then swung into the "So do you like the job? Do you think they like you?" bit and came in for the kill with a friendly "Oh, by the way" routine. Carla calculated that the whole conversation would take less than ten minutes.

Myrna couldn't have stuck to Carla's script better if it had been faxed to her in advance. She even fed Carla the lines she needed to segue into the real reason for the call by saying, "I get to talk to chemists and perfumers all the time."

"My, my," Carla replied in her most seductive voice. "Isn't that a coincidence? There you are surrounded by perfume experts and here am I with a friend who has a perfume problem. Sometimes she sneezes when she walks into a certain room. She doesn't smell anything, but she thinks perfume might be the cause. Could you ask one of the chemists if that's possible? I, er, she would be very grateful."

Flattered by Carla's friendly phone call, Myrna promised to relay the question to a chemist without asking why her friend's sneezing attacks were so important to Carla.

At one o'clock Carla strolled over to a fancy Northern Italian restaurant on East 48th Street. She usually stayed in the office to catch the lunch time surge of apps, but today she had an important date.

"Mother, you've got to learn the truth about Tony's marital status." Nancy Miller's voice escalated into a whine, thought better of it and fell back to its normal register. "You'd kill me if I dated a guy for a while without getting the facts straight about his marital status."

"You're right, Nancy, but I'm your mother and you're my daughter and what's right for mothers isn't always right for daughters."

When Nancy mentioned that she had the day off from classes at the CIA in honor of the birthday of a famous French chef, Carla invited her for lunch. Now she regretted making the date. Mothers don't like to be chastised by their children. Carla picked up the piece of bread that she had promised herself she wouldn't touch.

"I think Tony is a great guy, Mother, but he did pick you up in an elevator. Suppose he's a murderer or a rapist or a burglar or…"

"Don't talk nonsense, Nancy." Carla dipped the piece of bread into a dish of seasoned olive oil before she stuffed it into her mouth. "I think he has something on his mind and I don't want to pressure him with a lot of silly questions."

"Silly?" Nancy pressed a piece of grilled salmon onto her fork. "These aren't silly questions, Mother. You have to assert yourself. You can't sit back and humbly accept any crumb a man hands you. This isn't the Middle Ages."

"Oh, I don't know..." Carla stabbed at her penne bolognese like an eeler going after the catch of the day. Smart ass answers from her daughter, she did not need.

Nancy gently patted Carla's hand. "How about another bottle of wine?" She signaled to the short, barrel chest waiter, who reminded Carla of an Emperor penguin. "This is a fantastic chardonnay. It's a Santa Margherita. Clean and elegant, don't you think?"

Carla shrugged. "It's very nice, dear, but what do I know? Actually, I get a headache from white wine and I don't usually drink at lunch, but since you ordered it, it's fine. And I don't want any more. I have to go back to work." She tried to cover her glass with her hand, but the penguin was too fast. Like it or not, her cup runneth over.

"Go back to work? The thought of you finding jobs for other people makes me laugh." Nancy made an unsuccessfully attempt to muffle her braying laughter by pressing her hand hard against her cherubic mouth.

"That's not funny. I'm good at advising other people what to do. Didn't I recommend that you enroll in the Culinary Institute when you decided not to go to college? And you like it, don't you? You always loved to cook." A vision flashed in Carla's mind of ten-year old Nancy in the kitchen whipping up a gourmet meal that put her puny efforts to shame.

"I didn't ALWAYS love to cook, Mother. I learned to cook in self-defense. How else could I get a decent meal in our house? I love you very much, but let's face it, you are a lousy cook."

Carla frowned. Why did her friends and relatives harp on her lack of culinary talent? When did a person's cooking ability become the measure of her worth? Could Abraham Lincoln cook?

"And yes, Mother, the Culinary Institute of America is great."

Nancy's grudging admission brought a smile to Carla's face. "Now why didn't you say that before? I'm happy that you'll be doing something you love, just like your brother. And listen, Nancy," Carla switched gears, "speaking of your brother, do you know why the place where he works is called Silicon Valley? I don't dare ask him."

Nancy shook her head at her mother like a nursery school teacher placating a three-year old. "Because most computer companies are headquartered in northern California."

"But what's the connection with silicon?"

Nancy's shoulders tensed. "Everybody knows that silicon is used to make the...the computer chips, that's it, the chips are..."

Carla blinked, "And what do the chips do, Nancy?"

"Well, you know how to use a computer, so you know that the chips are the little things that, well the things that...you better ask Robbie the next time you talk to him. He can explain it better than I." Nancy took a long swig of her wine.

"You don't know either, do you?" Carla smiled like a happy Cheshire cat.

"Mother, I should have known that you were putting me on. You were, weren't you?

"But of course, darling." Twice a year Carla surrendered to an unmotherly desire to show her children that they didn't know everything. Today Nancy's number came up.

"Well, stop it right now, because I have something important to ask you. Will you come to the CIA?"

"I wish you wouldn't use that expression. It sounds like you're mixed up with spies."

Nancy's back stiffened. "Stop it, Mother. You know very well that I mean the Culinary Institute of America, not the Central Intelligence Agency. We're having our annual Renaissance Feast next weekend and I'd love you to come. I'm doing boar with truffles. It takes days to prepare." Nancy's eyes sparkled with enthusiasm when she added, "First I clean its ears, then I brush its teeth. It's real neat."

"Oh, Nancy!" Carla shuddered at the thought of her little girl working inside a dead pig's mouth. "I've tried to be a good sport and taste your gourmet concoctions, even marinated tongue, but I definitely will be ill if I eat something whose ears and teeth you've cleaned. It would be like eating a friend."

Nancy hissed without a hint of humor, "Don't be silly, Mother, a boar is only a boar. I don't get personally involved with it."

Carla stared across the table at her daughter. She knew that she couldn't disappoint her in her moment of triumph. "I'll come, but please don't tell your grandparents that you cooked a pig, and could we change the subject while we eat?"

"Sure, but what's up with your dumb friend, Aldyn? She acted real weird at your party."

A small piece of pasta stuck in the back of Carla's throat. "She's not dumb and what did Aldyn do to you?"

"She didn't do anything to me. In fact, she pretty much ignored me, but while I waited in the hall to use the bathroom, I overheard her and Uncle Harold having an argument in your bedroom. She said, 'You know you'll give it to me.' Then he said, 'Drop dead. I'll break your neck if you...' That's when Nellie came out of the bathroom, so I went in and by the time I came out, they had left. A few minutes later I saw Aldyn on the terrace talking to your weird furrier friend and he didn't have a smile on his face. Boy, nobody likes her. That lady could wind up dead someday."

Blame it on Nancy's bombshell or too much wine, but Carla felt the room spin and had to clutch the edge of the table to steady herself. "Aldyn can be overbearing, but I'm sure her arguments didn't mean anything. You know your Uncle Harold has a short temper. He probably flew off the handle when she told him she didn't like his new line of shoes. As for Jack Demmer, maybe she came on to him."

Carla stumbled through her invented explanation before she changed the subject. "How's whatshisname? You know who I mean, the guy who runs a bee motel. You brought him to my party," she added as though Nancy might have more than one beekeeper friend.

"Whatshisname? The guy at the party? Mother, how can you?" Nancy squawked like a turkey. "He's an apiarist and he owns an apiary, which is not a bee version of a roach motel. And would you please try to remember his name. It is William, Will for short, Elliott Wonderman." The name rolled off Nancy's tongue smooth as chocolate mousse.

"Sounds like Willie Wonka to me." Carla drained her glass.

"That's not nice."

"Nancy..."

The damn penguin poured more wine into Carla's goblet.

"Yes, Mother?" Nancy's eyes opened wide.

"Get a new boyfriend."

Chapter 19

That evening Carla made a detour on her way home from the office to the garage under Aldyn's high-rise apartment building at 73rd Street and Third Avenue. "Hello." She tapped a quarter on the window of the cubbyhole office to attract the attention of the attendant who sat behind a battered gray metal desk. He reluctantly glanced up from a copy of *Penthouse* magazine. "Make and color?" he asked, his greasy hand extended for the claim check.

"I'm not here to pick up a car. I want information about renting space."

"Like what?"

"Like what's the monthly rate and is the garage open 24/7?" Carla knew nothing about renting garage space. Her former house in Merrick had an attached three-car garage the size of a Manhattan studio apartment.

"Yeah, we're open all the time and it'll cost you four hundred and ninety bucks a month plus tax."

The garage attendant lifted his Ray Bans to get a better look at the lady who had asked the dumb questions. All the while his watery piggy brown eyes stared at Carla, his Carl Malden nose sniffed the air like a bloodhound searching for a scent.

"What's the matter? Don't cha' have a garage in your building?" he demanded.

"No, I don't. That's why my friend Aldyn Sheridan recommended this one to me. She parks here. Could I have a spot near hers, Gus?" Carla squinted at the name embroidered on his green jumpsuit.

"If it's open, it's yours. Lemme check." While Gus thumbed through his log book, he mumbled an unintelligible chant. At last the mumbling turned into words. "Hey, you're in luck. Follow me." Gus hauled his ample girth out of the chair and headed into the bowels of the underground garage.

Carla trotted behind the attendant to the rear of the garage. "See, you can be right there."

She barely glanced at the empty space where he pointed. Her eyes were fixed on the Alpine White four-door BMW with New York license plate AS-1 parked in the space beside it—twenty-three hundred pounds of solid proof that Aldyn Sheridan did not drive her car to her vacation destination.

"That's your friend's car, isn't it?" Gus ignored the shocked expression on Carla's face.

"Yes, it is. Have you seen her recently?"

"Not for three, four days." Gus scratched his head. "No, that ain't right. She takes the car out every weekend, come rain or snow, either late Friday afternoon or real early Saturday morning, but not this weekend."

"Are you sure? Maybe you were busy with another car and didn't see her."

"No way. I'm here all weekend and I never miss nothin' that goes on. If I say she didn't take the car this weekend, she didn't take the car." Gus' voice turned icy cold at the implication that he had missed something.

"Well, could she have gone away in someone else's car or taken a plane?"

"How should I know, lady? You wanna' gossip about Miz Sheridan or do you wanna' rent a spot for your car?"

"I'll think about it and get back to you," Carla called over her shoulder and fled the garage.

Chapter 20

Once out on the street, Carla realized that she had chosen the wrong shoes to wear today. Her favorite Stuart Weitzman beige pumps with the three-inch stiletto heels looked great, but they weren't meant for walking the nearly twenty city blocks to her apartment, which is exactly what she planned to do to clear her mind of the growing evidence that Aldyn had not gone on vacation to Hilton Head, but lay dead somewhere in or around New York City. At East 60th Street and Second Avenue Carla leaned against a tree to massage her aching feet, and decided that things couldn't get worse.

Not true.

She unlocked her door, hobbled into her apartment and screamed. The foyer rug was moved halfway into the living room. The couch cushions lay scattered on the floor. The French doors to the terrace and the kitchen cabinet doors stood ajar. Her apartment had been ransacked!

Should she flee the apartment or should she call the dreaded police? The cold hand of fear clutched at Carla's chest. A terrified scream threatened to explode in her throat. Then she heard "*Old MacDonald Had a Farm...*" and she ran down the hall to follow the song to its source.

She flung open the bathroom door.

The tall, thin, twentysomething hunk in Carla's bathroom froze like a deer caught in the bright glare of a car's headlights. He dropped the large towel he was using to dry himself. "Holy shit, can't a guy have some privacy?"

"Robbie? It's you! Oh, you've changed."

"Mom!" In one rapid motion Robbie retrieved the towel from the floor and wrapped it around his naked mid-section.

"I mean you've grown."

"Mom!"

"Taller, yes, that's it. You're much taller than the last time I saw you," Carla stammered.

"Please get out of here, Mom, so I can get dressed." Robbie firmly pushed his mother out of the bathroom.

Carla grinned when she heard him lock the bathroom door. How could she have failed to recognize the familiar signs that her son had come for a visit? Smart, handsome, sweet, kind and honest but still not housebroken described her son. She pitied the woman who would take on that job.

While Robbie dressed, Carla put the apartment back in order. The living room and kitchen took less time than she anticipated, but restoring her bedroom to its former serene state proved to be a daunting task. Her son had moved her slipper chair clear across the room and had pushed her carefully arranged collection of porcelain boxes into one small corner of the bureau to make room for his books and laptop computer. His clothing spilled out of an over-sized green duffel bag parked in the middle of the floor. The worst part of the disarray proved to be her queen size bed where Robbie had snacked and napped. Two corners of the crumb dotted fitted bottom sheet were pulled off the mattress. The huge twisted ball on the floor was the top sheet and duvet. Her collection of needlepoint pillows that made the bed look so inviting, were flung to every corner of the room.

Carla restrained herself from charging back into the bathroom and strangling her son. Instead, she efficiently remade the bed with fresh linens. As she struggled to hoist the bulky duvet back into place, a white envelope fluttered to the floor. The words CARLA MILLER typed dead center stared up at her.

Numb with fear, seconds passed before Carla forced herself to open the envelope and read the message typed on a single sheet of white paper. "*Stop being nosey or you will lose more than your nose,*" it warned. Even without a signature, she knew that it came from the East Side Cat Burglar. He must have left the envelope on her pillow and when Robbie flung aside the pillows it landed in the jumbled mess of the duvet. Carla slid the missive back into its envelope and hid it under the scented liner in her bureau drawer.

"Sorry, if I scared you, Mom," Robbie announced when he found her in the kitchen preparing a pitcher of instant ice tea.

She stood on her toes to tousle his dark auburn hair. "And I'm sorry I barged in on you, but I got so excited when I heard your song that I flung open the bathroom door without thinking." Carla taught Robbie to sing *Old MacDonald Had a Farm* for his third birthday. As far as Carla knew, he didn't know any other song from beginning to end.

"That's okay, Mom. Forget it. Guess you've seen me without clothes a couple of times before." Robbie's face turned a bright shade of pink that clashed with his auburn hair.

"I guess we've both apologized enough, so let's chat in the living room." Carla poured the ice tea into two tall glasses.

After they made themselves comfortable—she on the couch and Robbie stretched out in Tony's favorite chair—Carla said, "I had lunch today with Nancy, but if you had let me know that you planned to be in the city today, I'd have switched our date to dinner so you could join us. It would have been nice—just the three of us."

Robbie blushed again. "It wouldn't have worked, Mom. See, I met this girl Tammy at a computer convention a couple of months ago and we've been text messaging back and forth ever since. She lives in Manhattan."

"Text messaging doesn't sound romantic"

Robbie held up his hand to protest Carla's objection to his form of communication. "Sure it is. It's great. We talk all the time, and think of all the postage we save. I have to be in Boston tomorrow morning for a seminar, so I detoured to New York to have dinner with her tonight. I stopped here to take a shower and hang out with you until it's time to meet her. That's okay, isn't it?"

"Sure. Are you coming back here to sleep? Carla resisted the urge to point out to her son that he hadn't come to visit her, but to use her apartment as a pit stop.

"Mom!"

"I'm not being nosey, er, curious." Carla stumbled over the word that appeared on the threatening note. "I just want to know if I should wait up for you."

"How about I call if I'm coming back?" Robbie's sly smile indicated that Carla shouldn't expect his call.

Carla took a long sip of tea before she changed the subject. "How did you get into my apartment? The key that I gave you wouldn't have worked because I installed a new lock a little bit ago."

"Yeah, I found that out. The doorman let me come up because he had a copy of the letter you wrote to the management company giving permission for Nancy and me to come up anytime. When my key didn't work, I figured you had changed the locks. Then I remembered that you used to hide a spare set of keys outside our old house, so I thought that's what you did here. Now, if I had this pad, I'd have taped the keys to the top of the door frame, but since you're so short..."

"I am not short, Robbie. I'm petite." Carla indignantly corrected his description of her diminutive size.

"Okay, Mom, you're petite. But petite or short, you still can't reach the top of the door, which is why I ruled out that hiding place. Then I spotted the table near the elevator, and sure enough I found two keys taped to the back of it.

"So it's not a good hiding place."

"It depends if you're the hider or the hidee." A wide smile slashed Robbie's handsome face then quickly faded. "What's up, Mom? Why are you so nervous? Maybe you need to get another dog for company." He stared hard at his mother.

"I'm not nervous and I'll never replace Bonkers. His presence is always with me, and I have plenty of company, thank you very much." Carla didn't add that some of the company came into the apartment without an invitation. Despite her bluster, her hand trembled when she put her glass down on the cocktail table.

"Come on, Mom, tell me what's up. You're strung tight as a cat and you just put your glass on the table instead of using one of those stupid coasters. You always had a screaming fit if any of us didn't use them. You said we'd ruin the table tops. Now you're doing it. So what gives?" Robbie pointedly put his sweaty ice tea glass on one of the silver rimmed glass coasters that Carla kept stacked on the cocktail table.

"You're reading too much into nothing, Robbie. When people get older, they tend to forget things. Be more tolerant of your old mother," Carla stammered through her answer.

"Yeah, sure, like you're old. My buddy Ira has something going with a foxy lady who's your age. Robbie flashed a radiant smile that showed off his incredibly straight, white teeth. "Hey guess who I saw?"

Carla didn't care to indulge her son by playing a guessing game with him. She disliked them as a child and she especially disliked them when adults played them. "I give up, Robbie. Who did you see?"

"Uncle Mervin. I saw him walking up East 56th Street near Second Avenue. I called to him from the cab, but he didn't see me."

"Probably deep in thought, as usual. You know how serious he is about…what's this?" Carla recoiled from the envelope that Robbie placed on the cocktail table.

"Why are you so upset about a dumb envelope? You must have dropped it in the hall near the bathroom. At least, that's where I found it. I didn't mean to scare you."

"I'm sorry if I overreacted. It's been a long day." Carla gingerly turned the envelope face up. "Isn't that strange, it's a telephone bill for my neighbor Mrs. Callahan. How do you suppose it got into my apartment?" The thought entered Carla's mind that the cat burglar had left both envelopes.

"Maybe the mailman put it in your mailbox by mistake then you dropped it in the apartment."

"I never saw the envelope before," Carla insisted.

"Don't make a big deal over it, Mom. Just give it to Mrs. Gallagher."

"It's 'Callahan' and you're right, it's no big deal." Although Carla agreed with her son, she decided to return the envelope to the mail carrier rather than give it to her neighbor and risk an unpleasant run-in with her.

"Great. Now I gotta go. It's late. Thanks for everything. I'll call you in a week or so, and promise me you'll think about getting another dog or maybe a cat. Yeah, a cat would be good. One more thing, Mom, please call me Rob. Robbie is for kids." Rob retrieved his duffle bag from the bedroom, hoisted it on his shoulder, kissed Carla on the cheek and hurried out the door.

Chapter 21

"Listen, Mimi, finding Aldyn's car in the garage clinches it. She's dead. But what can I do? The police don't believe anything I say and I can't file a missing person report because I'm not a relative."

Carla paced her bedroom as she spoke on the phone to her friend. Right after Rob trekked off for his date with his computer generated girlfriend, she called Mimi to update her on the progress of her investigation.

"I know how touchy you are about the police, but why don't you call them again?" Mimi asked. "Maybe this time they'll believe you. You have Aldyn's credit cards and you can show them her car in the garage."

"No. I told you before, I'm not going to the police. Even if I do, they'll explain away my fears by saying that Aldyn pretended to go away alone because she is with a married guy, which explains why she didn't need her car and hasn't missed her credit cards or cash. And you know what? If I hadn't seen her body, that explanation would sound logical to me." All the while Carla spoke she had a mental vision of Aldyn's crumpled body in the trash room and the jewels in her kitchen air vent.

"...Mervin."

"What?" The mention of Mimi's husband jerked Carla's thoughts back to the present.

"I said that this could be the time to talk to Mervin."

"No, Mervin only wants hard facts. If the police don't believe me, why should he?"

Carla glanced around her bedroom. Ever since she discovered the jewels in the air vent, she constantly examined the apartment for signs that someone had paid her a visit while she was away. Today she found those two envelopes. Yesterday a roll of toilet paper and a couple of cans of tuna fish disappeared. But why would a cat burglar steal toilet paper and tuna fish?

"Well, since you're so sure that Tony is innocent; why not talk to him about your problem?" A drop of rare sarcasm dripped from Mimi voice.

"I would, but he's away." Carla's voice softened. "I'm sorry that I snapped at you. Her reflection in the gold leaf mirror that hung above her dresser surprised her. Her face looked drawn, yet her eyes glowed with the steely glint of determination—a trait that she lacked in her old life.

"You'll never guess who visited me today." Carla artfully switched the conversation from Tony to Rob.

A long pause followed after she related the details of her short visit with her son before Mimi said, "You better change your lock again."

"I just told you that Rob—he asked me to call him Rob instead of Robbie—visited me and all you can say is that I should change my locks. Don't you think the important part of the story is that Rob came to see me?"

"No, Carla, what's important is that Rob got into your apartment without any trouble, which means that you're still not safe. You have to get a keyless push button lock. It would take a thousand years for someone to figure out the six digit combination, unless you use stupid numbers like your date of birth. The twins installed keyless locks on their apartment doors and now they're as safe as if they still lived at home."

Everyone referred to the Berks' sons, Lester and Leroy, collectively as "the twins," never by their individual names. Carla suspected that Mimi somehow arranged to get her child bearing over with in just one quick trip to the maternity ward. It saved so much time.

"I'll think about changing the locks. By the way, have you spoken to Nellie? Mimi, are you there? Did you hang up?" Carla asked a dead line. Damn it. Mimi had finished what she wanted to say and had hung up.

Carla returned to the living room to test the terrace doors. She looked out at the warm peach glow of the setting sun. A soft breeze sent the leaves of the potted plants swaying like hula dancers. The beautiful evening invited her to come out. Perhaps a walk would calm her down enough to sleep well tonight. She turned to go into the bedroom to change into shorts and a T-shirt then abruptly changed her mind and stepped out on the terrace. Soon the terrace would be wrapped in a shroud of darkness and offer cover to a burglar who might swing down from the roof or climbs up the outside of the building like Spider Man. Carla snapped on the outside light. It sputtered on for a second then went out. She snapped the switch down and up—nothing happened. *Damn it! The bulb is burnt out.* Carla unscrewed it and left it on the kitchen counter as a reminder that it needed to be replaced.

Minutes later she walked out of her apartment building and turned onto Sutton Place lined with solid rows of elegant apartment buildings. The incessant rumble of cars traveling high overhead on the Queensboro Bridge greeted her when she reached 59th Street. At East 63rd Street and York Avenue—Sutton Place becomes York Avenue under the bridge—she jogged up the cantilevered ramp that leads to the East River pedestrian walkway. Carla felt safe here surrounded by other joggers and the hundreds of cars that whizzed by on the adjacent FDR Drive, sometimes known as the East River Drive.

Her jog turned into a leisurely stroll the better to allow her to watch the yachts, oil tankers and smelly garbage scows that traveled up and down the waterway. Her combination jog and walk would take her to Carl Schurz Park, a terraced riverfront woodland that runs parallel to the Drive from East 84th Street to East 90th Street. Originally the private garden of Gracie Mansion, the mayor's residence, it offers breathtaking views of the East River and the Triboro and Queensboro Bridges. By the time Carla reached the park the evening sunset had given way to the gathering darkness. The mist rolling in off the river reminded her of Carl Sandburg's poem about the fog coming in on little cat feet.

Carla sensed a shadowy presence close by on the nearly deserted walkway. When she stopped to pretend to retie a shoelace she thought she heard the echo of footsteps. She turned around quickly. A figure huddled in a hooded black sweatshirt stood at the guardrail staring out at the river. *Who wears a heavy sweatshirt on a warm night? A mugger, that's who.* Carla asked and answered her question.

She considered her options. She could continue to the end of the deserted promenade and hope to find a security guard near Gracie Mansion. She could scream and pray that someone would come to her rescue. Or, she could leave the park through the broad curved stone staircase that beckoned to her. She hurried to the stairs.

Carla congratulated herself on making the safe choice. Under the comforting light of a street lamp she saw a straight path with flat treeless lawns fanning out on either side—all open space with no hiding places. As her foot touched the last step, the lamp imitated her terrace light—it went out—plunging her surroundings into foggy darkness. Carla stumbled blindly ahead until her eyes adjusted to the darkness. Through the mist, she could dimly see that the straight path became a meandering trail bordered by dense bushes. Above the thump, thump of her heart, Carla heard the sound of footsteps coming up behind her. She broke into a sprint. She had to get to the 86th Street exit. People would be there. She ran and ran. The red glow of the light above the exit gate greeted her. She'd be safe in a moment.

She smelled the sweat and garlic that oozed from her predator's pores barely a second before he tackled her to the ground. She tried to scream as he dragged her into the bushes, but could only make a pitiful mouse squeak. Her assailant's thick legs straddled her body. His strong hands grabbed tight on either side of her head. He breathed heavily and shook uncontrollably. He tipped off balance. Carla willed strength into her legs and kicked him as hard as she could. Her aim proved true. A loud howl rocketed out of his foul breath mouth. Carla's assailant doubled over in pain, clutched his groin, hopped up and down, yelped like a crazed hyena, then scurried away in the fog.

Carla sunk back to the ground sobbing with combination of fear and relief. She had nearly been raped or killed or both and she had herself to blame. She should have known better than to walk alone in a deserted place after dark. She was dumb, dumb, dumb—but she had survived.

"Are you all right?"

Carla's tears stopped as the sound of another voice.

"Fritz and I heard your screams." A young woman dressed in a designer warm-up suit stared down at her. A large German shepherd on a leash stood attentively at her side.

"I didn't scream. The mugger did. I kicked him."

"You kicked him? That's terrific." The woman broke into a hearty laugh, her hand extended to help her up. "Are you hurt? I'll take you to the hospital."

"No, I'm fine, except for a couple of bruises and a sore neck. I'll take a cab home."

"Do you need cab fare? I have money." The woman patted a gold fanny pack slung low on one hip.

Carla shook her head. "I have plenty. I always carry mugger money in my pocket, in case someone tries to rob me when I'm jogging. See." She pulled out a neatly folded twenty dollar bill from her shorts pocket.

"Boy, oh boy, you're one tough New York lady."

Carla smiled at the compliment.

"Not only did you kick a mugger, but you carry mugger money. At least, let me hail a cab for you. Hold Fritz."

Carla's would-be-rescuer opened her mouth, pressed two fingers on her lower teeth and let loose an ear-piercing whistle that brought two cabs to a screeching halt. The woman gave Carla a smart military salute as her cab sped away.

Chapter 22

All the while the cab sped downtown, Carla questioned herself about her near assault. Was the guy in the hood Aldyn's murderer? Was he connected to the jewels in the kitchen? Or, was he just an ordinary mugger with no connection to anything in her life? Carla favored the "ordinary mugger" theory, though a small voice inside her head whispered, "Don't be so sure." Midway home, she reached one firm conclusion—under no circumstance would she tell Tony or her children about her latest adventure. Why give them the opportunity to say, "I warned you to be careful."

For the rest of the cab ride Carla fixated on taking a luxurious soak in a hot bubble bath to wash away the grime and stench of her encounter with the attacker. It never happened. Her cab turned onto East 56th Street, and came smack up against a solid wall of police cars and television news vans. "I'll get out here." Carla shoved her twenty dollar mugger money into the plexiglass drop down cash box and jumped out of the taxi, leaving the driver to back out of the street or thread his way through the mess.

Carla ran down the block to her apartment building where she found her doorman mingling with the excited crowd of onlookers that gazed up at the roof. "What's going on?" she asked.

"The cat burglar paid us a visit. Not to worry, though, Miz Miller, it wasn't your place. He got into Penthouse A. Herself is down here now.

She can't go back till the police are done up there.

"I'll sue. I'll sue the building the city, the mayor."

Carla recognized the deep voice of Caitlin Oliver, the world-famous model. Even if she didn't speak a word, Caitlin could not be missed. She had a waist-length cascade of blue black hair, flawless alabaster skin, gray-green cat eyes and a drop dead figure. Every inch of the lady's fabulous six-foot body earned its keep—from her Estee Lauder face to her Calvin Klein legs to her Victoria's Secret breasts to her Dolce & Gabbana feet.

"After I took Chin Chou for his walk," Caitlin lovingly pattered her wrinkled Shar Pei's head, "I opened my safe to get the jewels I planned to wear tonight—and that's when I discovered they were missing." The model wrung her lovely Neutrogena hands, while poor Chin Chou furrowed his brow deeper than its normal three-inch rut, as though he feared he might be the cause of his mistress' distress.

"I won't allow that cat person to get away with it" she wailed. All my jewels—my Jackie Kennedy Onassis sapphire bracelet, my diamond tiara, my jade pendant, my diamond and ruby earrings, my emerald earrings, my beautiful 'Black Beauty' pearls, a gift from Prince…oh, it's too much."

"When did you last wear the pearls, Caitlin?" a reporter from the *Daily News* shouted.

"At the AIDS benefit the evening before I left on a photo shoot in Brazil. What a glorious evening. The photographers crawled over a dozen celebrities to get a picture of me wearing the pearls. They're a magnificent color. Really more gunmetal with a blue/green cast than black, and the diamond clasp is unbelievably beautiful." Caitlin forced a pale shadow of her dazzling smile for the television cameras clustered around her.

The model continued to wail, but the reporters had shifted their attention to a rotund silver haired man who came off the elevator accompanied by two uniformed officers. "Detective Moran," a Channel 2 reporter shouted, "could the robbery be the work of the East Side Cat Burglar?"

"Of course. Who else could it be?" Caitlin answered for the detective. "And I think I saw him at the party."

Carla saw Detective Moran's bushy eyebrows shoot up for a split second before he whispered something to Caitlin and walked out of the building, leaving the two police officers in the lobby. Whatever he said did nothing to halt Caitlin's tirade. Without stopping to take a breath, she continued, "How could this despicable person sneak into my bedroom, open my safe and take everything? I've nothing left! I'm naked!" Despite the torrent of fresh tears that cascaded down her sculptured cheeks, Carla observed that Caitlin's makeup remained intact.

While sympathetic hands reached out to soothe the model and a cameraman grinned as he savored her last statement, Carla stepped into the elevator. She had nothing to fear in her apartment now. Her mugger didn't know her address; besides he'd probably run back to his rat hole to nurse his wounds. And why should the cat burglar be out and about now? He'd left Caitlin's loot in her apartment a while ago. Carla recognized the pearl choker with the diamond encrusted clasp from Caitlin's description as the one she saw in the velvet box that had her address stuck to it.

If Caitlin's inconsolable grief truly reflected the enormous value of her jewels, then her insurance company would have to send her a very substantial settlement check—a lot larger than she was legally entitled to. Though Carla saw the "Black Beauty" choker and one of the model's diamond and ruby earrings in her air vent, she didn't see the "stolen" tiara or Jackie Onassis' bracelet. It appeared that the famous model planned to pull off a little insurance fraud. Carla surmised that the other gems in the air vent belonged to other victims.

Carla's bravado lasted just long enough for her to unlock her door. The apartment seemed too dark and too silent. She ran through the apartment to turn on every light in the place then she dashed back into the living room to flick on the sound system. Someone had Georgia on his mind. When she switched on the bedroom television set and heard the news flash about the cat burglar's latest heist, the rage that had been boiling in her gut all evening erupted as violently as Mount Vesuvius on a good day. Damn the mugger, but especially damn the cat burglar!

Parking strangers' jewelry in my air vent is one thing, but how dare he hide my neighbors' things here. I'm not going to take it anymore. This is war!

The shrill ring of the telephone bell interrupted Carla's silent battle cry. She stared at the instrument, as though it were a snake poised to bite her. It rang three more times before she picked up the receiver. "Hello." Her defiant voice dared anyone to dispute her greeting.

"Hello to you, too. I almost hung up. I thought you'd gone out." Tony's voice warmed Carla from her head to her stomach and down to her shaking knees.

"It's you."

"Of course it's me. What have you been up to?"

"You won't believe what's happened. There's been a robbery, the model in the penthouse, the cat burglar..."

"Whoa, slow down, Carla. What are you talking about? Who's the cat burglar? Are you okay?" Tony's voice was filled with concern.

"Never mind, it's too complicated to tell you on the phone."

"Are you sure? I'm in Washington at the L'Enfant Plaza. If you decide you want to talk, call me on my cell phone." Tony rattled off a string of numbers that Carla scribbled on a napkin. "Otherwise, we'll talk when I get back. I should be here another couple of days. Is everything else all right?"

"Not exactly, the light on the terrace isn't working." Carla knew she sounded like an airhead for using that lame excuse for a problem, but she would resort to any ploy to keep Tony on the phone. The sound of his voice made her feel so safe.

"Try changing the bulb."

"I will, but should the light switch be on or off when I do it?"

"Off, of course, otherwise you'll get a nasty shock. Look, I've gotta go. Talk to you later."

"Don't hang up yet. I want to tell you about the… Tony, do you hear me?" Carla stared at the telephone receiver. *Damn. Why does everybody hang up on me? I hadn't finished talking.*

Carla dialed Tony's cell phone number and got a Chinese restaurant. It took two more wrong numbers to convince her that she'd transposed some of the numbers and there wasn't a chance in a million that she could come up with the right combination to get Tony back on the line. Determined to speak to him, she got the hotel telephone number from Information. As Carla waited to be connected to his room, she debated with herself as to how much she should tell him about the cat burglar.

At last the operator came back on the line. "I'm sorry, but I can't connect you to your party."

"His room doesn't answer?"

"No, Ma'am. Tony Vitale is not a registered guest in our hotel."

The words pierced Carla's heart sharp as a knife. She slammed down the phone and fled to the pitch black terrace. How many more disasters would strike her today? She flung herself down on a lounge chair. Wrapped in a cloud of gloom, she tried to figure out why Tony wasn't registered in the hotel. She refused to believe that he had played a sick joke on her.

When no logical explanation popped into her head, Carla stomped into the apartment, grabbed a handful of chocolate chip cookies then stomped back to the terrace to wallow in her snit of bad temper. *Oh damn,* she snarled aloud. Her foot had caught on something. She snatched up the offending object, ready to vent her anger on it. Then her eyes softened with recognition. *Where is he, Bonkers?* She fingered the metal links of her beloved dog's leash like worry beads.

Soon a comforting thought crept into Carla's head. *Of course, Tony changed hotels but there was no reason for him to tell me because he thought's I'd call him on his cell phone.* She gently laid the leash back beside Bonkers' empty water bowl, went back into the apartment, flung herself across the bed and fell into a deep, dreamless sleep.

Chapter 23

The call from Myrna Verde came early the next morning. "I'm sorry it took so long to get back to you, Mrs. Miller, but I think I have the answer to your friend's question." Myrna twisted her announcement into an apologetic whine. "Dr. Rupert's assistant said, well, wait a minute. You don't know Dr. Rupert, do you?"

Myrna liked to run around left field before she answered a question. For example, if someone asked her for the time, before she looked at her watch she would explain that she bought her fake Rolex watch on the street for twenty dollars because who wants a real gold watch that can get lost or stolen when a cheap one tells time just as accurately. And by that time, the time would be five minutes later than when she began her convoluted explanation.

Carla tugged impatiently on a lock of hair while Myrna rambled on. "Dr. Rupert is the head of research here at the Council, but I don't know him real well yet, so I asked Joey, his assistant. It's okay that I told Joey about your friend, isn't it, Mrs. Miller?"

"Of course it is, Myrna. No problem, but what did he say?" Carla had a sinking feeling that Myrna would never get to the point.

"He? No, Joey is a she, not a he. I should have used Joey's real name. It's Jessica, but she doesn't like it, so we call her Joey. Come to think of it, I don't know why she calls herself Joey. Joey isn't the nickname for Jessica, is it?"

Carla stared at the clump of amber hair clutched in her hand. Heavy tugging will do that every time. "No, I think it is Jessie, but if Jessica likes the name Joey, that's fine with me. And speaking of Joey," she seized the opportunity to push Myrna back on the right track, "what did she say?"

"About what? Oh, yeah, I forgot. Your friend sneezes a lot and all that. Well, Joey thought that first I should explain about the notes. It's like this: Every perfume has what they call in the business notes—three of them. The top note is generally floral, the middle note combines spice, herbal and woody scents with the floral while the base note, which is made up of essential oils like sandalwood, musk or patchouli, stabilizes the scent." As Myrna repeated Joey's explanation, an unfamiliar voice of cool authority replaced her usual whine. *A little knowledge can be more than dangerous. It can be intoxicating.*

"So how does that help me, I mean my friend?"

"I told Joey this stuff would be too technical for you." An impatient sigh traveled from Myrna's phone into Carla's ear. "You'll understand in a minute, but first Joey said to ask if your friend gets a rash when she sneezes, because then it could be an allergic reaction. Does she?"

"No, no rash. Just sneezes."

Out of the corner of her eye, Carla saw Bernadette Saxon, her least favorite app, wiggle waggling a blue scarf at her like a one-armed sailor doing signal flag duty. Bernadette always color coordinated her outfits. Today she wore blue from the perky azure blue bow tied around her blond corn rowed hair to her navy blue suit to her four-inch high electric blue suede platform shoes. Carla motioned to her to sit down.

"Well, then it could be psychological." Myrna continued. "Scent stimulates the limbic system, that's the part of the brain associated with memory and emotion. Like if your friend dislikes somebody who wears a specific perfume or cologne, then it's possible that she will sneeze whenever she smells that scent. The scent could remind her of an unpleasant experience. Maybe she's not aware of the smell but it's there and it bothers her. Does she smell anything?" Myrna asked.

Carla recalled the very faint woodsy smell in the kitchen whenever she had a sneezing attack. "You know, now that you mention it, she said something about a vague odor."

"Well, that's it. Scent lingers a long time—up to eight hours. The person wearing the scent could be miles away when your friend smells the base note hanging in the air. See, that's why Joey had me explain the notes to you. The base note is probably the culprit."

"I don't understand what you mean, Myrna." Carla's response turned one level above plaintive. She wondered how she could have considered herself well-educated and yet be so stupid about perfume.

"Don't you remember, Mrs. Miller? I just told you that the base note—the essential oil—is usually musk, sandalwood or patchouli. Well, those scents linger the longest, so any one of them could make your friend sneeze. If your friend wants to know anything else, give me a call."

"Yes, I certainly will. Thanks a lot, Myrna. I appreciate it and thank Joey for her help. My friend owes you both a lunch."

"That's okay. Call me anytime you want to know something about perfume." Myrna abruptly ended the conversation.

Carla leaned back in her chair to digest Joey's information. *Allergies are not the cause of my sneezes. I sneeze because I don't like the cat burglar or a memory that his scent triggers, which means that I'm right—I know him.* Carla's thoughts were interrupted by a flutter of blue wagging in her face.

She straightened her shoulders to face her nemesis. "I don't have anything for you today, Bernadette. Call me later in the week. I'm sure something will come in by then that will suit you."

Carla kept a wide grin on her face until Bernadette trotted out of the office, then she let it collapse into a pout. Somewhere in the five boroughs of New York City there had to be a job for her.

For the next half hour Carla played catch-up with paper work while she mentally rehearsed her speech.

"I have a doctor's appointment at ten thirty. I'll be back in an hour. Is that okay?" Carla announced.

"Sure, just get back in time for the noon stampede of apps."

Kitty sat as close as she could get to her eight strength magnifying mirror, intent on performing a morning ritual. Oblivious to Carla's rapt attention to her chore, Kitty held her eyelid taut with her left hand while her right hand carefully laid a false eyelash across it. She squinted into the mirror to make sure that the little devil lay properly in place, then she repeated the process on the other eye.

"I'll be back in plenty of time. The doctor is very prompt. It won't take long at all. I want him to look at the bruises I got from the mugger." Carla disliked lying, but she had detective business to take care of.

"I said it's okay, Carla, so go." Kitty inched closer and closer to her mirror to proceed to step two. Not satisfied that her lashes resembled thick wooly caterpillars, she stroked layer upon layer of ebony black mascara on them to make them appear thicker yet. By the time she applied the seventh layer, she'd come so close to the mirror that her breath fogged the lens. "Damn! You made me smear my eye. Why do you have to go on and on like that? I don't need a fancy song and dance."

"Well, I thought you would like to know..."

The furry black caterpillars perched on Kitty's upper lids blinked at Carla.

Carla bolted out of the Career Steps office, determined to finish her two reconnaissance missions within the allotted time. Instead of taking a down elevator, she got into one headed up and pressed the button for the twenty-eighth floor—Tony's supposed destination on that fateful morning when they met.

The elevator doors opened directly into the offices of Dellridge, Denver & Saugerty, a heavy duty accounting firm. The large mahogany paneled reception room was tastefully furnished with comfortable burgundy leather Queen Ann chairs and three-seater couches upholstered in a tartan plaid. Side tables offered a varied selection of magazines. An open hunter green leather guest book was carefully angled on the reception desk. There was no utilitarian water fountain in view to disturb the clubby atmosphere.

May I help you?" a dour-faced receptionist demanded as her beady dark eyes swept over Carla's chic black silk suit and crisp white blouse.

"I hope so. I'm Carla Miller. I'm an employment counselor at Career Steps. We're downstairs. May I speak to your personnel manager about the services we can provide to your firm? Here's my card."

The receptionist gingerly held Carla's business card between her thumb and forefinger while she took an incredibly long time to read the four simple lines of print.

The moment the woman picked up the phone to tap in an extension number, Carla launched into her plan. She held her breath, then forced a couple of long wheezing coughs. While her shoulders heaved up and down, she stabbed at her throat.

"Hang on. I'll get you a glass of water." The receptionist understood her hand signal. After she scurried down the hall, Carla flipped backward through the guest book to the date she met Tony. A lot of people visited

Dellridge, Denver & Saugerty that day, but not Anthony J. Vitale.

"Drink this." The receptionist forced a tiny pointed bottom paper cup into Carla's hand.

"My asthma is acting up. I'll come back another time when I'm feeling better." Carla took a tiny sip of the water, wheezed one more time and retreated into a down elevator.

Chapter 24

The dented wreck of a cab, held together with baling wire, sticky tape and staples, sped across the Queensboro Bridge carrying Carla to her brother's Shoe Heaven corporate headquarters. If asked to rate the comfort of this ride on a scale of one to ten, Carla would have given it a minus three. The coils in the passenger's seat had collapsed into themselves like giant Slinkies and half the padding had squirmed out of the plastic through a long gash made by a sharp instrument, the likes of which Carla did not wish to contemplate. So there she sat barely six inches above the debris-littered floor, while she tried to balance herself on the edge of the deflated blob that passed for a car seat and stared at her knee caps. Each time the cab lurched, she toppled over onto the slippery, dirty black plastic seat.

"Could you go a little slower, please? You went through a red light back there," her thin voice pleaded.

"Nize day, lady."

The cab continued to speed across the bridge.

"Excuse me, sir," Carla squinted to read the driver's name on the little card attached to the passenger's side of the dashboard, "er, Mr. Toorkninian, please slow down."

"You like Yahnkeez bezebill team?"

Mr. Toorkninian turned up the volume on his tape deck higher and higher until Carla found herself wrapped in the stereophonic bang, bang, eeck, eeck, boom, boom, clank, clank, clanking that blasted through four speakers.

"I don't know anything about baseball and I don't like heavy metal music. How about a little Rod Stewart, please?"

"Clunk, clunk, eeck, eeck," boomed from the speakers.

"Josh Groban?"

"I drink your blood, I kick your face," an angry voice snarled above the clunk, eeck, clunk, eeck.

"Mr. Toorkninian! Pleeeze turn off that music! It makes me sick."

Mr. Toorkninian's reply, a sudden sharp right turn off the bridge, forced Carla into the tattered remains of an armrest.

"Feck." She cringed back from the neatly chomped wad of gray gum that clung to her palm. It took all her courage to tentatively flick it to the floor.

"That's it, I've had enough. Stop the music." Carla pounded on the partition.

Mr. Toorkninian flashed a gold toothed smile at her in the rear view mirror. His hands merrily pounded the steering wheel in time with the music. "Nize, very nize lady. You relax. We here soon."

The cab rattled along at a steady sixty-five miles an hour all the while Mr. Toorkninian maneuvered around Grand Canyon-size potholes.

Mr. Toor…"

Carla's fists fell to her lap. Frustrated but not defeated, she withdrew a small bottle of aspirins from deep within the dark cavern of her super size tote bag. She neatly bisected the wad of cotton thoughtfully provided by the manufacturer, stuffed the pieces in her ears and triumphantly returned Mr. Toorkninian's rapturous smile.

"Mr. Toorkninian, I would love to make you listen to three hours of Andrea Bocelli," she shouted.

"Nize, nize," the cabby grinned back.

"...and then I would implant a tape in your head of all the songs ever recorded by Tony Bennett."

"Good, Lady. See, we here." The cab lurched to a dead stop.

Carla squinted through the dust encrusted cab window at the red neon Shoe Heaven sign high above an ugly cinder block building. "Thank you, Mr. Toorkninian, we must do this again sometime." She yanked the cotton from her ears, pulled her shoe free from the sticky grip of the same wad of gum that had clung to her hand just moments ago and gracefully climbed out of the cab.

"Carla, glad to see you, kid. Hope you don't mind if we get right to the point of your visit. I'm crunched for time and you're five minutes late." Harold Weinstein greeted his sister in the dingy reception room of his corporate empire with a brotherly blast of cigar smoke in her face and ushered her into his cluttered windowless office.

The place looked worse than Carla remembered. Ugly plastic shoes of every description plus some that defied the imagination merrily danced across the top of Harold's faded blue couch. They crowded their way in front of framed family photographs on the credenza. They huddled on bookshelves and perched on filing cabinets. She saw orange ankle straps with five-inch rhinestone heels, fluorescent green four-inch platforms, yellow and pink plaid high-top sneakers, magenta flip flops with monkeys and cats clinging to the straps, and a nifty little gold pump with plastic goldfish floating inside the see-through heels—and that was the daytime collection. The evening collection—don't ask.

The furniture equaled the awful caliber of the shoes. Harold bought it all at ten cents on the dollar from his biggest competitor after he had gleefully forced the poor man into bankruptcy. He used the money he saved on furniture to purchase the red ball head pins stuck on the wall map that marked his one hundred Shoe Heaven stores.

"What a dump! Why don't you fix it up?" Carla pushed half a dozen sample shoes off the lopsided chair Harold offered.

"Do I look like a Class A jerk, like our cousin Bernie? He spends his money on a fancy store with a fancy office and fancy clothes, but has he got a dime?" Back in high school, on the football field and with the ladies, Bernie had been Harold's arch familial rival. He owned the Carpet Heaven chain of one hundred and fifty discount rug stores.

"Why shouldn't Bernie spend money on nice things? He does very well and he's saved his nickels and dimes." Carla rose to her cousin's defense.

"Dimes he's got, kid." Harold peered over his half glasses. "But does he have bucks? I mean big bucks at the end of the year after he pays his fancy shmancy decorators, heavy overhead for those stores and don't forget the alimony he pays to five ex-wives." He sucked on his cigar.

"Come on, Harold, you pay alimony to three ex-wives. Is money the only thing that interests?"

"What's bad about that?" Harold flicked the long ash of his cigar and, as usual, missed the ashtray by two inches. "What's happened to my baby sister? Did she become a Commie in her middle age?" Harold used Communism as a comeback whenever someone accused him of being too wrapped up in amassing a fortune to enjoy life.

"Me, a Communist? Fat chance, but damn it, Harold, why does everything you do have to be related to money?"

"Because it's a fascinating commodity that no one can do without. But you didn't schlep out here to discuss my office decor or argue about money or Bernie, so what's up, Carla? Why are you here?" Harold looked at Carla with those warm puppy brown eyes that masked his shark soul.

She shifted in the uncomfortable chair. "Well, Harold, it's business, so I thought it would be better to see you in person instead of calling on the phone."

"What kind of business?" Harold's eyebrows rose like quarter moons on his forehead. "Hey, wait a second, say no more." His anger melted. "I should have guessed. Okay, you caught me. You want in, right? How much?" Harold rolled his cigar around in his mouth.

"In? How much? I don't know…" Beads of perspiration peppered Carla's upper lip. *It's Harold. My brother is the cat burglar.*

"Don't play coy. You're my sister, you know I'll cut you in."

"How could you? What drove you to it?" Carla's throat went dry, angry tears threatened to spill down her cheeks. "Is the business in trouble? Are you gambling again?" Carla forgot her promise to Mimi not to do or say anything rash until she contacted her, and continued to wave her red flag of accusations in Harold's face. "Are your children on drugs? How could you have sunk so low as to…"

"Sunk so low? What the hell are you talking about? What's wrong with going public? Don't you want some?"

"Some what?"

"Stock, you dummy! Don't you read the papers? Shoe Heaven went public last week. I'm franchising all over the place. It's the only way to go. The stock opened at eight and a quarter. Now it's up to fifteen." Harold's chest puffed with pride. "The damn stock will triple in a couple of weeks. You can make a killing. I made a bundle going public. I should have done it years ago."

"That's wonderful, Harold. I'm so glad that you didn't... I mean...that's not what I meant to say..."

"Sure, sure, I know what you want. You want a franchise. Right? What woman wouldn't love to own a shoe store? You're a damn centipede. Can't get enough shoes and now you can have your own place. It'll be great for you, kid. I've got a prime spot in Merrick that you can have cheap. You'll be back with all your friends. Do you a world of good. I told Larry just the other day that I don't think living in Manhattan is good for you."

"You spoke to Larry?" Carla attempted to leap up from the chair but her skirt was caught in a crack in the plastic seat and each time she stood up her skirt pulled her back down.

"Sure, Larry and I talk all the time. Don't blame me. You're the one who nagged me until I gave him my accounting business. I've been meaning to thank you for that. He's damn good. Never could understand why you two got divorced." Harold shook his head.

"Anyway, he bought a franchise. He doesn't run it. It's just an investment. He also threw in a few thousand on the first offering. Dad did, too. Say, didn't anybody tell you anything?" He noticed her blank expression. "I thought somebody would. Mom? I was too busy to call, but it's not too late." Harold rushed on, embarrassed by his oversight, "You can still make good dough on the deal. So how about it?"

"No, Harold, I don't want any damn deal you have for me," she snapped.

"Well, that money grubbing friend of yours sure wanted in."

"What friend of mine are you talking about?" Carla asked though she suspected from Harold's choked voice who he meant.

"Aldyn Sheridan, of course." Harold confirmed her hunch. "Do you think I meant Mimi the Amazon or Nellie Goody Two Shoes? After the witch read about the offering she wanted a franchise in a prime location. She had the guts to say she'd pay all cash if I gave her a discount. I told her no way."

Harold's reaction to Aldyn's demand baffled Carla. Her brother never passed up money. Something wasn't right. "I didn't think you knew Aldyn, although I wondered why you argued with her at my party."

"Listen, you're a big girl now what with your divorce and a new guy—one hell of a guy that Tony of yours—so I figure I can tell you. Aldyn and I had a thing three-four years ago," Harold confessed. "I was between wives and was looking for a bachelor pad. She showed me a half a dozen apartments. Didn't buy from her, but we had some good times together, then I sort of ended it. But she's one hard lady to shake."

Though furious that Harold thought Tony needed his stamp of approval, Carla kept her mind focused on his newest revelation. "What did Aldyn do? Did she keep calling or did she write nasty letters?"

Harold swiveled his dilapidated leather chair around a hundred and eighty degrees, which forced Carla to ask her questions to the chair. "None of the above. She'd pop up once in a while with some sad story about being short of cash, so I'd give her a coupla' hundred..."

"Come on Harold," Carla cut in, "you don't give anybody anything including your own family. Did she have something on you?"

"I'll be perfectly honest, Carla, yeah, she did. See, I didn't say goodbye to her till after I'd been married a couple months, and since Bunny had a mean temper, I paid Aldyn to keep quiet." Any lingering doubts that Carla had about Aldyn's side profession vanished. From the looks of it, Aldyn carried on her blackmailing business with half the guests at her party.

Carla became fascinated by the mushroom spiral of cigar smoke that hung above Harold's chair. She couldn't decide if it looked like an atomic cloud or a tornado twister. Both were extremely dangerous phenomena, the same as her brother when someone crossed him.

"Excuse me for sounding stupid, but which Bunny do you mean?" she asked.

"The last Bunny, not the new Bunny," the chair answered.

"But if you paid her, why were you arguing with her at the party?"

"Because the vicious witch recognized my new Bunny. She saw her in Vegas a couple years back when Bunny dated an important guy. He is, you know, well connected."

"You mean your new wife, my sister-in-law, had a Mafia lover?"

"Let's just say he is important and leave it at that. He's away and won't be coming back, but Aldyn threatened to spill the beans to the press."

"That's ridiculous, Harold. You aren't important enough for the press to care about, so why did Aldyn think she could blackmail you again?"

Carla felt stupid holding a conversation with the back of a chair, but she knew that Harold preferred to speak without looking the other person in the eye. It made it easier for him to lie.

"I'm running for president of the Manmade Shoe Manufacturers Society. The witch found out about it and thought it would ruin my chances of winning the election if it came out that my wife isn't exactly on the up and up. But I laughed in her face and told her to shove off because nobody cares about that stuff anymore. Look at all the crap they try to stick on politicians, but they still get elected."

"How did Aldyn take it? Did she threaten you?"

"Yeah, sort of. She huffed and puffed about how she'd make it hot for me then she walked away. I think she spotted another customer."

"Did you recognize the person?" Carla asked in a forced calm voice.

"No. Aldyn nailed me on my way to get Bunny a fresh drink. I knew she'd be pissed if I stayed away too long, so I headed for the bar and didn't pay any attention to what Aldyn did after that."

A new cloud of smoke rose above Harold's chair. "Now answer a question for me, Baby Sister. Why all the questions about Aldyn Sheridan? Is she blackmailing you, too?" The chair spun around. Harold's eyes locked on Carla.

"Don't be ridiculous. I told you, when I saw the two of you arguing I wondered what it could be about. That's all," Carla stuttered.

"You're sure about that?"

Carla nodded.

"Okay, so let's get back to the reason you took a twenty buck cab ride to see me. What do you want?"

"Well, what I want is," Carla fought to regain her composure, "you know that I work for an employment agency..."

"Yeah, Mom said something about it. What do you do? Send out the mail, answer the phones, that kind of crap?" Harold chomped on the turd between his teeth while he absent-mindedly scanned the computer printouts scattered all over his desk.

"Give me some credit, Harold. I'm an employment counselor. That's why I'm here. Will you give me an exclusive?"

"An exclusive what?"

"The exclusive right to provide Shoe Heaven with all its secretarial help." Carla thought her story sounded plausible and maybe Harold would give her some business.

"Why?"

"For a commission, why else? In return for saving you the trouble of advertising and screening applicants, you pay my company a commission of..."

"Hold it right there." Carla had struck the money nerve. "What do you think I am, a jerk?" Harold definitely was not a jerk. Though he had an M.B.A. from Harvard Business School, he talked and acted like a dope to fool anyone who tried to get the best of him.

"But, Harold..."

"No buts, kid. I hire my own help. They come and go so fast that no one ever gets a paid vacation because that means working here a full year. Can't say I blame 'em. Who'd want to work in this dump, even with a discount on shoes?" Harold nodded toward the tiny cubicles in the outer office crowded with sullen faced women pounding away on first generation computers.

"Well, maybe we could work out a trial offer. How about if I send you one free secretary? If you like her, we can go from there."

"For free you got yourself a deal. Been nice talking to you, come to the house sometime for dinner. Bunny would love to see you again." Harold smiled for the first time, happy that the meeting had turn out to be profitable. Maybe only marginally profitable, but that's better than if it had cost him something.

"Oh, one more thing." Carla sniffed the air. She tried to catch a whiff of Harold's cologne but the stench of his cigars over-powered every odor on earth, with the exception of skunk in the summer.

"What should I get Dad for his birthday?"

"Get him a nice sport shirt." Harold shrugged.

"No, I don't want to give him another sport shirt. I thought cologne would be nice, but I don't know what kind to buy for him. Since you have such good taste..." Carla bit her lip on the lie. "What do you wear?"

Harold tilted back in his faded burgundy leather chair and chomped his cigar. "Canoe," he said affirmatively.

Carla blinked. "What do boats have to do with Dad's birthday present?"

"Not boat canoe, dummy. Canoe, Canoe. You asked, I told you. That's what I wear. Been wearing it for thirty years. Didn't you ever smell it on me? It has a certain distinction. Nice, classy citrus scent, yet not overpowering like some of that sissy stuff they make for men now. Here, take a whiff." Harold opened the bottom drawer of his desk and pulled out the familiar bottle with the signal flags on the label. "Great isn't it?" He spritzed the air.

No sneeze.

"Good, Dad will love it." Carla smiled. She crossed Harold off her mental list of suspects.

"Wrong," Harold said. "He wears that junk that Mom gets wholesale for five bucks a gallon. So don't waste your money on cologne. Take my advice, Carla, a nice shirt from Bloomingdale's. Bright colors, short sleeves, size Medium. I had Bunny get three for him. He'll love another one. You can't go wrong."

Chapter 25

"Hi! I'm back." Carla collapsed into the rattan peacock chair in Kitty's office. Last night's dreamless sleep and her visit with Harold left her exhausted and emotionally drained.

"So, what he'd say?"

Kitty looked up from the latest issue of *Vogue*. A quick glance through the fashion magazines stocked for the apps satisfied Kitty's desire to keep up with the fashion scene. She rarely shopped in stores. Her extensive collection of custom-made tent dresses and dyed to match Reeboks carried her through the four seasons.

"Who do you mean?" Carla almost forgot the story she had told her boss. "Oh, the doctor. He said everything is fine, nothing serious."

"Yeah, I knew the mugger didn't hurt you much, but are you pregnant?" Kitty's periwinkle blue eyes stared at Carla's stomach.

"Me, pregnant? What gave you that idea?" Carla defensively ran her hand down the front of her slim pencil skirt.

"Well, I know you've been dealing with a lot of problems what with thinking you saw a body and Tony's disappearing act, but you have to admit that you've been acting nuttier than usual so I thought being pregnant, especially at your age, might explain…" Kitty's raspy voice trailed off. She called 'em the way she saw 'em, and today she saw Carla pregnant.

"At my age! What do you mean by at my age? I'm not that old and I'm still capable of being pregnant, but I'm not. I can't believe that you would think…" Carla caught herself. No matter how far off base Kitty might be, Carla had to play it cool. As the owner of Career Steps, Kitty had the power to toss Carla out of a job that she needed and loved. "No, I'm not pregnant. I'm tense. I'm sorry I got so upset."

"It's forgotten, honey. I'm sorry I upset you, but if you get into trouble, no matter what, let me know." Kitty reached across her desk to give Carla's hand a motherly pat, the same as Nancy did a couple of days ago. "And speaking of trouble, I've got good news for you. Charlie is ready to give you that reading he promised. He'll do it after work today for free, and then everything will be all right." Kitty's broad smile indicated that she believed Charlie's psychic reading would make all of Carla's troubles vanish.

Carla forced a weak grin. "I appreciate that Charlie wants to help me, but how can he? His lips are sealed. And I did I tell you that I don't believe in things like ESP or tarot card readings, so if it's all the same to you, I'll pass."

Kitty's face drooped longer than its normal sag. She didn't like to be refused. "You don't understand. He's going to tell you things about yourself, not anything about Aldyn, so his dumb code of ethics doesn't hold. Look, honey, I can't explain exactly what Charlie does since he won't do a reading for me. Says it won't work because he knows me too well, but I know he's good. No, change that—he's great! He's been written up in all the best magazines—*New York, Playboy, the National Enquirer*, you name it. And it's free, so what have you got to lose?" Kitty had made her point.

Carla waited nervously to be admitted to the only seedy town house on the otherwise gentrified Upper West Side block. Charlie had lived alone in this West End Avenue house for years before he married Kitty. Now he used it as his office and as a getaway when he needed space from his beloved. The door opened on the fourth gasp of the asthmatic buzzer. The Seer to the Stars greeted Carla with a wispy smile.

"You are right on time, my dear. I admire promptness in a woman, although my darling Kitty has yet to learn that virtue. Come in."

Charlie continued to prattle on about punctuality all the while he escorted Carla down a dark, narrow hallway that led to his oak-beamed consultation room. Flickering votive candles revealed a room jammed full of massive furniture and murky paintings, all badly in need of restoration. The combination of heavy damask draperies, dusty Oriental carpets plus the over-powering odor of tobacco and mold reminded Carla of a crypt, though she'd never visited one.

"Come right this way, my dear." Charlie led her deeper into the gloomy room.

"What are you going to do?"

"Have no fear, Carla. I'm quite good at this. You will feel better in no time."

Right. Sure. Carla became apprehensive. They were alone in this big, old gloomy house, and nice as Charlie appeared to be, who knows what he might do once he put her under a spell?

Charlie gently eased her into a black leather Eames chair, an incongruous piece of modern furniture in the otherwise Gothic room. He stood over her. "Let your body float. Close your eyes." As his long fingers exerted light pressure on her forehead, the mask of numbing pain behind her eyes slid away. "You feel better now, don't you?"

"Oh, much, thank you. But before you start to do whatever it is you do, I have to be honest and tell you that I never…that is, I don't…"

"You don't believe in seers, ESP or astrology." Charlie finished her sentence. "Of course, you don't. Most people don't, but they read their horoscopes every morning. I'll bet you do, too." Charlie's voice turned gently indulgent.

"Well, once in a while." Carla blushed.

"You see, you are not as much of a skeptic as you pretend to be. So, if you read your horoscope, then you know that our lives are influenced by outside forces—some good, some evil. Think of me as the postman who delivers messages to you from these forces. I tell you what is happening around you so you can take action. Based on what I tell you, you can alter your future."

Even as Carla told herself that Charlie was either a nut case or a scoundrel, her head nodded in agreement with his sales pitch.

"Excuse me, Carla. I must wash my hands before I receive the messages."

"Of course, you don't want to get the messages dirty." Carla made a nervous joke of what she assumed was Charlie's old fashioned way of saying he needed to use the bathroom.

A pained expression clouded his face. "I thought you understood. Messages are transmitted to me through waves of energy. They go into my brain. Now if you will excuse me."

Charlie lifted the lid of a Capo Di Monte porcelain candy dish festooned with cavorting naked cherubs and removed a packet of moist disposable towels similar to the ones gambling casinos hand out to gamblers after they trade in their dirty slot machine coins for paper money. He meticulously wiped his hands three times before he tossed the towel into an overflowing wicker wastebasket.

"Now we are ready."

Charlie lowered his fragile bones into a worn emerald velvet chair. His gnarled hand dug his old meerschaum pipe into an oilskin pouch filled with sweet smelling tobacco. He pushed and kneaded the tobacco in the bowl until it had just the right texture, then he lit the pipe with a wooden match and sucked hard on the stem till his parchment-thin cheeks threatened to collapse inward. All the while he performed this ritualized task, Charlie's unblinking eyes stared at Carla, who in turn stared back at him and wondered what the hell he was doing.

His regular clients knew that Charlie would not proceed until he received a divine message. The stare-out between seer and client would continue for ten seconds or ten minutes or however long it took for a message to travel from outer space to the West Side of Manhattan.

"Aha!" After three minutes, Charlie slapped the side of his chair with a rapid rug beater motion that sent a thick cloud of dust spiraling toward the beamed ceiling. *"Friends have secrets to tell. You will be shocked by what you hear, but listen well."* Charlie sat ramrod straight, his head cocked to one side. "*Danger, grave danger surrounds you. You must be careful.*" His soft voice accelerated to a roar, his eyes bore into hers. "*Beware of a man who is very close to you. He wears two faces. Do not trust him.*" Charlie puffed hard on his pipe.

"Who is he?" Carla demanded.

"I can't say."

"Then tell me how I can save myself," she begged. Charlie's grim warning erased her earlier skepticism about his mystical powers.

"There is nothing you can do." Charlie paused to let the gravity of his words sink in before he continued, "*Another controls your fate. You will be dragged and*

carried toward danger, but an unexpected loved one will rescue you."

You have to give me a better description than that. Who will save me? A relative? A man? A woman?" Carla's husky voice changed to a terrified squeak. Her eyes pleaded with Charlie to give her another clue to her rescuer's identity.

The Seer to the Stars puffed three times on his pipe. "*He is short and has white hair.*"

"My Uncle Ben, who lives in Florida, is going to save me? He can't. He's seventy-six years old and walks with a cane."

"That's all I have to say." Charlie slumped back in his chair.

"Well, what about Aldyn? Where is she?" Carla pleaded, but Charlie's eyes looked beyond her. The session had ended.

Chapter 26

Carla debated with herself whether to take a cab or a couple of buses to return home from Charlie's town house. A cab ride was expensive and fast. Public transportation was cheaper, but she'd have to take two buses to get to the Upper East Side—AND walk from West End Avenue over to Broadway to catch the first bus, then she'd have another one-block walk to her apartment after she got off the second bus. Between walking to the bus stop, waiting for two buses and walking the rest of the way home, her trip could easily take forty-five minutes. The heck with the cost, Carla hailed a cab.

"Let me off at 53rd and Third," she instructed the driver as the cab whizzed through Central Park. She'd stop at the shoemaker and save herself a special trip there tomorrow.

"New lifts, new tips and a shine and they're good as new. That'll be thirteen bucks." The shoemaker offered Carla her repaired beige shoes for inspection before he slipped them into a plastic bag.

"Thanks." As she turned to leave the shop she glanced through the large front window in time to see Caitlin Oliver strutting down the street. Whenever they met, the model found something to complain about, which made her the last person in the world Carla wanted to walk home with today. She turned her head quickly so as not to be seen, then counted to twenty before she left the shop.

By the time Carla walked down East 53rd Street to Second Avenue in the gathering darkness, Caitlin was a block ahead of her at East 54th Street. Her waist-length black hair and her famous catwalk strut made her easy to spot. A man wearing a gray warm-up suit and a New York Yankees baseball cap pulled down low over his eyes, suddenly cut ahead of a middle aged couple and jogged slowly behind Caitlin. Carla feared he might be stalking Caitlin the same way the foul smelling mugger stalked her. Her apprehension dissolved when he suddenly sped ahead of the model.

Heavy evening traffic careened wildly up First Avenue as Caitlin approached the intersection. A few feet back from the curb the man in the warm-up suit jogged in a circle while he waited for the red "Don't Walk" sign to flash to green "Walk." A delivery truck speeded up to make the changing light just as Caitlin reached the curb.

Carla saw the jogger sprint toward Caitlin. His shoulder knocked her. There was a blood chilling scream, the sickening thud of a body being hit, and the long shrill screech of brakes.

"Stop him. Please stop him. He went that way," Carla screamed to a guy on roller blades as she helplessly watched the jogger bolt down First Avenue.

"Where, lady?" He looked where Carla pointed. "I don't see anybody, but I'll give it a try." The skater took off.

Carla pushed her way through the crowd gathered around Caitlin. The model lay in the street covered with a passerby's khaki jacket. Her head rested on a pillow made from a rolled up white sweater. Both oozed blood.

"Caitlin, it's Carla Miller. Carla knelt beside her. "Can you hear me?" She spoke to the model's left cheek, the only part of her once beautiful face not smashed and bloodied.

"Yes," she whispered. Carla held her hand. It felt cold.

"Do you know who pushed you?"

"Him. He wore…" The sound of wailing sirens drowned Caitlin's words.

Three police cars and an ambulance screeched to a stop inches from the crowd of spectators. Within seconds an emergency medical team had Caitlin hooked up to an IV. A police officer spoke to the horrified truck driver. He sat on the sidewalk, his head in his hands, repeating over and over, "It's not my fault. Somebody shoved her."

An EMS technician loaded down with more medical gear pushed Carla away from Caitlin's side. Minutes later a detective approached her. "Did you know her?" he asked.

"'Did'? She's dead?" Unexpected tears spilled down Carla's cheeks—the same as when she'd discovered Aldyn's body. She wondered why death reversed her feelings about people.

"Can I take your statement now, ma'am?" Carla realized the detective was still speaking to her. "Then I'll have someone to drive you home. You okay?" the officer asked, but he knew "okay" did not describe her.

"Sure," Carla whispered her lie and fought hard to keep her emotions under a tight rein. She was in a state of shock. Her body trembled with fear. She looked like a tiny child shrunk deep within her blood smeared clothes.

Carla told the officer about the man in the warm-up suit and the rollerblader who gave chase. He didn't comment on anything she said, but glanced up from his notebook when she told him about Caitlin's earlier allegation that she could identify the cat burglar. She wondered why Officers Ramirez and Murkowski weren't on the scene. The only time she had a real body and her cop friends didn't show up.

The promised ride in the patrol car marked the second time Carla returned home in a police cruiser. The first time she was a sobbing seven year-old, who became lost in the zoo and came home with a balloon, ice cream and flashing lights. Forty years later, Carla only got awkward small talk from the cop who chauffeured her back to East 56th Street.

Cliché or not, bad news does travel fast. The doorman and Timmy O'Grady, the super, greeted Carla with glum faces when she got out of the patrol car. "The cops, they've been here already, Miz Miller. And I'm that sad about Miz Oliver. A lovely lady." Timmy lied. He despised Caitlin for her constant complaints, but, now that she'd no longer be around to pester him, he could afford to be charitable. "And what's to become of that sweet dog of hers, waiting patient as a lamb for his mistress to walk and feed him?"

"Chin Chou? Can't you walk him?"

"Me? Walk a dog?" Timmy screwed up his fat round face like he'd been asked to eat a rat. "I would do it gladly for the dear Miz Oliver, but don't you know I'm allergic to the fine little animals."

Carla didn't believe one word of his excuse. If anything, his allergy had to do with the New York City's pooper scooper law, which mandates that dog walkers must pick up after their pooches or pay a fine—if they're caught. "Well, how about the doormen? Can't one of them walk Chin Chou?" she asked hopefully.

"Against the co-op board rules. If someone in the building doesn't walk the dear dog, he'll have to wait till a family member comes for him, and that could be who knows when. Maybe by that time his dear little bladder will burst."

"I'll do it," Carla snapped.

The grin on Timmy's face told her sure as any spoken words that she'd been duped. Bad enough she didn't like the Shar Pei, but she'd never walked a dog on a leash and certainly never picked up after one. When Carla lived in Merrick, she opened her back door and said "Go" to Bonkers, who obediently trotted out to the fenced in yard, did whatever he needed to do, then returned indoors without the need for her to join him in the cold, rain, sleet or snow. Periodically, Larry the Louse or the monthly gardener walked gingerly through the grass to scoop up his accumulated droppings.

"That's real nice of you, Miz Miller. I already explained the situation to the cops and they gave permission for the dog walker to go into the apartment. Here's the keys." Timmy dropped them in her hand.

"So who is coming for Chin Chou?"

"That'll be her brother Ned. He'll be coming as soon as he's arranged her er, you know, so's all you have to do is feed the dog and walk him now and maybe later depending on when himself shows up."

"Only twice. How nice."

Carla changed into jeans and a shirt, then tossed her bloody clothes down the trash chute on the floor below, just as she disposed of the shorts and top that she'd worn when she nearly got raped.

The keys that the super gave Carla for Penthouse A slid effortlessly into the locks. An interior designer had done the apartment in a sophisticated Art Deco style. Neutral colors were used throughout the apartment, occasionally accented with black or turquoise. Black lacquer, ivory and crystal accessories complimented the blonde furniture. A zebra skin rug partially covered the polished parquet living room floor. A talented landscape architect had transformed the terrace into a Japanese meditation garden.

Carla expected to find Chin Chou waiting at the door ready to attack her or to give her a friendly greeting. The dog did neither. He lay on Caitlin's king size bed, snoring loudly. Carla's hand hovered over his head, ready to waken the orphaned dog. *Don't be a fool, this is your opportunity*, she told herself. Her hand dropped. Carla would search the empty apartment for clues that might lead to the identity of the mysterious man at the AIDS party. She reminded herself not to touch anything in case the police dusted for fingerprints.

The living room and kitchen held no visible secrets. No surprises in the bathroom either, only a lot of expensive cosmetics plus some over-the-counter and prescription medications. She tiptoed back into the bedroom. A mirrored tray in the middle of the bureau held a collection of Lalique perfume bottles. Carla sniffed each one without touching the stoppers. They were all grassy scents. She also sniffed a pile of clothes dumped on the floor. They smelled of the same fresh fragrances.

Carla wrapped a tissue around her hand before she opened the door to what she assumed would be a small apartment-size closet. It was a closet, but it wasn't apartment-size. The closet was the size of a bedroom. Actually, it had been a bedroom until Caitlin's architect transformed her two-bedroom apartment into a one-bedroom plus a huge walk-in closet. Carla inspected the racks, shelves and bins crammed with Caitlin's enormous wardrobe. All the garments hung on padded hangers, covered with clear plastic cleaner's bags. An index card pinned to each bag listed the accessories to be worn with the garment. Countless handbags stood at attention on rows of padded shelves, while dozens of hats flipped and flopped on hat stands on a shelf above the racks of clothing.

Clear Lucite boxes allowed Carla to see but not touch Caitlin's enormous collection of shoes. She owned day shoes, evening shoes, summer, winter and fall shoes, beach shoes, rain boots, snow boots, fashion boots plus shoes for various sports. She had stiletto, high, medium and low heel shoes, also open toe, close toe, sling back, slides, sandals and thongs. She owned shoes in every imaginable color; a few were even multi-color or print. Her black and beige shoes came in every heel height and every style. The rows and rows of boxed shoes reminded Carla of her brother's showroom, except Caitlin's collection did not include any shoes fashioned from manmade material.

Carla walked deeper and deeper into the closet. Achoo, achoo, achoo. She sneezed. *He's been here.* Carla forced herself to continue her search. At the farthest corner of the closet her nose picked up another smell that didn't make her sneeze. It had a familiar musky odor. Carla's eyes swept the tiny space until she spotted a swatch of gray fabric caught on a raised floor board. The scent of Opium and the fabric were unmistakable—they belonged to Alydn Sheridan. *This is where the cat burglar brought her body after Carla left the trash room.* Carla slipped the bit of fabric into her pocket and continued her search.

She was on her knees examining a small black safe welded to the floor when something scratched her thigh. Carla spun around ready to battle another attacker, then she smiled. "Chin Chou, you scared me half to death," she stuttered. The wrinkled dog stood behind her. He alternately scratched her with his paw and trotted in and out of the closet. When he guided her to the leash that hung from a hook beside the front door, she caught on to his charade. He wanted to go for a walk. Conversation in the lobby stopped the moment Carla and her four-footed charge walked out of the elevator.

She pushed thoughts of murder out of her mind to allow herself to concentrate on her dog walking duties. "Up and down the block once, then home. Okay?"

Chin Chou did not obey her command. He pulled her down East 56th Street, across Sutton Place and up East 57th Street. The dreaded "it" happened after they turned onto First Avenue. Without warning, he squatted and made a large night deposit smack in front of the bank at the corner of First Avenue and East 57th Street. Carla looked from the mound to the dog and up and down First Avenue. Not a pooper scooper patrolperson in sight. "We're out of here." She tugged on Chin Chou's leash and ran with him back to the apartment building. Their return to the lobby didn't rate a second glance from the doorman or concierge.

Carla froze at the sound of a male voice when she and Chin Chou walked into the apartment. *It's Caitlin's brother*, she thought before she realized her mistake. The voice came from the answering machine. She listened intently to the end of the message: *"And about the AIDS benefit at Dawn's place, no one can put a name on the man you described. He either crashed or came with that group from the record company. The police questioned Dawn about him, too, and she's mad as hell that you think someone at her party stole your Black Beauty pearls. You should apologize to her. I'll call back next week."*

The message would have been of no help to Caitlin, but it helped Carla. Now she knew that the cat burglar looked good enough to be invited to a fancy party—or crash it without causing any suspicion, which eliminated her mugger. His bad breath and body odor wouldn't get him further than the front door of any place except a third rate hotel.

A whack on Carla's leg interrupted her thoughts about the phone message. Chin Chou had returned. "Okay, I'll feed you, if you'll show me where to find your food."

The dog understood. He nuzzled his nose against a bottom kitchen cabinet that indeed held cans of dog food, cartons of biscuits and three bowls inscribed with his name. Carla obligingly filled the bowls with water, a lamb and rice combination and biscuits.

"I'll be back later," she told the dog. He ignored her farewell and began to chow down his dinner.

Chapter 27

Carla heard the phone ringing as she opened the door to her apartment. She bypassed the kitchen phone and dashed into her bedroom to catch the call.

"Well, it's too late." A loud *tut* crackled through the telephone line as soon as she picked up the receiver.

Carla's stomach tensed. Immediately after Charlie warned her about danger surrounding her, she witnessed a murder. What more could go wrong today? "Too late for what? What's wrong, Mother? Today isn't Monday."

"It's too late for you to get a free fur coat from Jackie. That's what's wrong,"

Carla relaxed. No trouble in Florida, only that damn coat again.

"I told you that coat isn't exactly free and why is it too late?"

"Because Jackie is in jail. I just got off the phone with Jessie Demmer. She is beside herself." Mrs. Weinstein *tutted* her way through the last sentence.

"What did he do?"

"She kept repeating that Jackie has problems because something is all over. Poor Jessie was crying so hard that even though I could hardly understand her I still sympathized with her because I know how broken hearted I'd be if God forbid Harold got arrested."

"Never mind Harold, what happened to Jack?"

"Let me finish, dear. I told Jessie that no matter how upset she is, she shouldn't assume that nothing can be done for Jackie. He can always appeal. *Tut.*"

"Are you sure that Mrs. Demmer said 'all over'? Could she have said 'Aldyn'?"

"Mrs. Demmer definitely said 'all over' but she got the story from Jackie and maybe he said 'all done'."

"No, Mother, Jack didn't say 'all done.' He said 'Aldyn.'" Carla pronounced the name "All din." "That's a woman who can cause a lot of trouble. Tell me exactly what Mrs. Demmer said."

"I'm trying, dear, but you keep interrupting. You've done that ever since you learned to talk. I don't know who you get it from, certainly not from me."

"I swear I won't interrupt anymore, if you just tell me everything that Mrs. Demmer said. It's important."

"There's not much more to tell because Jackie could only talk for five minutes. This 'all done' or 'all din' person turned him into the IRS for cheating on his income tax returns. It's awful. They took all his records and closed the store. This is worse than the last time he got arrested."

"The last time? When?" Carla knew nothing of Jack's previous arrest.

"Three years ago and don't interrupt," Mrs. Weinstein warned and picked up the conversation where she left off. "He kicked one of the IRS agents. That's when they dragged him off to jail, like a common thief. *Tut.*"

Carla couldn't figure out if Mrs. Weinstein's *tut* indicated concern for Jack or the decked IRS agent.

"Did Jack say why he's so sure that Aldyn turned him in?" The bedroom spun at a crazy speed as she envisioned Jack, dressed in a black cat suit and a Lone Ranger mask, pursuing Aldyn. If Aldyn threatened to turn Jack into the IRS, he had a good motive to kill her.

"He told Jessie that 'all done' threatened to call the IRS if he didn't give her a lot of money but he didn't take her seriously. Of course, when the agents showed up just as he opened the store this morning, he knew that she meant business. Turn on your TV, it's probably on the news right now."

"Too late, Mother, the news is over. I'll catch it at eleven o'clock."

"Are you all right, dear? Your voice sounds strange."

"I'm fine. Just a little tired."

"That's good, dear, and speaking of voices, your father has been elected the president of the new choral group at the Golden Age center, you know, the Liberation Chorus."

"What kind of name is that for a senior citizens group? Who came up with it? It sounds like a Marxist organization." Carla fought to keep her mind focused on her conversation with her mother.

"I named the group. It was either that or the Alter Kakers Korus, and I thought it sounded…"

"Mother," Carla interrupted, "how's Uncle Ben?"

"All of a sudden you're the dutiful niece, asking about your uncle. He's fine. *Tut.*"

"So his arthritis is better?" Perhaps he could save her from Charlie's predicted danger.

"No, I mean he's doing fine walking with two canes." Mrs. Weinstein's voice trailed off then came back strong with a new topic, "Now about Nancy."

"What about her?"

"Does she have to get personally involved with a pig?" Mrs. Weinstein bristled. Without waiting for Carla's response, she continued, "Heaven knows, your father and I don't keep a kosher house. And although we eat shell fish, we don't ever touch pig."

"Are you talking about Nancy's Renaissance Festival? She's grilling or stewing or doing something to a boar and she has to clean its teeth. I know all about it."

"Yes, she said it's a boar, but I'm not stupid. I know that a boar is just an ugly overgrown pig. Your father and I talked it over and we decided that you should tell Nancy that if she must brush an animal's teeth for her party, then she should go to the butcher and get a nice kosher chicken."

"Chicken don't have teeth, Mother, and why should I tell her that she shouldn't be a pig's dental hygienist? Why don't you do it?"

"I don't want to hurt her feelings. You do it. You're her mother!"

Click.

Carla stretched out on her bed. She needed time to think about the latest turn of events. Maybe Jack did kill Aldyn, but he couldn't have killed Caitlin. The IRS took him to jail before she was pushed in front of the truck. And what about Charlie's predictions? It didn't seem likely that Jack could be the person he warned her about. Why did the killer leave Aldyn's body in Caitlin's apartment? Where is it now? Carla punched her pillow. Where had all her running around gotten her? She wasn't one step closer to finding the cat burglar than before.

During the next few hours Carla pushed Mimi's speed dial number over and over, but always hung up before the phone rang. She couldn't bear to relate the events of her horrendous day to her friend. When gnawing hunger pangs reminded her that she hadn't eaten since noon,

Carla trudged into the kitchen in search of any edible leftovers that might be lurking in the refrigerator.

"Achoo, achoo, achoo," a trio of sneezes exploded when she crossed the kitchen threshold. Carla didn't need Charlie's ESP to know what she would find when she climbed up her kitchen ladder and peered inside the air vent. "Damn," she shouted. What glistened in the light didn't surprise her—enough bracelets, necklaces and earrings studded with precious stones to make Elizabeth Taylor hyperventilate.

"Damn, damn, damn," she shouted over and over as she closed the vent and scrambled down from her perch atop her ladder.

The cat burglar had been here today. He might have been walking away from the area when he seized the opportunity to kill Caitlin. Carla shivered. Compared to his reaction to Caitlin's hint that she could identify him, the threatening note he left in her bedroom seemed downright friendly. Her appetite disappeared.

Carla returned to Penthouse A to take Chin Chou out for his last walk of the day. As she started to put the key in the lock, the door sudden burst open.

"Who are you?" Carla and a tall, dark, handsome man asked in one voice.

"Carla Miller."

"Ned Oliver."

"I walked and fed Chin Chou. I've come back to walk him again."

"I'm Caitlin's brother that is I was…"

"I was with her…"

"I know. The police told me. Thank you."

"Can I help you with anything?"

"No. I'll be all right. I'm taking Chin Chou."

"Then I'll go. Goodbye."

"Goodbye."

They smiled.

Carla left.

CHAPTER 28

Caitlin's death rated barely two inches of space in the Metro Section of the *New York Times* with the unimaginative headline *Model Killed by Truck*. The *Post* and *Daily News* juiced up their front page coverage with photos of Caitlin and more creative headlines. One read *Model Mashed By Truck*; the other *Famous Model Mowed Down*. The inside stories speculated that she may have been killed by the East Side Cat Burglar. Carla became upset when she discovered that both tabloids identified her as an eye witness to the accident, though one who hadn't see the killer's face. They also got her age wrong.

Between repeating what she knew about Caitlin's murder and denying that she was forty-nine years old to everyone who called the office, Carla got very little work done. Tony, the only person she wanted to speak to, didn't phone. He hadn't called last night either.

Late in the afternoon she stopped at the Seventeenth Precinct to sign the statement she made at the accident scene. "Have you read it carefully, Mrs. Miller? Is it correct?" the detective asked.

"Yes, it's exactly as I told you." Carla used his black Bic pen to scrawl her name at the bottom of the page.

"Well, thanks for coming in." The detective hesitated as he rose to escort her out of his tiny office. "Is there any connection between what happened yesterday and the two bodies you reported to the precinct?"

"What?" Carla feigned indignation and prayed the detective could not hear her wildly pounding heart.

"It's like this, Mrs. Miller, I ran a routine check of your name in our computer and came across the reports you made about those two bodies that turned out not to be bodies. So my question is, are you sure you saw someone push Ms Oliver? We located the skater, but he said he didn't see the guy. None of the other witnesses saw him, either."

"The truck driver did."

"It's to his advantage, isn't it?"

"Are you implying that I imagined seeing someone push Caitlin Oliver into the path of the truck?"

"Not exactly, ma'am. I'm only trying to get the facts straight."

Carla smiled. She had considered telling him abut the strange goings on in her apartment, but now she knew to stick to her first instincts—D*on't tell the police anything.* "I told you exactly how the accident happened. If you don't have any other questions, I'll be going."

A large easeled portrait of Caitlin banked with fresh flowers and twinkling votive candles greeted Carla when she strode into the lobby of her apartment building. Timmy, resplendent in the first suit and tie Carla had ever seen him wear, stood by the door acting as the host of the impromptu wake. A supernatural talent allowed him to blink out a crocodile tear each time he solemnly greeted a resident with a sweaty handshake and a mumbled "Tragic loss to the world." Unwilling to endure his phony display of grief, Carla joined a group of people who had already passed through the receiving line and were headed for the elevator.

Two simultaneous sounds greeted Carla when she opened her apartment door—a door closed and the intercom buzzed. "Miz Miller, Mr. Vitale is here to see you," the doorman announced.

"Oh, oh, my goodness. Send him right up."

Carla pinched a bit of color into her pale cheeks a moment before the door bell rang. She flung open the door and everything turned navy blue pinstripe.

"Hello, Beautiful. I missed you," Tony whispered.

Wrapped in the warm blanket of his embrace, her head nestled against his chest, all her questions about where he'd been for the past few days disappeared. Her arms slipped under his jacket to caress his tight rear end. "You feel delicious," she murmured. Her hands took the slow path up to the small of his back.

"I want to…" She pulled away from him. "What's that?" she cried.

"That? It's nothing to be concerned with. In my rush to here, I forgot to put it away. I've been meaning to tell you about it." Tony tried to pull Carla back into his arms, but she kept her arms crossed in front of her chest to protect herself from his touch.

"Sc-sc-ared? Why should I be sc-sc-scared?" she stuttered. "You disappear for days at a time. You use a credit card to unlock my door and now I discover that you carry a gun."

"Trust me, Carla. I can't tell you what's going on now, but when I do you'll understand. All those questions about the cat burglar, you think I'm him, don't you? I'm not. Honest, I'm not."

Carla nodded. "Yes, I know you're not the cat burglar because you don't smell."

"I don't what?"

"I mean you don't wear cologne. The cat burglar wears cologne and he's someone I've know for a long time. That also eliminates you. It's very complicated."

"I'm glad we both agree that I'm not your cat burglar. You know I'm just an ordinary guy."

"Hah! Just an ordinary guy who carries a gun." Carla scoffed.

He returned her doubt with a lopsided grin. "Bad choice of words, I guess. If you'll calm down, I'll explain the gun."

Carla blinked three times before she opened her eyes wide, not as a coded assent, but as a way to fight back the storm of tears that threatened to brim over her eyes. "How can I believe you?" An uncooperative tear rolled down her cheek.

"Why not? Did I ever lie to you?" Lines of concern creased his brow. "Sit down and tell me what's bothering you." Tony maneuvered Carla into the living room, then gently guided her to the couch.

"A lot of things are bothering me, like when I called you at the hotel in Washington and the operator said you weren't registered."

"Why didn't you call me on my cell phone?"

"Because I jotted down the wrong number, so I called the hotel direct. I got the number from Information."

Tony's mouth tensed so slightly that Carla might have missed his reaction to her answer had she not been staring directly at him. "Did you spell my name?"

"No." Tony had her on the defensive.

"That explains it. She probably thought you said 'Battale' or 'Natale'. Happens all the time. Look, I'll show you the bill." He reached into the inside pocket of his jacket.

"Never mind, I believe you. I've never caught you in a lie before, but sometimes I think you're not telling me the whole story."

"I admit it, I'm guilty. I do leave out things, but it's for your protection." Tony put a strong arm around her shoulder for emphasis.

"You have a gun because I need protection? Or are you a cop or the FBI or what?"

Tony ran his hand through his hair. "Well, you sort of hit on it. I'm not a business insurance broker. I made up that story because I thought you might be uneasy if I told you the truth. Years ago I was an FBI agent, but now I'm on my own."

The quizzical look on Carla's face forced him to expand his explanation. "I have a corporate investigation agency in Jersey. My office is there instead of Manhattan to keep a low profile. And before you ask, I'll tell you that sometimes I use the broker story as a cover. That's why I have that business card. I'm also a security consultant."

"A what?"

An FBI agent Carla could accept even though Tony's Roman profile didn't fit the Robert Redford look she imagined for an agent. But a security consultant? What the hell is that? Sounded fishy to her. She would not tolerate a shady prospective lover. That would be too much of a compromise, even if she believed an article that concluded with the sobering prediction that the odds of a woman of her age finding an eligible man are close to zilch.

"Honest, I didn't make it up. I have ten full-time operatives. They're former CIA, FBI and IRS agents, some lawyers, some accountants—all professions.

"You better begin at the beginning." Carla didn't like that ominous word "operatives" or the way he threw around connections with the CIA and the FBI.

Tony smiled at her the kind of smile that offered an apology. After a long pause he said, "Here's the short version of my life. I grew up in the Bath Beach section of Brooklyn near the Verrazano Bridge. The day after I graduated from high school I joined the army and got shipped to Vietnam. But by that time the war had about come to an end so I spent most of my enlistment back in the States. After I got discharged, I enrolled in NYU. The day after I graduated from law school, I married Dolores then…"

"And speaking of Dolores," Carla interrupted to ask that nagging question, "How do you explain the fact that Victor Reynolds birth name was Ricci, the same as Dolores' maiden name?"

"What are you talking about? It's a common name. I don't know the man. Who is he?"

"He owned this apartment. Don't you remember that I told you I bought it from his daughter?" Carla didn't like being put on the defensive, so she nudged him back to his story. "What happened after you graduated from law school?"

"My plans made a 180 degree change. I seriously considered a couple of offers from big name corporate law firms until I saw an ad in the *Times* for FBI agents. The job description sounded like fun and I had all the qualifications, so I said why not. I spent a couple of years at the Vegas office, then Philadelphia. I'd been at 26 Federal Plaza about a year when I got a call from Washington. They wanted me to…"

"Who's 'they' and how did 'they' know about you?"

"They, them, whoever. Come on, stop interrupting. Let me tell the story." The unexpected sharpness in Tony's voice scared Carla into silence. "…the agency offered me a job as a Special Investigator. They needed guys like me who had special skills." Even though Tony didn't offer to name the agency that wished to employ him, Carla suspected that most everyone referred to it by three initials, same as the FBI. And she wondered why he didn't explain what special skills he had or where he learned them.

"I spent most of my time in DC, but I also drifted around the Middle East and Africa."

"Some drift."

"Knock it off, Carla." Tony's voice turned sharp again. "You asked, so let me tell the story my way."

She nodded.

"Two years ago I took early retirement." Tony's hand idly stroked her arm.

Carla broke away from his touch. She wanted to throw herself into his arms, kiss the tiny laugh lines around his eyes and run her tongue across his deliciously sensuous lower lip but if she did, all of what he had been leading up to would end in another half-finished story.

Half-finished stories were a way of life with Carla. A telephone call interrupted Rose Weinstein just as she started to tell sixteen-year old Carla what Cousin Stella did that forced her to move from Philadelphia to Terre Haute, Indiana. After the call Mrs. Weinstein said she had a headache and never finished the story. Larry the Louse didn't leave a story unfinished; he did worse by not finishing his marriage proposal. He had an asthma attack right after he said "Carla will you…" so he never officially asked her to marry him, although Carla assumed that's what he meant when he slipped a two carat diamond ring on her finger. Now Tony would pay for the sins of omission of others. Tonight Carla would learn the whole truth about him, no matter how awful it might be.

Chapter 29

"If this is going to be a long story, how about a drink?" she asked.

"I thought you'd never ask. How about a vodka and tonic and make it heavy on the vodka, light on the tonic." Tony took off his jacket and loosened his tie.

Carla watched in silence as he removed a gun from the back of trousers. She regained her voice after he put it on the console table in back of the couch. "Okay, so you're retired from some Washington agency and you're a corporate detective or whatever, but why that?" She pointed to the gun, which had she asked, Tony would have identified it as a .357 Magnum Smith & Wesson with a four-inch barrel. Since she didn't, it remained the unnamed "that."

"Well, most of the time I'm paid to dig up dirt on the heavies who are jockeying to take over my clients' companies or track down hidden assets of disposed dictators. My operation is similar to Kroll Associates, but smaller." He named a giant corporate investigative agency. "Sometimes I get cases that are tricky, for example the one I'm working on now, which is why I've been away so much. I've been tracking a guy who sells pharmaceuticals."

"There's a law against that?" Carla handed Tony his drink and curled up close beside him on the couch.

He took a long sip before he answered, "Sure, if they're stolen from a client's warehouse and are sold on the street."

"Shouldn't you call in the police or the FBI or CIA instead of going after these people yourself?" As Carla casually spoke about the FBI and CIA, visions of the strange people she'd met since her divorce paraded across her brain. There was Kitty with her collection of former husbands and her current psychic husband, her alcoholic neighbor Mrs. Callahan, Bernadette Saxon, the color coordinated Amazon, and now Tony, the gun toting investigator.

"I'll call in the DEA as soon as I've built up a strong enough case. This guy is the comptroller of the company, so he's no dummy and his business associates have a good supply of Uzis, which makes the case more interesting and more dangerous than most. But hey, let's not forget that I can also get hurt keeping company with a nutty redhead who carries a mean looking nail file."

"And do you recall that YOU broke into my apartment like, excuse the expression, a thief."

"But you nearly scared the pants off me," Tony laughed. "I only wanted to surprise you. Who knew you'd turn into that guy in 'Psycho'. Promise never to do that again, Carla. I could have had a heart…" Tony's words trailed off.

"What's wrong? Are you all right?" She put her arms around him.

"It's something I try not to think about."

"You had a heart attack? Is that what's wrong?"

"No, not me. Dolores. That's how she died."

Carla sank back in the deep cushions of the couch. At the most unexpected moment she got the answer to the question that had troubled her for weeks. "Maybe we should talk about Dolores now because, I don't know how to say this…" She hesitated, the sentence left unfinished.

"What is it, Carla?" The lines in Tony's forehead deepened.

"It's Dolores. I'm not sure she's gone and sometimes I think that's why you haven't shown me your house."

"What are you talking about?" Tony's eyebrows shot up to meet the lock of salt and pepper hair that fell across his forehead. "I don't know whether to apologize to you or tear my hair out. You make me crazy, but maybe part of this is my fault. I should have told you about Dolores' death but it is…" He hesitated while he searched for the right word "…embarrassing". He got up from the couch and began to pace around the room.

"How can death be embarrassing? It can be sad or traumatic or painful but not embarrassing."

"It can be, trust me. I'll tell you the whole story if you promise not to interrupt until I'm finished. Deal? Tony took Carla's hand in his. His soulful brown eyes pleaded that she grant his request.

"Deal," she said. "I won't say a word until you're finished."

Tony returned to the couch but turned his face away from her so they couldn't look at each other. "Dolores and I hadn't been getting along for years. Among other things, she didn't like my line of work. She also didn't much like sex. I think the statue of the Virgin Mary that she kept on a shelf over our bed—it glowed in the dark—had something to do with it. It probably inhibited her. The little lady put a damper on me, too. No disrespect," he added hastily.

"Sometimes when I made love to Dolores, I'd look up at the statue's little upraised hand and I'd crumble." An uncomfortable laugh caught in his throat.

Carla fought the impulse to laugh.

"Anyway, one Saturday three years ago—the kids were on their own by then—she decided to make a special dinner. She spent the whole day cooking minestrone, lasagna imbottita with sausages, hard cooked eggs, lots of ricotta, Parmesan and mozzarella cheeses and, of course, meat sauce." Tony's eyes lit with pleasure as he recalled his wife's last supper. "She made it all from scratch, didn't use any of that prepared junk stuff."

"She must have been a terrific cook." Carla smiled weakly. The basic ingredients for her meager repertoire of recipes included all that 'prepared junk stuff'. "Sorry, didn't mean to interrupt," she said, remembering her vow of silence.

"Dolores was terrific in the kitchen. I have to say that for her. We drank two bottles of Chianti during dinner." He looked at his empty glass, went to the bar and mixed a fresh drink before he continued, "By ten o'clock we were pretty well loaded and were hugging and kissing and pulling off our clothes like we did when we first got married. We ran up stairs and jumped into bed. And this time I swore I wasn't going to look at the damn statue. I was just going to…well you know what I was going to do."

Carla's lowered her eyes. She didn't want to hear how Tony made love to his wife, but she couldn't tell him to stop because she had insisted that he tell her the whole story. Carla hoped that if she held her breath she wouldn't hear about Dolores and Tony's love making. Unfortunately, lack of breath does not affect one's sense of hearing. Carla heard every word that Tony said.

"Poor Dolores, she was panting and holding me tight and kissing me like she did when we first got married. I felt her body arch—I thought she was having the biggest orgasm of her life. I said, 'Dolores, are you coming?' I had to ask," he explained. "She hadn't come for such a long time, I wasn't sure what was going on. Well, Dolores didn't say anything.

She panted one more time, then she went still. She was gone. She had a heart attack right in the middle of making love."

"Oh, Tony, that's so sad. I'm sorry," Carla said softly.

"Come on Carla, don't interrupt. This is tough enough without having to back track all the time. She was dead in bed. I had to call 911, but first I dressed her in a nightgown. She was very modest and she'd have been mortified to be taken away naked. You understand, don't you? Just nod, Carla, don't say anything."

Carla nodded solemnly.

"That's why I've never taken you to my house. I should sell it, but I haven't gotten around to it yet. I'm too busy. How can I show you the bed where it happened? Of course, I don't sleep in our bedroom anymore and I put the little statue in a drawer. You know, she always had her hand up saying 'no."' Tony gulped down his drink. He nodded permission for Carla to speak.

"That's the saddest and nicest story I've ever heard." Carla sniffed back a tear. "You shouldn't feel guilty about Dolores. Think how happy she must have been when she left you right in the middle of making love—that's so nice. It's as though that night of ecstasy was her farewell. It happens like that sometimes. I remember this friend of my father's finally managed to take his secretary away for a weekend and just as he was about to..." The strange look on Tony's face warned Carla to hold off telling him the story of Jacob Goldfarb's untimely demise.

"I never thought about Dolores' death quite that way." He softly stroked her hair while he thought about Carla's take on his wife's death. "I was broken up after she died. No one wants to see the mother of his children go like that. It was rough, but now I'm enjoying life and I..." He took Carla into his arms and covered her cheeks, her nose, the curve of her throat with tender kisses that sent sharp quivers all the way down to her toes.

Carla nuzzled her head into his chest. Feather light wings of happiness lifted the heavy stone of doubt from her heart. So what if a religious statue put a whammy on his marriage, so what if he worked for the FBI and possibly the CIA, so what if he carries a gun and maybe plays dirty tricks, so what if she had a gnawing feeling that she forgot to ask him an important question. At least she knew the truth about Dolores.

Chapter 30

Carla purred like a contented cat. Tony had his arms around her. He'd answered her questions. Life is good. No, it isn't! "I'm in mortal danger," she announced without preamble and broke free from his embrace.

"What are you talking about? What have you done?" Tony sat straight up, sputtering like a frizzling firecracker

"Nothing, but I must tell you what's going on here." Confession time or not, Carla decided to tell only what she could prove. She told Tony about the jewels in her kitchen air vent and Caitlin's murder because she had the evidence to make him believe her story—the padded air vent with its secret stash of jewels and the newspaper accounts of Caitlin's death. But she knew it would be useless to tell him about Aldyn's disappearing body without proof that she had come to a horrible end. And she held firm in her resolve not to tell Tony about the mugger.

"So I made up a list of suspects—the men who came to my party. I've smelled most of them without sneezing. But when I find the one who makes me sneeze, then I'll have the cat burglar and maybe the murderer. You believe me, don't you?" She looked at Tony for reassurance.

"Sure I do." His arm reached out to caress her. "I hear stories every day. Some are cover-ups and some are true. It's my job to know which is which, and I know that something screwy is going on in your apartment. The jewels, your proof, you said they're here. Can I see them?" Tony's dark eyes stared hard at Carla.

"Sure, follow me." All the while she pushed him toward the kitchen, Carla prayed the cat burglar hadn't repossessed her evidence

She clutched her screwdriver in her hand as she scampered up her stepstool like a squirrel scurrying up an oak tree. It occurred to her when she unscrewed the air vent grill that since she and the cat burglar opened it so often one of them should switch the screws to Velcro.

"Hold out your hands." She tossed out a necklace. "Catch this." An earring flew out of the air vent. "And here's more." Brooches, bracelets, rings, earrings whizzed through the air like colored flying saucers.

"Holy Mother, there's a fortune here." Tony gawked at the jewels spread out on the counter top. "You better call the cops."

"No! I can't. Can you imagine what will happen when I show them the jewels? They'll say that I'm an accessory or an accomplice and besides, they don't believe that I saw someone push Caitlin. And it will be all over the newspapers and television that the cat burglar's loot has been found in my apartment, then there goes my *laissez faire* relationship with him."

"You're not thinking rationally, Carla. If the person who's hiding his stash in your apartment killed Caitlin you're already in danger. He's a killer. Cat burglars don't kill. This guy is hiding his real motives behind the mask of a cat burglar."

"He doesn't know that I've found his loot. I'll be safe as long as I keep it that way."

"You're wrong. You can't trust a thief. The cops will protect you. If you're afraid to call them, I'll do it for you. I've got friends in the department. It'll be okay." He tried to soothe her.

"No!" The word bounced off the walls before it slammed into Tony's head hard as a racquetball. "I won't talk to the police. It scared me when

I thought you might be the cat burglar, but I'm okay now, really I am." A tiny tear drop clung to Carla's long eyelashes.

"That's not the point. The cat burglar may have plans for you."

"Plans? What kind of plans?" Her eyes opened wide.

"Anything. He could use you as a hostage if the police close in on him while you're in the apartment. It could be dangerous."

Now it's you who is over-reacting. He's in and out of the apartment all the time and he's never bothered me, but..." Carla stopped in mid-sentence. The cat burglar could come into the apartment and do any of the horrible things that Tony insinuated. She grabbed his arm. "I never thought about it like that before and what about my jewelry?"

"Your jewelry is very nice, but it's not the type that would interest the cat burglar." Tony nodded at the gold Florentine hoop earrings that dangled from her ears.

Carla glared at him. "I've got plenty that he would love to get his hands on."

"You do?" She thought she heard a gasp catch in Tony's throat.

"Absolutely," she said. "Larry liked to buy fine jewelry. That's the only thing he enjoyed buying besides cologne that came with free duck umbrellas. He called jewelry 'hockables' for the 'what ifs' in life."

"What the hell are 'what ifs'?"

"Serious problems that you have to be prepared for, like what if you need a lot of cash fast to settle an IRS claim or something like that." Carla thought that a collection of "hockables" would be very useful for Jack Demmer right about now. "Larry said stock and real estate can lose their value, but that rarely happens to jewelry. As I said, he kept it as a hedge against the time when he might need a lot of money fast. That's why there's so much. I've convinced myself that Larry let me keep it all after we split up because he felt genuinely guilty about leaving me. No one knows about it, not even my lawyer. Do you want to see it?"

"It's all here?"

"Sure. I'll get it." Carla retrieved the squat brown pot from the coat closet and plunked it down on the kitchen counter. "I used to keep it up there," she pointed to the shelf above the cabinets, "until I found the jewels in the air vent."

"It's amazing." Tony shook his head. "The cat burglar probably leaned on the little sucker a dozen times when he opened the vent. "That's funny." His eyes crinkled as he laughed at the image of Carla and the cat burglar stashing their jewels side-by-side.

"That's why I moved it to the closet."

"Do you think that's the best place for your jewelry collection?" Tony pointed to the crock pot.

"It's a great hiding place. I planned to give the pot to a thrift shop until I realized that it made a perfect storage place for my jewelry. Ugly little thing isn't it?" She gave the pot a friendly pat. "Larry got it as a give-away from some bank. I think he had his choice of a sun lamp or this pot so…"

"I don't care about the pot's genealogy." Carla detected a hint of irritation in Tony's deep voice.

"Sorry, but I want you to understand why I use it instead of hiding the stuff in a drawer. When I put the pot on the shelf, I didn't know that I'd be sharing my kitchen with a cat burglar. Do you want to see my jewelry collection?"

Tony's jaw dropped when she lifted the pot's heavy lid—rings, bracelets, necklaces, and earring barely steps below the grandeur of the cat burglar's latest collection. "This isn't your regular run of the mill collection of jewelry. I didn't think accountants did so well."

"Some do," she sighed. "Larry knew how to bargain. A lot of his clients were jewelers. They always gave him a good price on a ring or a necklace, especially around tax season when they needed cash to pay Uncle Sam. Sometimes he accepted a ring or bracelet in place of a fee."

"Shrewd guy."

"Guess so. He begged me to wear the jewelry to our country club dances or when we went out with friends, but I refused. I only wore the stuff around the house for fun—never outside." Carla's shoulders lifted then fell back, like she wanted to do a samba, but thought better of it.

"It must cost a bundle to insure the stuff." Tony picked up a flawless emerald ring that blazed like a spark of green fire.

"Of course it does, but none of it is insured now. I can't afford to pay the policy. Before our divorce, Larry figured that we'd never lose all the jewelry, so he only insured the diamond necklace, which is the most expensive piece. He said that if I lost something, he would put in a claim for the necklace, then he'd find a way to sell the necklace and make out double on it. But I outsmarted him. I never lost anything."

"Larry is a real piece of work." Tony's brow creased while he considered the ethics of Carla's former husband.

"I told you he's a jerk, but he's not the problem now. What should I do with my jewelry?" She stuffed it all back into the crock pot.

Tony gave her a devilish wink that under less trying circumstances would have thrilled Carla from the top of her head to the tips of her pedicured toes. "Hate to offer obvious suggestions, but why not sell the jewelry or put it all in a safe deposit box? That would make more sense than leaving it in the apartment for your friend to steal."

"I can't sell my 'hockables'," Carla said indignantly. "And safe deposit boxes aren't safe. Didn't you read the article in the *Post* a couple of months ago about the robbery at a Queens bank? The burglars drilled through from the Laundromat next door, got into the vault and opened all the safe deposit boxes. They took all the jewelry, cash, bonds, everything. So, no thank you."

"Come on, Carla, you're talking about a one in a million shot. But okay, forget banks, forget the police. I know I'm going to regret asking, but what do you want to do with your jewelry?"

"Well, this it only a temporary solution until I figure out something better, but in the meantime…"

"Quit stalling. What's your plan?"

The sound of Tony's foot doing an impatient tap dance on the tile floor forced Carla to cut to the heart of her hastily conceived plan. "All right, this is it, I'll leave the cat burglar's jewelry where it is. I'll pack my stuff in my big green bag—it looks like alligator only it isn't, it's pressed leather and has long straps…"

"Carla, I don't want a damn fashion commentary. Just tell me what you're going to do with your jewelry."

"Well, I thought you'd like to know how I plan to carry the jewelry, but you're obviously not interested. As I started to say, I'll take my stuff to Mimi."

Tony shook his head. "Not a good idea. That means going to the Penn Station. There are too many crowds there and too many chances for a purse snatcher to make off with the jewelry."

"You're right," she conceded. "What I'll do instead is take a cab to Mervin's office. You know Mervin, he's Mimi's husband, the lawyer. That's it. I'll ask Mervin to keep everything in his office safe until we decide how to catch the cat burglar." She flashed a broad self-satisfied smile.

"We? All of a sudden 'we' are going to decide," Tony said quizzically.

"Well, I just assumed that you would want to help me."

"I do." He grinned and added, "How well do you know Mervin? Do you trust him?"

"Oh, for heaven sake, I've known him for twenty years. He isn't going to steal my jewels. He's a very successful attorney. Before he opened his own law firm, he was an associate at one of those mega blue chip places with a name a yard long." To hide her indignation that Tony questioned Mervin's integrity, Carla scooped three measures of coffee into the Braun coffee maker.

"What's the firm's name?"

Tony added the water and turned on the coffee maker.

"I don't remember. Mimi and Mervin always referred it by its initials, like XYZ or LMNOP, something like that. I wouldn't know the name if I heard it now. Is it important?"

"No, just curious. Let's get back to our plan. Make an inventory of your jewelry before you go to Mervin. Tell him that you want to leave the jewelry there until you can rent a safe deposit box, but don't tell him your theory about safe deposit boxes not being safe. That should do until we figure out where to go from there. And promise me that you won't try to find Caitlin's killer."

"I promise."

"Great. And now I don't know how to tell you this..." Tony hesitated.

"Tell me anything but don't tell me that you're leaving town again, because I don't want to hear it." Carla slumped against the refrigerator, her hands clasped over her ears.

"Carla, honest, I feel like a heel leaving you again, but I have to catch the last shuttle back to DC. I've got an important meeting at eight o'clock tomorrow morning. I can't postpone it—too many people are involved." Tony tried to hug her but she pulled free of his embrace.

"Don't look at me that way that."

Carla blinked; her hands still clasped over her ears.

"Hey, your plan is damn good. Honest it is. Everything will be fine. Let Mervin take care of your jewelry, but don't tell him about the cat burglar. The fewer people who know about him, the better." Tony rambled on as though his encouraging words would ease the shock of his leaving. "And let's hope our friend doesn't pull another heist till I get back. I'll call you from my hotel before the meeting. I'm staying at a different place this time," he added. "You'll be okay." He kissed her lightly on her cheek.

"Yes, I'll be fine. I'll take the jewelry to Mervin tomorrow," she said in a stone cold voice.

Why would he walk out on me when I need him so much, she asked herself. Three options raced through her head: *He's keeping a young bimbo in Washington. Hhe doesn't want to get involved in my problem. He's telling the truth.*

Tony smiled. "That's the ticket. You can do it. And you know what?" He cupped her face in his hands to stare into her eyes. "I feel sorry for the cat burglar, because I know you're going to make him wish that he'd never messed with you or your apartment."

Carla pulled free from Tony. When she spoke, her impersonal tone could have been meant for a stranger. "Since you're in such a rush to return to Washington, go right now." She took a scalding hot sip of coffee from her "Have a nice day" mug.

"I guess I should."

Tony walked out of the room. When he returned to the kitchen, he wore his suit jacket and his gun was back in its hiding place. He offered Carla a slip of paper. "Here's my cell phone number in case you need to reach me. Otherwise, I'll call you from the hotel." His lips sought her mouth, but Carla turned her head in time for his kiss to land on her ear lobe.

"See you," she said.

"Take care of yourself," he said.

Carla banged her clenched fist hard on the counter when she heard the door close. The pain of the impact jarred her memory, and she remembered the final question she wanted to ask him: Why didn't his name appear in the Dellridge, Denver & Saugerty guest register?

Chapter 31

"Yes, anytime today will do. No, I won't be long and yes, I'll speak quickly. Please. I really need to see him. One thirty? Terrific. Thank you, thank you very much, Miss Charrington. You're an angel."

Carla had promised herself that she would grovel, whine, wheedle or beg to get an audience with Mervin. As it turned out, she needed to do all of the above to win a few precious minutes of his time. Now she had one more hurdle to face. "Hate to ask another favor, but..."

"Yeah, I know, but you will," Kitty snarled. What with the heartburn she had from her breakfast onion bagel, *agita* from Carla she didn't need. "Are you ever gonna give me a whole day of work? This is a full time job, you know, not a filler-inner between doctors' appointments and lunch dates with your daughter."

For the first time since she began working at Career Steps, Carla encountered her boss' testy side, and her words stung her like a slap across the face. But Kitty was right, she had been spending too much time on her personal problems and not enough time on her job. *The minute I find the cat burglar, I'll work straight through every day without going out to lunch,* she solemnly vowed.

"Honest, Kitty, this is important and I promise not to ask for time off again." Carla crossed her fingers. "The cat burglar left more jewels in my apartment and I'm afraid he'll find my jewels so I want to take them to my lawyer for safekeeping."

A fast glance at Carla's mournful face melted Kitty's gruff exterior right down to her Cool Whip soft heart.

"Sure, sure, go. But first tell me, what kind of jewels do you have?"

"Larry gave them to me. You know, they're 'hockables'."

"I know what you mean. Always like to have some around. But wouldn't it be easier if you put the stuff in a safe deposit box?"

"Won't work. You wouldn't understand." Carla nervously fluffed her hair till it stood out like the fuzz on a dandelion head.

"You're right. I won't. Just go."

"It won't take long. Mervin's office is a couple of blocks away, at Fifty-sixth and Park. I promise I'll be back in less than an hour."

"Mervin? Fifty-sixth and Park? Hey, that's funny." Kitty eyes squinted shut while she considered the coincidence.

"What's funny? Mervin is my lawyer. He's my best friend's husband. You know her, Mimi Berk."

"Yeah, your friend Mimi. You're always talking about her, but honest honey, her last name never registered with me. Is your Mervin Berk around forty-five, forty-eight, kind of tall, maybe six two, sharp dresser and bald as a hard boiled egg?"

"I don't believe it, that's my Mervin. You know him?"

"That's real funny." Kitty slapped her chubby bejeweled hand against her thigh. "He's my Mervin, too. We've got the same lawyer. Mervin is the lawyer I told you about—Julius' lawyer, remember?"

"Sure, the lawyer who helped you, but I never thought to ask his name. Didn't you see him at my party?"

Kitty shot Carla an uncharacteristic sheepish look. "To tell you the truth, kiddo, my feet were killing me that day, so I got myself a plate of shrimp and a glass of Chardonnay and plopped myself down on your bed.

I let Charlie to do the mingling for both of us. You didn't notice when we ducked out early. I think you had a problem with the music. So I guess with me being in the bedroom most of the time and leaving early, I didn't run into Mervin. He'll crack up laughing when he finds out that us two crazy broads work together. Be sure to tell him I said hello. Now get back to work or you won't have any money or jewelry to worry about." Kitty waved her hand to dismiss Carla, then changed her mind. "By the way, how are you getting along with the Amazon app, you know, Bernanette Sexy?"

"You mean Bernadette Saxon? Fine. Terrific. She gave me her five-pound weights after I told that my three-pounders are too light. I plan to exercise in the morning but I haven't gotten around to using them yet." Once again Carla had rambled on, leaving her listener exasperated.

"I don't give two shakes about her weights. All I want to know is when you'll find her a job," Kitty snapped.

"Don't worry about a thing. I'll have her placed before the end of the week."

To demonstrate her determination to make the placement, Carla turned on her computer. But instead of scanning job orders she absent-mindedly typed the words cat burglar, jewelry, air vent, perfume, Tony, why, who, who, who.

"Have a seat, Mrs. Miller." Mabel Charrington, Mervin's ultra private secretary, ushered Carla into Mervin's large corner office. Feisty, short and squat, she reminded Carla of her crock pot. She wore a no nonsense shapeless black suit with a white buttoned-to-the-neck cotton shirt and red patent leather pumps with four-inch heels. Carla suspected that she had a dominatrix outfit complete with black leather pants and a whip hiding in her bedroom closet.

"No, no, not there," Miss Charrington sputtered in her bone chilling voice when Carla headed toward the butter soft black leather coach. "That is for Mr. B's nap.

"But I want to sit…"

"No! Here, is for guests." She pointed to a high back black wooden chair designed for a basketball player with ostrich length legs.

Carla obeyed the command and sat ramrod straight on the edge of the chair, her shoes planted firmly on the thick gray carpet.

"Mr. B will be right in," Miss Charrington barked. Carla assumed she meant Mervin was in his private bathroom. A while back Mimi told her that after Mervin joined a gym he commandeered the small file room for a private bathroom/dressing room so he could change in and out of his workout clothes in private.

"You wouldn't like coffee or tea while you're waiting, would you?"

"Yes, I would."

"No? Good." Miss Charrington scurried out of the room with a gloriously triumphant smile smeared across her face.

Carla's hesitant smile dropped into a frown. She slumped forward and stared at the dove gray suede walls. She never admitted to anyone that she disliked formal one-on-one meetings with Mervin. All the odd bits of arcane information that he tossed around as free as bird seed made her feel inferior. He could rattle off the population of Tibet and explain the difference between an alligator and a crocodile without breaking a sweat. When the door finally clicked open, Carla clutched her green satchel to her chest, re-straightened her back and primly crossed her ankles.

"Carla! What a nice surprise."

Mervin strode into the room. In the split second that his face came close to hers to land a dead fish kiss on her cheek, she detected a faint masculine scent. She didn't sneeze. Not that she believed Mervin could be the elusive cat burglar, but you never know.

"It's been too long." A faint smile flicked across Mervin's tan face before he sat down in the oversized black leather executive chair positioned dead center behind his desk.

Carla wished she could say something astute like "Will the Chinese ever achieve true capitalism?" or "Do you subscribe to the theory that the increase of starlight toward the center of Galaxy M87 suggests the existence of a black hole?" Instead she opted for "Hi."

"How have you been? How are you enjoying your apartment? Robbie and that beautiful Nancy, what are they up to? Mervin asked his questions while he scanned the telephone message slips neatly lined up on his otherwise empty desk.

"It's Rob now, not Robbie."

"Certainly, Rob." Mervin acknowledged Carla's correction and barreled on, "Mimi told me someone tried to assault you. How terrible. I read that you witnessed a horrendous murder and can identify the murderer. How are you holding up?" Mervin fired questions at her fast as machine gun fire.

"No, I didn't see the murderer's face. I only saw my neighbor get pushed into a truck. Otherwise everything is fine."

"Then what is your problem?" An inquiring frown creased his forehead. "Miss Charrington said it is urgent. Frankly that's the only reason I agreed to see you. Excuse me a minute." Mervin pressed his intercom button. "Miss C, did you find those papers?" he snapped.

Miss Charrington's defiant voice replied, "I didn't find them, because I didn't lose them, Mr. B. I told you before, I never saw them."

"Keep looking." Mervin turned his attention back to Carla. "I'm really crunched for time today. I'm just back from a long luncheon meeting with an important client and I have another outside meeting scheduled in an hour." While he spoke his hooded gray eyes remained riveted to the outline of her full breasts revealed under her jersey dress.

"I'm sorry to bother you, Mervin. I have what you may think is a strange request."

"Nothing you do is strange," Mervin said. But, of course, he knew that she did do weird things, like the catered Thanksgiving dinner she and Larry the Louse gave for family and friends every year on the third Thursday in September. Her rationale for the early celebration being that the weather is much nicer in September than it is in late November.

"What do you want?"

Carla leaned forward in her uncomfortable chair to whisper, "I want to borrow your safe."

"My safe? Whatever for?" Mervin's thin lips puckered.

"Because my crock pot won't do any longer. It's not safe. That's funny, not safe." Carla wanted to laugh at her feeble joke but couldn't. Her parched lips were stuck to her teeth. She took a deep breath instead. "So I want to use your safe."

"Did I miss something? I don't understand what my office safe has to do with your crock pot. In fact, as I recall, you don't cook." Mervin drummed his fingers impatiently while he discreetly glanced at his Piaget wrist watch.

"It's my jewelry, Mervin. Larry gave me a lot of jewelry."

"And why didn't I know about it when I drew up the divorce settlement?" he demanded.

"What difference does it make now? The point is that I'm afraid to leave the jewelry in the crock pot any longer because of the cat burglar.

You've heard of him, haven't you?" Carla added when she noticed the quizzical look on his face.

"Yes, of course. Reports about him have been on television and in the newspapers forever. I don't understand why he hasn't been caught. Either he's damn clever or the police are very stupid. I'm inclined to believe the latter."

"You're right, so will you keep my jewels until I either get a safe deposit box or the cat burglar is caught?"

"You still haven't explained what the cat burglar has to do with you."

"Weren't you listening?" Carla's breasts heaved. "I already told you. The jewelry that Larry gave me is in the crock pot that used to be in the kitchen. It's worth more than one hundred thousand dollars, or that's what he told me."

"More than one hundred thousand dollars worth of jewels stored in a silly little pot! Incredible! Well, I…I would assume…you, like any normal person…in a safe deposit box…no, you didn't did you?" Mervin stammered.

"I told you, I don't have a safe deposit box, but I'm going to get one because I can't leave the jewelry in my crock pot any longer. The cat burglar…" Carla took a deep breathe and willed the pounding in her heart to subside. "You see, my apartment is his hiding place."

"Extraordinary." A flame of interest lit Mervin's cold eyes. "I find that extraordinary. Why don't you start at the beginning?"

"It's a long story, Mervin, but, well, he, the cat burglar keeps his loot in my kitchen air vent."

"Does Mimi know about this?"

"Nn-oo." Carla turned her denial into a two syllable word. She chose not to tell Mervin that she'd confided in his wife because she feared she might also stumble into telling him that Mimi also knew about her plan to sniff out the cat burglar—a plan that he would certainly scoff at.

"You didn't tell anyone?"

"Of course, I told Tony, he's my boy, er, my friend," Carla corrected herself. The "boyfriend" tag sounded too juvenile. But what could she call him? Certainly not her "beau," too Victorian. "Lover," not right, that is not yet. "Friend" would do. "Don't you remember? You met him at my party."

"Yes, and he seemed pretty straight forward, but who knows? He could be your cat burglar." Mervin tapped a yellow legal pad with a capped Mont Blanc fountain pen.

"Don't even hint at that about Tony."

"Why not? You must to suspect everyone. You told Tony about the cat burglar and the jewelry, but what do you know about him? Mimi said he is rather mysterious and he disappears at odd times."

"He is not mysterious at all," Carla insisted while icy fingers of doubt clutched at her heart. "I know everything I need to know about him, but what are you implying, Mervin?" It occurred to Carla that despite their long friendship, Mervin was treating her as an ordinary client. While he sat in a comfortable chair behind his desk, she sat in an uncomfortable chair in front of him. She would have preferred that he turn this meeting into a friendly chat and inviteher to join him on the couch where they would be equals.

"I'm implying that you should be careful. Terrible things can happen to naive women who live alone in the city. You are so inexperienced, Carla. Now that you are divorced, I feel responsible for you."

That admission caught her off guard. She didn't think Mervin felt responsible for anyone, not even Mimi or the twins. "Oh, Mervin, I am sorry that I've being so defensive," she apologized, "but the past weeks have been difficult and I'm tired of being warned about Tony. He is not the cat burglar. I'll stake my life on it," she said defiantly.

"You could be right, Carla, but what if you're wrong?" Mervin's words trailed away, leaving the outcome to her vivid imagination. "Think about what I've said, and, as your attorney, I am compelled to advise you to tell the police what is going on."

"No, no police! Not until I catch the cat burglar."

"Don't be ridiculous. You can't catch a thief who has eluded the authorities for years. You must contact the police immediately." Mervin gave an irritated tug on his monogrammed shirt cuff. So much for genuine concern. He had reverted to his usual pompous ass self. "If you don't care about the legal aspects of the situation, think about your safety. Something could happen to you. Carla, I must insist…" Mervin rose from his chair.

"No, Mervin, you can't insist. I won't call the police until I either catch the burglar or identify him, and right now I have nothing to back up my claim."

"You have the cat burglar's jewels. That should be proof enough. Go to the police."

"I can't do that. They'll keep the jewels as evidence and moving them will tip him off that I know what's going on." Carla knew that Mervin had lost patience with her the moment she saw his eyebrows rise nearly as high as his non-existent hairline and his face turn the same pinkish purple as the crocuses that once grew in her mother's garden.

"If you feel uncomfortable doing this favor for me, I'll find another place to hide my jewelry." She picked up her green bag and rose from her chair.

"Don't leave." Mervin's command forced her back into the chair. "Please, Carla, stop." His voice softened to a polite request. "I didn't mean to be sharp, but I can't allow you to run through the streets of New York with all that jewelry. I'll keep them in my safe until you decide to go to the police. And when you do, I'll be right there beside you."

"Oh, Mervin, you do believe me! I can use your safe?" Carla's hand flew to her chest in a gesture of gratitude.

"Of course, you can. I'll give you a receipt for your property." He sat down in his chair and rolled his chair around to face the computer on a shelf behind his desk.

"Don't bother. I have an inventory. Tony insisted that I make one." Carla waved her hand-written description of the rings, bracelets, necklaces and earrings that once snuggled comfortably in her crock pot next to the cat burglar's unique safe.

"Splendid. Most efficient of your friend. Charming." Mervin sneered at the smiling sun face at the top of her note paper. His eyes scanned the inventory before he scribbled his signature at the bottom of the page.

"Now I'll take your jewels." Mervin came around to Carla's side of the desk. "Watch what happens." He pointed above the couch to the huge canvas splashed with a profusion of secondary colors. At the tap of a hidden button, the painting slid back on recessed tracks to reveal a wall safe. Mervin approached the safe, spun the dial four times to the right, once to the left. The door swung open. "Put your bag in there."

"This is so exciting." Carla pushed her bag into the safe to join some thick envelopes, records books and three neat piles of cash. "I feel better already." Her earlier feeling of hostility toward him had faded. "You are the best lawyer in the world. Oh, I almost forgot, you won't believe who knows you. My boss, Kitty Larsen, is one of your clients."

"Kitty Larsen? Larsen? Of course, Julius Silverberg's wife, Kitty. The light of recognition illuminated his face. "Lovely lady. Send her my regards. I understand that she had a break-in not too long ago. She spoke to Miss C about it." Mervin closed the safe.

"Probably the cat burglar. Same M.O. as the other jobs."

"M.O., Carla? Quite the professional, aren't you."

"Well, you know what I mean—the police use those initials all the time. Anyway, there was no forced entry and he knew the combination to her safe like all the other jobs, but this time he got a surprise—no jewelry."

Mervin's laugh came sharp as an ax. "You have a vivid imagination, but take my advice—don't play amateur detective. It could be dangerous, and by the way you can execute your new will tomorrow." He picked up his pen to make a notation in his appointment book.

"Tomorrow isn't good." Carla couldn't ask Kitty for more time off. Besides, executing a new will could wait. She didn't foresee dying in the near future.

"Then pick a convenient time with Miss C. Now, if you'll excuse me." Mervin ushered her out of his office.

Chapter 32

Carla felt light as a feather when she left Mervin's office. She had found a safe haven for her jewels on this unseasonably sunny and hot early autumn day. Nothing could upset her now. There would be time enough tomorrow to think about the two murders.

"Carla? Is that you?" A soft voice barely made itself heard above the Park Avenue hubbub.

"Nellie? Carla's second best friend suddenly appeared beside her. "What are you doing outdoors? It's nearly ninety degrees." Nellie hated the heat and hibernated in her air conditioned house whenever the temperature rose above eighty degrees. Only a major occasion like Carla's apartment warming party could drag her outdoors in the sultry heat.

"I had an important meeting this morning and I had some time to kill before my train so I visited Saks." Nellie waggled two signature Saks Fifth Avenue shopping bags at Carla to underscore her shopping excursion. "I can't believe that I ran into you right here on Park Avenue, of all places. I've been meaning to call you. We have to talk." A nervous laugh caught in Nellie's throat. "Please, can we go somewhere quiet? It's important. I need your help." She tugged on Carla's hand like a frightened child.

"I'd love to, but I can't. I'm due back at the office right now," Carla said, mindful of her solemn promise to Kitty.

But her resolve shattered when she noticed the tension lines at the corners of Nellie's mouth that the nightly application two hundred and twenty-five dollar an ounce wrinkle cream couldn't erase. "Okay, let's go across the street." Carla nodded toward the Waldorf Astoria Hotel.

The prestigious hotel had the best Ladies Room in town—actually, several private mini rooms, each with a marble sink and toilet. The opulent Art Deco lobby provided great opportunities for celebrity watching. A couple of months ago Carla spotted Angelina Jolie when she detoured through the block square hotel to get from Park Avenue to Lexington Avenue. At least, from across the lobby the beautiful lady with outrageously full lips looked like Angelina Jolie.

Carla and Nellie propelled themselves around the lobby like two little schooners under full sail until they found a vacant claret velvet settee tucked away in a secluded corner that they claimed as their own. Nellie's tiny hand plucked at an imagined thread on her dress while she gathered her courage to plead in a fragile voice, "Promise not to repeat to anyone what I tell you, not even Mimi."

"You know I'm a sphinx," Carla whispered to emphasize that she appreciated the need for discretion.

Nellie continued to play with her dress for a couple of seconds before she moaned, "Oh, Carla, I'm miserable. I feel terrible about what's about to happen." She nervously fanned her face with a white lace-edged handkerchief.

"What's wrong, Nellie? What's so terrible?"

Wild thoughts of a fatal illness, bankruptcy or death flashed through Carla's mind until Nellie confessed in one rambling sentence, "I'm leaving Eddie, I'm in love with someone else, and I've never been so happy and so miserable at the same time."

Nellie's admission turned Carla mute. How could she and Mimi have misjudged her so badly? "I don't believe it. Mimi might fall for another man, but not you," Carla stammered after she regained her voice.

"I know it's hard to believe, but at last I've found someone who needs me. It isn't as though I have children to take care of." It did seem ironic to Carla that Nellie, the former kindergarten teacher, and Eddie, the obstetrician, had two large Persian cats instead of children.

"Well, that's true, you don't have children." Carla nodded. "But how about Eddie?"

"Eddie will be fine. He only needs pregnant women. He says that when he delivers a baby he comes as close as a man can ever be to giving birth. He swears that he feels the labor pains and that his body is sore for hours afterward from pushing and contracting. Isn't that weird? It's so metaphysical." Nellie's eyes blinked wide-open like a bisque doll.

"I guess so, but what does 'metaphysical' mean?" Carla didn't hesitate to question Nellie, although she rarely asked Mimi to explain anything. Whenever she did ask her friend for an explanation, Mimi made her feel dopey. But not Nellie. She was as dumb about some things as Carla.

Nellie shrugged. "I don't know. Someone once described having a baby as a 'metaphysical experience' and it sounded good to me. Maybe that's not the right word, but you know what I mean."

Carla nodded. She understood Nellie.

"Anyway," Nellie picked up the thread of her conversation, "Eddie and I haven't made love for years. He's never home. The delivery room is his home. This man, the man I love, makes me feel alive. He's unlocked the real me. I can't control myself when I'm with him. I become a tiger, a sex machine." Nellie blushed. "I would do anything for him; follow him anywhere." Carla noted that when Nellie spoke about her lover, she underwent an amazing metamorphosis. Her voice grew stronger, her body tensed and the light of animal desire glowed within the depths of her doll eyes. "But I can't continue to live a double life. How many trips to spas and visits to relatives can I pretend to take so we can be together?"

"That's where you've been, away with him?" Carla's eyes grew to the size of large Russian amber beads.

"Yes. We've been together for almost two years." Nellie's voice cracked and a tear rolled down her ivory cheek.

"But how can I help you?" Carla didn't know if she wanted to add Nellie's problem to her current list of dilemmas. Tony, the cat burglar and the murders occupied most of her thinking time, leaving only odd moments for considering Rob and Nancy's predicaments, politics and the national debt.

Nellie plucked at the corner of her handkerchief. "You are my only friend who is divorced, so I thought that I could confide in you. I'm so confused. I don't know if I should tell Eddie before or after the party. What do you think?"

"About what, Nellie? What party and what does a party have to do with when you tell Eddie that you don't love him anymore?"

"Don't you know?" Nellie looked confused. "My sister Midge is giving us a twenty-fifth anniversary party at the beginning of next month and I don't know if I should tell Eddie before the party or wait until it's over."

"Under the circumstances, how can you think of going through with the party?"

Nellie twisted one leg around the other like a pretzel, then she leaned closer to Carla to continue her confession. "Well, you see Eddie bought me a gorgeous five-carat diamond ring for our anniversary. I know because I picked it out. We got it wholesale so he can't return it and Midge will lose her deposit if she cancels her contract with 'Affairs by Andre'.

She's having a tent set up on her lawn. She hired 'Ricky and the Rascals' to play '70s and '80s music. Did you get your invitation?" Now enthusiasm for her approaching party erased Nellie's concern about the breakup of her marriage.

"Oh, that invitation. What with moving, getting a job and my own party, I forgot all about it. I'm so sorry." Carla neglected to mention a couple of murders, the cat burglar or the disappearing jewels. "Can I bring Tony?"

"Sure, no problem. You see how hard it will be to cancel the party. But if I go through with it and I don't tell Eddie until afterwards, then he'll feel like a jerk. I don't want to hurt his feelings, and there's another problem," she added sheepishly. "My friend is married, too, so I have to consider his wife. They'll both be at the party. Oh, it's such a terrible fucking mess. What should I do?" Nellie stuffed a wad of chewing gum into her mouth. A loud crack filled the air each time she chomped down on it. Never before during their twenty-year friendship had Nellie used that four-letter word or chewed gum. Carla decided that her mysterious friend had loosened quite a few of her already unhinged screws.

"Well, what does your friend want you to do?" Carla threw the sticky little ball right back into Nellie's court. A voice deep inside Carla warned her not too give her friend too much advice because often when people ask for help all they really want is too hear themselves talk.

"He wants me to go through with the party. He's not ready to make a break from his family. I know he loves me and eventually everything will work out, but I think if I leave Eddie now it will be the push he needs. I hope you don't mind if I don't use his name."

Carla nodded. "That's fine with me. I don't want to know who he is. Maybe your friend has to tie up some loose ends, like get rid of his stuff or say goodbye to his wife. It all takes time. How does he feel about telling his wife?" Carla felt queasy when she caught the similarity between Nellie's affair with her lover and Larry the Louse's affair with Cybil.

"Oh, he's got it all figured out and that's what is taking so long. He's very honorable. He wants to take good care of his wife. He's going to liquidate his assets, set up a trust fund for her and their children then transfer the rest of his money to a bank in the Cayman Islands. Once it's all in place, he'll Fed Ex her a letter that explains us, the financial settlement, everything. It will arrive after we are out of the coun…" Nellie caught herself. "I didn't mean to say that." She slapped her mouth.

"Leave the country? Isn't that kind of drastic? Why don't you just move to another city?"

"No, he said we have to start all over some place new. We'll be like Adam and Eve entering Eden."

"Entering? Nellie, Adam and Eve where in Eden until they got kicked out." Carla shook her head. She wondered how Nellie managed to twist that story all around.

"Whatever. I'll send you a post card, if they have post cards," she said softly.

"Where are you going? I'm dying to know." Carla leaned closer to Nellie to catch every word of her unbelievable story.

"Well, I don't know its name, but it is a tiny island in the Caribbean. There's a man up in Canada who sells islands all over the world and my friend bought one. I think that means that when we move there he'll be the king or president and I'll be the queen or first lady." Nellie added, "Of course, I don't want a title," yet her nervous giggle told Carla that she certainly did want to be the queen or first lady of a tiny pimple in the middle of the Caribbean Sea. "The island is very beautiful and peaceful.

Maybe I'll write poetry or paint again." Nellie's pretty face glowed with happiness.

"Whatever happens, I hope you will be happy, but you should tell Eddie before the party. It would be awful if after everybody sings 'Happy Anniversary to You,' you say 'Screw you Eddie.'"

Nellie considered Carla's logic. "You're right, but how can I tell Eddie if my friend doesn't want me to say anything just yet?"

"Beats me." Carla stole a furtive look at the dozens of tourists, businessmen, shoppers and Ladies Who Lunch who populated the Waldorf lobby. She wondered how many of them were involved in murders or anything as crazy as Nellie's predicament,

"If only the party could be canceled." Nellie chewed and cracked her gum for a full thirty seconds before she inhaled. "Of course, if I came down with a strep throat the day of the party, then it would have to be postponed."

"That's ridiculous. Eddie is a doctor. He'd know you're faking."

"He would not. He's an obstetrician. He doesn't know a thing about the throat. He believes that doctors should stick to their specialties. Trust me, Carla, he will never look down my throat."

"But Nellie, even if you fake a strep throat, that won't solve the other problems. What about the caterer and the band?" Carla rubbed the dull pain at the back of her neck.

"Carla, until I met you and talked out my problems I didn't see a way out but now it's very clear—a strep throat is a health problem, which makes it an Act of God, which is a legitimate reason to cancel a contract. Midge can cancel 'Affairs by Andre' and 'Ricky and the Rascals' and I'll tell Eddie to keep the ring for his next wife. Oh, I love you, Carla, you solved my problem." Nellie clapped her hands with delight and promptly swallowed her gum.

"I'm happy I could help, but there is something you haven't told me."

"What did I leave out?"

"How did the affair start? Did you wake up one morning and say 'This is it, I'm going to have an affair?"

"Don't be silly. I've known him for ages but I never felt an attraction for him until some dumb dinner party we both attended… I can't remember where. Our hands touched as he passed me a bowl of broccoli, and that was it." Nellie enunciated "broccoli" as though it had magical powers.

Dumb dinner party, indeed! Carla's mouth locked in the wide open position as she recalled the memorable scene at her next to the last "Thanksgiving in September" party where Nellie Cooper took the damn bowl of broccoli from Mervin Berk. Now she knew why he looked so happy when Rob saw him on East 56th Street—he and Nellie have a neighborhood love nest.

Nellie ignored Carla's frozen catching flies expression while she nervously twisted the chain on her Chanel bag. "I can't live without him and I can't live with Eddie any longer." She sobbed softly.

The dull pain at the back of Carla's neck accelerated to a full scale paralyzing tension headache. She didn't know what to do about the problem that Nellie just dumped in her lap. Should she tell her best friend Mimi that Mimi's second best friend is having an affair with her husband? Should she tell Eddie, her second best friend's husband, that his wife plans to leave him for Mervin, his best friend? Should she tell Tony what her friends do in their spare time? The answer came to loud and clear—*You can't tell anybody anything. You gave Nellie your word.*

"I feel so much better now that we've had this talk." Nellie blew her delicate upturned nose in her handkerchief. "By the way, I think that man seated in the blue chair is trying to flirt with you." She nodded her head toward a burly young man with slicked back black hair. "He's been watching you since we sat down."

"Who? Where?"

Carla turned to stare at the man Nellie had pointed out with another quick nod of her head in time to see him get up from his chair, walk quickly by them and approach an attractive young woman.

"Sorry, my mistake." Nellie blushed at her error. "Let's have a drink in Peacock Alley. My treat."

"I'd love it, but I have to get back to the office. I'm late. Kitty is going to have a fit and I've got a crashing headache. Must be the heat," Carla said through tightly clenched teeth. She gave Nellie a quick kiss on the cheek and dashed across the lobby.

Chapter 33

"Mervin said 'hi.'"

"That's nice, kiddo. There's a stack of phone messages waiting for you. Better get to them right away." Kitty peered at Carla over the top her rhinestone frame granny glasses, then turned her attention back to the app perched on the edge of the peacock chair nervously reciting her curriculum vitae.

Carla punched in the phone number on the first message slip. "So what you're saying is that the blond corn rows, green eye shadow, green dress with matching shoes are too much of a fashion statement for an economist's office. Well, what did you think of Miss Saxon's skills? That bad? Yes, I'll screen the next app more carefully." Carla tossed the pink piece of paper into the wastebasket.

Finding a job for Bernadette was proving to be more difficult than she had anticipated when she accepted Kitty's challenge. Before every job interview Carla retested Bernadette's computer skills and coached her on how to dress, yet she always showed up at her interview in an outlandish outfit and goofed up on her testing.

"Career Steps, Carla Miller, can I help you?" She picked up the other line.

"That you, honey pot?"

Carla recognized the voice. "Where are you, Dad?"

"At the airport. We gotta' talk."

"You're coming up from West Palm Beach just to talk?"

"No. I'm already here. I'm at that *farmishn,* you know crazy LaGuardia Airport. He may have been a great mayor, but he's got a lousy airport. I'll grab a cab and be at your office in twenty minutes, I should be so lucky."

"What's going on? Why didn't Mother come with you? Is she sick?"

"She's sick, but not in the way you think. Give me your address. We'll talk when I get there."

Carla assumed that her father's unexpected trip to New York was connected with an argument he had with a pinochle crony. He had a volatile temper and often called her after an eruption, secure in the knowledge that she would always agree with him—unless he had argued with her mother, then Carla stayed neutral.

"So how's my New York daughter?"

Sydney Weinstein's booming voice preceded him as he sailed through the doors to Career Steps—The Agency with a Heart. Resplendent in a rainbow of Palm Beach colors, he swooped Carla up from her chair and smothered her with bear hugs and kisses. Out of habit, she sniffed. He smelled of Gray Flannel, a sexy masculine scent that he'd worn for as long as she could remember.

"You look terrific, Dad, and I'm thrilled to see you, but why are you here?" Carla didn't tell her father the truth, for under his leathery tan her father looked tired.

"I want a divorce."

"A what?" An awful pain, as hard as an elephant's kick, shot through Carla's stomach. Murders and cat burglars she could handle, but the break up of her parents' solid marriage, never.

"Is there something wrong with your hearing, honey pot? I just told you—I want to divorce your mother." Though his voice sounded firm, his lifeless eyes betrayed his sadness.

"For heaven's sake Dad, you and mother have been married for more than fifty years. Why do you want a divorce?"

"Because she loves someone else and I don't want to stand in her way."

"You better sit down and tell me the whole story." Carla gently eased her father into one of the molded chairs used by the apps, and took the one beside his so she could hold his hand while they spoke.

"Dad, before you begin, I have to say that Mother would never look at another man."

"But it's true."

"Maybe you should start at the beginning. Do you want coffee, tea, water or soda first?" She nodded toward the mini-refrigerator visible in the coffee break room.

"Nothing. So, I'll tell you. You remember Morty?"

Carla nodded. She met Morty Gruber when she visited her parents after her divorce. He'd been a minor league comedian in the Catskills back in the 50s and 60s. Now he managed the Early Birder restaurant in West Palm Beach where the Weinsteins had five o'clock early bird dinner every night with eight or ten of their friends. Morty wore a bad toupee, dirty running shoes, loud shirts and polyester primary color pants.

"Your mother always liked him, but I never did. He's too loud and phony. He kisses the ladies' hands, like he's a count or something. During the past month your mother has become obsessed with him. It's Morty this and Morty that. She's on the phone with him twelve times a day."

"Women like to talk on the phone."

"So why does she make the calls in our bedroom with the door closed? And she takes Morty for rides in her new PT Cruiser. Me, she doesn't let step in the car. I have to drive our old Cadillac. On Sunday she took a box of Godiva chocolates to the restaurant for Morty. I know what I'm talking about." Sydney stabbed his finger at his chest. "Your mother is in love with Morty Gruber and I want your friend Mervin Berk to handle our divorce."

Carla shook her head incredulously. First Nellie and Mervin's affair, now her parents' ménage à trios. "What made you jump to such a ridiculous conclusion? Did you speak to her about it? Are you sure you don't want something to drink?" Carla took a long sip from a bottle of spring water. Since moving to Manhattan, she had acquired the habit of drinking straight from the bottle. It made her feel like a jock.

"I talk, she denies. The woman laughs at me. Maybe our whole life together has been a sham. Maybe she never loved me. Whatever happened in the past is past. I want to make her happy now. If she wants Morty, she can have him. There are plenty of woman in Florida who will snap me up in a minute. She'll be happy and I'll be happy. That's the way it should be. Let's talk to Mervin." Sydney Weinstein pounded his liver spotted fist on the table that held magazines. Fortunately, there was no one in the office but Carla to hear his outburst. Kitty had gone off to meet a prospective client and the steady stream of apps had stopped momentarily.

All the while her father enumerated the reasons for his desire for a divorce, happy memories of family celebrations flashed before Carla's eyes. Never once did she recall a hostile look pass between her parents. It couldn't be true that Rose Weinstein would betray her wonderful father for a jerk like Morty Gruber.

"Not so fast, Dad, first, Mervin doesn't practice law in Florida so he'd have to refer you to another attorney. Second, let me talk to Mother before you do anything crazy like register with an on-line dating service or hang out in a singles bar."

"Don't make jokes and don't call that woman." Sydney Weinstein made a half-hearted attempt to sound indignant, but it didn't fool Carla. She recognized his magnanimous act as his loving attempt to make her mother happy.

"Did you have lunch? You must be starving. Go to the deli around the corner and get something to eat while I talk to Mother. They make a great lean corned beef sandwich." Carla edged her father toward the door.

"Tell her I'll split everything fifty-fifty…" Sydney Weinstein stopped in the doorway to add, "…but I keep the piano. I need it for my singing."

"Sure, Dad, just go. Leave your suitcase here."

Rose Weinstein picked up the phone on the first ring. "Morty, is that you?" she asked expectantly.

The elephant in Carla's stomach gave her another whack. "Mother, it's Carla."

"Hello, dear, why are you calling?"

"Mo-th-er, do I need a reason to call?"

"No, but you usually do. *Tut.*"

"First tell me why you expected Morty Gruber to call."

"It's a free country. He can call. *Tut.* So why are you calling?"

"Dad is here and he's very upset about you and Morty."

"Your father is in New York? I thought he went to Washington with his Liberation Chorus to sing at an AARP convention. What is he doing in New York?"

"I told you, he's upset about you and Morty Gruber."

"What does Morty have to do with us?"

"Dad thinks you're in love with him."

"That's ridiculous. Morty wears a cheap toupee and white socks. You know I hate white socks. *Tut.*"

"Look, Mother, Dad said that you're spending a lot of time with Morty, that you talk to him on the bedroom phone constantly and that you take him for rides in your new car. He's upset and he came up here to get a divorce."

"*Tut, tut, tut.* That's the craziest thing your father has done all year. Why would he think I'm having an affair with Morty? I wouldn't know what to do with another man."

"Then what are you doing with Morty?" Carla knew she had lost control of the conversation, but that wasn't unusual when she spoke to her mother. Mrs. Weinstein could carry on an hour conversation without answering any direct questions if it didn't suit her.

"What I'm doing with Morty is my business. That's all I care to say."

"If you don't tell me, then I'll keep my promise to Dad and ask Mervin Berk to help him get a divorce. Is that what you want?" Carla stopped short when she realized that she sounded exactly like her mother when she used to scold her as a child. *Oh, my, I have become my mother*, she told herself.

"Stop that Carla. I don't want a divorce. I love your father. And if you must know, Morty is helping me arrange his seventy-fifth surprise birthday party. I hope you're satisfied now that you made me spoil the surprise. *Tut.*"

"That's wonderful." The elephant stopped kicking. Her mother still loved her father. "But if Morty is involved, then the party will be at the Early Birder."

"Of course, where else would it be?"

"Mother, the Early Birder is a cafeteria. You can't have Dad's birthday in a cafeteria."

"Why not?"

"It's tacky."

"We eat there every night with all our friends. Why should we go somewhere else? The food is very nutritious, and Morty is giving me an excellent price. That's why I've been spending so much time with him—to get the price down."

"But, you go to the Early Birder every night."

"That's why it will be a surprise. Your father won't suspect that he's having a party where he eats every night."

"Great. But couldn't you splurge on a restaurant with waitress service?"

"We live on a fixed income, Carla. I can't throw money away on fancy parties."

"Mother, your income maybe fixed, but it's large. You don't have to watch your pennies, especially with all the money you made when Harold's Shoe Heaven went public."

"Don't bring Harold into this, dear." Mrs. Weinstein slid right over Carla's allusion to the stock deal that she'd been excluded from. "Some day you'll understand about needing security in your old age and that no matter how large or small it may be, a fixed income, is a fixed income. *Tut.*"

Carla's stomach ache returned. "You're right, Mother. Whatever you say is right."

"I'm glad you agree. By the way, dear, Jessie Demmer told me that poor Jackie is still in jail. He can't pay his bail, so I think it would be nice if you would visit him. Bring a pastrami sandwich with potato salad and cole slaw or a turkey club with celery tonic. It's nice to be nice and maybe when he reopens his store, he'll give you the free coat."

"I don't think prisoners are allowed to have take-out deli sandwiches," Carla said sweetly then added through tightly clenched teeth, "And I told you before, I don't want the coat."

"You said you'd think about the coat. *Tut.*"

"I forgot. Yes, Mother, I'll think about it and I'll tell Dad to come home, but how do I explain Morty to him?"

"You'll figure out something, dear. You always had a vivid imagination. Be sure to let me know what time his plane lands here. I'll meet him at the airport in my new car. One more thing, tell your father to stop at Bloomingdale's before he comes home and get a couple of short sleeve shirts. Lillie Kravitz, you know, my friend from Scarsdale who calls me every week, said they're having a sale."

"He doesn't need to do that. Bunny bought him shirts for his birthday."

"She's very thoughtful. What are you sending him?"

"More shirts."

"That's nice, dear. But still tell him to buy some, in case he doesn't like what you send. *Tut.*"

Chapter 34

Carla had no trouble convincing her father to return to Florida on the five o'clock plane, especially after she told him that Rose Weinstein would pick him up in her new gold PT Cruiser. She kept a smile on her face all the while she rode down in the elevator with him and helped him into the cab that would take him to the airport. Once the cab disappeared into the heavy stream of Madison Avenue traffic, Carla's face clouded, the same as the once sunny sky had turned ominously dark.

Nellie's tangled life was all she could think about. She blamed Larry and the cat burglar for learning her friend's secret. If she didn't have the jewelry, she wouldn't have been worried that the cat burglar would find it, and then she wouldn't have visited Mervin and wouldn't have run into Nellie, who blabbed about their affair. And what should she do about her new problem—how to keep her cool the next time she spoke to Mimi? The best way to do that, she decided, would be not to call her until the shock of Nellie's revelation wore off enough for her to talk about mundane things without blurting out the sordid details Nellie and Mervin's affair.

Carla flicked on the television set as soon as she returned to the relative security of her apartment. She wasn't interested in listening to the news reports. She just wanted to hear the sound of another voice to keep her from focusing on Tony, Mimi, Nellie, the Cat Burglar, Aldyn and Caitlin.

"Wish Tony..." she said aloud in unison with the ring of the telephone.

"Tony?"

"How'd you know?"

"I recognized your ring." She wanted to stay angry with him, but his warm voice erased the hurt she felt last night. He probably did have an important meeting in Washington.

"I guess there's no use asking you to explain that." He laughed. "How'd it go with Mervin?"

"Good. I gave him the jewelry and told him about the cat burglar." Carla cradled her cordless phone between her shoulder and ear, the better to stride from the kitchen to the living room and curl up in the recliner that Tony favored.

"You told him about the cat burglar?" Tony's voice turned sharp. "Didn't we agree that the fewer people who know about him the better?"

"Yes, we did, but Mervin is different. I've known him for years," she explained.

"Did you also tell him about Caitlin's murder?"

"No. He knew about it."

"Be careful, Car."

"Honest, Mervin is okay. He doesn't smell like the cat burglar, but maybe I shouldn't have told him, especially since he and Nellie are planning to run off to the..."

"Carla," Tony shouted into the phone. "Listen, what's done is done, but from now on don't talk to anyone about the cat burglar."

"Don't worry, I won't." She felt no need to reveal that she told Mimi about her visitor. And since Tony didn't know about Aldyn's alleged murder, she didn't think it necessary to tell him that Mimi, Kitty and

Charlie all had a leg up on him in that respect.

"Remember, Carla, this cat burglar business is between us."

"Huh, what did you say? Between the thunder and the television, I can barely hear you. I'll turn down the TV. Oh, here comes the rain," she shouted into the phone.

"A violent storm dumped several inches of rain on the Capital this afternoon. Severe flooding on Pennsylvania Avenue caused the cancellation of an anti-abortion protest in front of the White House. The storm has moved up the coast to the New York City area and is expected to..." The newscaster's voice droned on in a near inaudible whisper.

"That's better. What did you say?"

"Yeah, it's raining very hard. Be careful until I get back."

"I'm okay, honestly. Don't worry. I'm in for the night. When are you coming back? Will you go with me to Nancy's Renaissance Feast?"

"I don't know." Tony hesitated. "My meeting isn't going too well. It may run into the weekend but if you need me, day or night, just call. I'm at the Willard this time. And get the number right. It's 1202..." He said the numbers very slowly so there would be no mistake.

"I don't like to bother you."

Carla found it difficult to call Tony to ask for help because Larry had discouraged her from calling him in the office with what he called "housewife problems." "Work it out yourself," he said after she told him that Nancy had broken her arm. And when she shrieked into the phone that her car had been sideswiped by a tractor trailer that subsequently tipped over and spilled a full load of tomatoes all over the Long Island Expressway, his response was "Well, you are a lousy driver."

"You never bother me, Carla. Remember, if anything happens, call right away."

"Sure, I'll call. Good night," she purred.

Carla sat on the kitchen stool toying with a couple of microwaved crab cakes while torrents of rain pelted the apartment windows and lightning bolts brightened the sky. She hoped her father's plane would out fly the storm.

Only a fool would be out tonight, she thought when a loud thunder clap rattled the dishes in the cabinet. A second later the doorman announced, "Your brother is here to see you." Carla's stomach tensed. It had to be bad news. She had the door open by the time he came tramping down the hall.

"If the police ask, say you don't know anything," Harold always cut to the important stuff. No words wasted on a friendly greeting like "Hi, sis. How's it going?"

"Hello. How are you, Harold? And what don't I know anything about?"

Rivulets of water ran down his face, dripped off his suit and sloshed out of his shoes. His fiery trademark, a smoldering Hauptmann cigar, had lost the battle to stay lit and hung on his lower lip like a dejected wet mouse. Harold abruptly pushed his way passed Carla and sloshed into the living room, leaving her to debate with herself whether she should ask him to take off his wet clothes or offer him a towel to sit on.

Harold solved her dilemma. "I can't sit down. I'm too keyed up. Fix me a scotch and water. No, make it a straight double."

He tossed aside the dead cigar and spat out the end of a dry one into a Lalique ashtray. Carla counted three spent matches before he got it going. He knocked back the drink she handed him "Thanks," he muttered.

"So, what is this all about?" Carla remained standing rather than sit and be forced to look up to her brother. Consequently, as she spoke she uncomfortably shifted her weight from one stiletto heel to the other. "Is something wrong with Bunny?"

"Forget her. No. It's this—she's dead! Don't you read?"

"Who's dead?" Carla asked.

"Aldyn Sheridan, you fool. She's dead." He waved a newspaper clipping under her nose.

The words jumped out at Carla "*...badly decomposed body found in New Jersey woods near the Meadowlands Sports Complex by members of a Boy Scout troop...identified as New York realtor Aldyn Sheridan, who...*"

Carla wanted to shout, "It's true, I did see her body." Instead she gasped, "That's awful, Harold. Poor Aldyn." She would not tell Harold anything until she knew why he feared that he would be accused of her murder.

"Yeah, terrible. But in the meantime, forget what I said about the broad. Do you understand? The cops will try to pin her murder on me if they find out about the blackmail business. If they ask you about me, keep your mouth zipped and I'll make it worth your while. A couple of hundred shares of Shoe Heaven stock will make a nice little nest egg, don't you think?"

"You don't have to bribe me. All you have to do is tell me the truth. Did you kill her?" Carla felt as though she'd taken three steps backwards. After eliminating her brother as Aldyn's killer, he had just incriminated himself.

"Hell, no." Harold flicked cigar ashes on the carpet. "Aldyn didn't amount to more than a mosquito bite on my rear end. Itch, itch, itch, that's all she did. A real pain, but I knew that eventually she would go away. Aldyn always had bigger fish to fry. Besides, you know that I never go to Jersey."

"When did you see it?" Carla pointed to the clipping.

"I had a late afternoon appointment back here in the city so I drove in from Queens, left the car in a garage and took a cab to...to the place where I had the appointment."

"And then?" Carla knew that whatever fib her brother told her about his appointment, Bunny IV's days were numbered. Harold had a new Bunny warming up in the rabbit hutch. Her sarcastic smile revealed her thoughts.

"Don't sneer at me. I'm over twenty-one and I can do what I want. Anyway after my meeting I stopped for a drink. Someone left a newspaper on the bar and the story about Aldyn getting herself murdered jumped out at me, so I ran over here to talk to you."

"The paper didn't say how she died."

"Come off it, Sis. Since when is it considered a natural death when you get planted in Jersey? What did she do? Strangle herself, dig a pit and cover herself with a load of grass?" Harold smirked at Carla through a cloud of cigar smoke.

Aldyn's awful swollen deep purple face flashed before her eyes. "Why did you say strangled?"

"Because it says so farther down in the article, you dummy." Harold tapped the clipping. "I'm wet and I'm cold, so just say that you'll keep your mouth shut, and I'll be on my way."

Carla debated if she should cover for her brother or tell the police that he had a motive to kill Aldyn. She disliked him nearly as much as she disliked Aldyn, but Harold was family and she had no proof that he was a killer.

"Sure, Harold, I promise. My lips are sealed."

"Thanks. I'm going. Say, did you send Dad a sport shirt?"

"I took care of Dad today."

"Oh yeah, I just remembered." Harold turned the doorknob to leave. "You better send flowers to Uncle Ben. I sent candy. The day he went to some second rate Miami hospital for a hip replacement, he fell and broke his other hip. He's going to be laid up for months."

"Oh, no," Carla gasped. "Poor Uncle Ben. That's terrible. Then he won't be here to help..." She caught herself, but she needn't have worried about her slip. Harold had sloshed out of the apartment without so much as a goodbye.

The news of Uncle Ben's accident turned Carla's insides into a shaky mound of quivering aspic. She collapsed into Tony's chair to consider who would take Uncle Ben's place as her rescuer. At last the simple answer came to her. If Charlie got it all wrong about Uncle Ben being her guardian angel, then the rest of his dire predictions were also be a bunch of baloney. No one had to save her. That happy thought cheered Carla until she recalled the two murders, the disappearing jewels and the cat burglar.

"Hello, Mimi."

Seconds of silence passed before Mimi responded to Carla's news of the discovery of Aldyn's body. "That's good. You're out of danger."

"Why?"

"Because now that Aldyn's body has been found, the murderer has more to worry about than you. He has to lay low. By the way, did you find any new clues in her Filofax?"

"I refuse to look at it. It's buried in a drawer under my winter sweaters, and that's where it's going to stay."

"Carla, I don't like what's going on. Maybe you should stop looking for the killer. He'll get caught eventually."

"Eventually isn't good enough. As long as he's using my apartment, I'm in danger. It's been nice talking to you Mimi." *Click.* This time Carla hung up first. She wanted to ask Mimi what she should do with the new crop of jewels in the air vent, but decided against it. She didn't want to lay such a trivial problem on her friend knowing that very soon she would be hit with a full load.

Carla surfed the local news programs from ten o'clock until eleven thirty. Exactly one newscaster reported the discovery of a woman's body in New Jersey—and Aldyn would have been furious that her name got edited out of the report.

Carla didn't have pleasant dreams that night, nor did the cat burglar.

Chapter 35

Miles away he is lying in bed. The lights are off, his eyes are open, his muscles are tense. He is getting ready to replay his mental video entitled, *Aldyn Sheridan Meets the Cat Burglar*. Damn shame that it can't be shown at a film festival. His homages to Hitchcock, Fellini and Stone are brilliant.

The opening scene

It's Carla's housewarming party. The camera picks him up as he mingles with the other guests. There is a close-up of his face when he spots Aldyn before she sees him. He dodges her a couple of times, but eventually they meet.

She nuzzles up to him. "We have to talk," she whispers.

He pulls away. "Don't bet on it," he growls.

"Remember, sweetheart, I always get my man." She laughs her awful cackle and slithers away.

Zoom in on a day-by-day desk calendar. The day is Monday. Montage of pink telephone message slips. All say "Aldyn Sheridan called. Urgent you return her call."

He doesn't.

Fast forward to Friday afternoon. Shot of a Manhattan high-rise...

He struts out of the fire stairs on the twentieth floor and ambles toward Carla's apartment. He has a thick black moustache glued on his upper lip and a dark wavy wig plopped on his head—he often wears a disguise when he takes on his cat burglar persona. He's come to retrieve his stash of jewels from her kitchen air vent. He must deliver them to his fence on Monday. He is not apprehensive that he might meet anyone in the hall. Most of the residents on that floor are gone all day, except for the old busybody, but he's prepared if she comes snooping around.

A blood curdling voice screeches his name. "What are you doing in that stupid get-up?" Aldyn Sheridan demands.

He doesn't like to watch the next scene.

He should have sweet talked her—he's good at that—but he panics. He wonders if he is getting too old to play the game. Whatever the reason, he grabs her by the throat and squeezes and squeezes until her screech gurgles down into silence. He drags her body into the trash room. He hesitates. Should he toss her down the chute like a piece of garbage? No, someone will find her. She has to disappear for good. He rings for the service elevator.

The simultaneous sounds of footsteps in the hall and the approaching elevator blend together. He steps behind the door seconds before it opens. It's Carla. She leaves. He's about to emerge from his hiding place when she opens the door a second time. He hears her sneeze. He peers through the sliver of an opening between the door and the doorjamb to watch Carla study Aldyn's body,

His heart pounds. His eyes blaze with anger. He stops the tape.

He relives the panic he felt as he watched Carla make her gruesome discovery. He has to do something about her. Too bad, he likes her. She has guts. But she's getting in the way.

He restarts the tape.

The floor indicator shows that the service elevator is still on the twentieth floor. He waits until he hears her footsteps tap, tap, tap down the hall before he drags Aldyn's body aboard the elevator and rides up to the deserted penthouse floor. Caitlin Oliver is away for another week on a fashion shoot. The other apartment on the floor is unoccupied. He takes his time using his tools to unlock her door. The dog comes up to him, sniffs his shoes, and saunters away.

Now comes the part that makes him laugh.

After he puts Aldyn's body in the back of Caitlin's crowded closet he leaves the building through the lobby. He strolls over to Bloomingdale's to buy some underwear. He almost bumps into Carla in the first floor Men's Department. She doesn't recognize him in his disguise. She sneezes. He follows her out of the store.

Fade out. Cut to Saturday afternoon

He is at the wheel of an old station wagon driving leisurely into the city. He does not wear his disguise. He stops at a Salvation Army thrift shop where he buys a pair of old jeans, a washed out shirt, peaked cap and a blanket. He changes clothes at a deserted rest stop.

He drives down East 56th Street and double parks until a car pulls out of a legal parking spot close to the service entrance to Carla's building. He pulls in, tucks the rolled up blanket under his arm and walks around the corner to the twin building on 55th Street. He opens the garden gate with a stolen key, follows the path that Aldyn took and unlocks the door to Carla's building. In less time than it takes to say "Here comes the cat burglar," he's in the service elevator where he calls Carla's apartment from his cell phone. There is no answer. Satisfied that she's not at home, he opens her apartment door with the key he made from the putty impression he took of her lock. He removes the jewels from the air vent, returns to Caitlin Oliver's apartment and wraps Aldyn's body in the blanket.

He smiles. The diversion scene is coming up.

He leaves Aldyn's body in the trash room while he runs down the hall and rings for the passenger elevator. When it arrives, he holds open the door with his foot. The camera zooms in on his finger hitting all the floor buttons plus the emergency button. He runs back to the trash room and boards the service elevator with his package.

The scene shifts to the lobby where the doorman and concierge are scratching their heads while they try to figure out what the hell is wrong with one of the passenger elevators. Their backs are to the TV monitor that covers the service entrance. The camera moves in for a close-up of that monitor. It shows him struggling to carry Aldyn's body out of the building.

Cut to the drive across town scene

This scene lacks the heart stopping chills of *The French Connection* car chase, but it's dicey enough for him.

He makes a right turn on Sutton Place, another onto East 55th Street and heads west toward the Lincoln Tunnel. A patrol car pulls up beside him when he stops for a red light at Park Avenue. His hands tremble on the steering wheel. He thinks the cops are looking at the blanket on the floor of the car. The patrol car stays right behind him until it turns off at Seventh Avenue. His hands are steady when he makes a left onto Ninth Avenue. At West 39th Street, a panhandler bangs his greasy squeegee on the windshield and demands payment for services not rendered. He throws a five dollar bill into the outstretched dirty hand, jumps the light and dives into the safety of the Lincoln Tunnel.

On the Jersey side of the Hudson River, he heads west on Route 3 toward the Meadowlands Sport Complex. One exit past Giant Stadium he turns south toward the dump. He leaves his cargo in a hastily dug grave, makes a U-turn and drives away. He turns off at a secluded dirt road where he changes back into his own clothes. He tosses the Salvation Army gear into a rest stop dumpster.

The final scene

He is sipping a pre-dinner cocktail. A distant bell tolls five.

Fade out

He holds down the "Reverse" button till he reaches the burial scene. He watches it again and again to reassure himself that he didn't leave any clues to his identity.

He knew that Aldyn's body would eventually be discovered, but he counted on it taking so long that the elements and furry animals would make identifying her body impossible. Damn those Boy Scouts!

CHAPTER 36

The heavy rain continued into the next morning. Carla tried not to think about the burglar's loot hidden just eight feet above her head as she sipped her black coffee and flipped through the pages of ads in the *New York Times*. Here it is barely the middle of October and the newspaper is thick with ads for winter clothes and fall mark downs. Right after the Fourth of July the stores replace all the summer clothes with fall clothing; Halloween cards pop up on display racks the day after Labor Day, and by the second week in November, tinsel and holly are everywhere.

Carla wondered why retailers fast forwarded time. Instead of rushing ahead, she wanted to turn back the clock to her last telephone conversation with Aldyn Sheridan. Perhaps if she had stuck to her guns and refused to meet her, Aldyn would still be alive. Carla shook her head as she put her coffee mug in the dishwasher. No, whatever happens is meant to happen.

She had no sleuthing plans for the day and just one item noted on her calendar—drop off a batch of clothes at the cleaner after work. On her way to retrieve the soiled skirts, sweaters and dresses from the bedroom, Carla's eyes fixed on the floor-to-ceiling mirror at the end of the hall. The reflected console and mirror in the foyer always appeared dead center. Today, part of them looked chopped off and too much wall showed.

She cautiously approached the mirror to scan it top to bottom and sideways. *What's going on? Why isn't it flush with the wall? How'd it get tilted out?* Carla wondered. She gingerly pressed on the gilt molding trim. Then faster than she could say *Through the Looking Glass*, the mirror made a half spin to reveal a dark hallway. Now she understood why her new locks couldn't keep out the cat burglar. He had free access to her apartment through this secret door.

Carla walked into the darkness. *Not so fast*, she warned herself. She'd watched enough Discovery Channel adventure programs to know that she needed to secure her escape route. She went back into the apartment to get one of Bernadette Saxon's eight-pound weights to use as a door stop. After she reassured herself that it was heavy enough to keep the door open, she took a hesitant step into the unknown.

"So, you've finally came to visit me, missy."

Carla felt bone crushing pressure on her shoulder.

Evelyn Callahan swayed from side to side. Her arthritic hand clung to Carla for support. Her breathe smelled of gin and tobacco.

Carla reeled back. Could Mrs. Callahan be the cat burglar and murderer? Logic told her "no," yet circumstances suggested "yes."

"Don't stand there in the hall. Come into the living room so we can chat. What time is it? The battery died on my damn watch." Mrs. Callahan's slurred voice intruded on Carla's thoughts.

"It's eight fifteen." Carla peered into the dark as midnight apartment and added "That's eight fifteen in the morning."

"Morning all ready? Well, isn't that a kick in the old whatzis."

Mrs. Callahan switched on a table lamp, and Carla was horrified to see that her living room was filled with more clutter than Charlie Blumenfaux's unforgettable study. Piles of books, newspapers, magazines and correspondence covered every surface. Half a dozen empty Bombay gin bottles stood by the front door. The stench of stale tobacco hung heavy in the air.

"I thought it was night when I dropped in to visit you, but I guess it was morning." Mrs. Callahan didn't appear to be dressed for socializing. She wore a loose floral printed muumuu, ripped stockings rolled below her knees and fuzzy blue scuffs.

"You haven't been in my apartment since my party a couple of weeks ago, Mrs. Callahan."

"Listen, little lady, I came into your damn apartment just a bit ago. Came through the connecting door like I used to do when I visited Wilbur's mamma, the old witch, may she rest in peace. I wanted to ask to borrow a bottle of gin, but you were in the shower. I heard the water running. I would have taken it myself, but I couldn't figure out how to open your damn bar. I guess I left the door open." Mrs. Callahan's lowered her stiff bones into a wing chair covered with cigarette burns.

"Who else knows about this door? Mrs. Callahan, can you hear me?" Carla shouted into her neighbor's ear.

The old woman's eyelids fluttered and threatened to close.

"No need to shout. I'm not deaf, you know." Mrs. Callahan's eyelids snapped wide open to reveal her bloodshot eyes. She picked up a cigarette from the table beside her, lit it and took a deep drag. "Everyone who lived or worked here when Wilbur and I bought the two apartments knew about it, but they're gone or retired now." The old lady fell silent for a moment to remember the ghosts of past friends.

"We bought one apartment for us and one for Wilbur's mamma, the old witch. She wanted the connecting door. But I had the last laugh on her when I insisted that we put a lock on our side. Did that ever make the old witch mad." She cackled at her revenge on her mother-in-law, before she closed her eyes.

The bubble of spittle that collected in the corner of Mrs. Callahan's mouth fascinated Carla. It expanded and contracted in perfect unison with her irregular breathing. Carla might have spent the morning watching the phenomenon if Mrs. Callahan's eyes hadn't snapped open again.

"What the hell are you staring at? Sit there, missy," she commanded.

Carla pushed aside piles of newspapers from a faded couch to clear a space for her to sit down. "Think hard, Mrs. Callahan. Does anyone come into your apartment? Does someone clean for you?" The apartment looked like it hadn't been cleaned in years, but who knows? Carla figured the dirt might be Mrs. Callahan's idea of casual living.

"I told you, nobody visits me. Wilbur is dead, you know. But I talk to my friends on the phone every day, except for the Malcombs'. Lovely people. Do you know them? Wilbur and I used to have dinner with them once a week, regular as clockwork. They came here or we went to their apartment. It's around the corner on Sutton Place. All my friends live on Sutton Place, you know." Mrs. Callahan took another deep drag on her cigarette. "The Malcombs' live at Number Forty-Seven."

Carla's eyes opened wide in surprise at the mention of Kitty's Sutton Place address. "Do you know Kitty Larsen?" she asked.

"Only from your party. Not my type. A bit loud, if you know what I mean."

"She's a lovely person." Carla leaped to her employer's defense, although she knew Mrs. Callahan would never overcome her innate snobbery to accept Kitty as her social equal. "But why don't you talk to the Malcombs' anymore?"

"You're not listening. I didn't say I don't talk to them anymore. I don't talk to them now because they are in Europe for six weeks, but I get post cards from them. My friends send me post cards when they travel." Mrs. Callahan stopped talking long enough to wipe her mouth on the shoulder of her mummu. "My friends are very rich. I show him all their cards. He loves to look at them and he loves to hear about their jewels and apartments."

Carla felt a knot in her stomach at Mrs. Callahan's admission that she had a regular visitor who knew about her friends' travels. "Who is he?"

"He's that nice young man who comes here. Didn't I tell you about him? He pays my bills and deposits the checks that come in every month. Wilbur left me a lot of money, you know. I leave the mail over there and he takes care of everything." Mrs. Callahan pointed a shaky finger at a cluttered Chippendale desk.

"What's his name?"

"I don't remember. Why are you asking so many questions?"

"I'm interested in your story." Carla hoped that Mrs. Callahan wouldn't nod off before she finished pumping her.

Mrs. Callahan swayed from side-to-side in her chair. "Well, if you must know, he's been coming here so long that I've forgotten his name, but he's very nice."

"How do you get in touch with him?"

Carla kept a wary eye on the cigarette that Mrs. Callahan held precariously between her gnarled fingers, and lunged for it just as it threatened to fall on a pile of newspapers. Her hand shook as she stubbed it out in an overflowing crystal ashtray.

"Why should I do that? He's comes here once a month. I think it's once month."

Carla jumped to a key question. "Does he know about the door to my apartment?"

"I think I showed it to him a long time ago after Wilbur died. Mamma had gone to her heavenly rest and no one lived in the apartment. You know what?" She waited for Carla's response.

"What?"

"Right after I showed him the secret door, Vic Reynolds showed up and made me an offer on the place. Poor man. I miss him. He would stop in to say hello whenever he came back from Florida."

"Did you also tell him about the door?"

"Shoot, no. If he took out the mirror, he'd have found the door. When he told me that he would keep the mirror, I figured why tell him. I just locked the door and didn't open it again until last night."

Mrs. Callahan shifted uneasily in her chair. "Hell, that's not right. I went into your apartment a couple of weeks ago. I needed toilet paper in the middle of the day, and I didn't feel like paying three dollars for the supermarket to deliver one lousy roll of toilet paper, so I opened the door with my key. I found a roll in the cabinet under your bathroom sink. I also took a can of tuna fish from the kitchen. I didn't think you'd mind me taking them."

Another mystery solved—Mrs. Callahan appropriated her missing groceries. "Sure Mrs. Callahan, you did the right thing. It's stuffy in here. Do you mind if I put on the air conditioning?" The acrid smell of stale sweat and cigarettes made her feel light-headed.

"Make yourself right at home, missy, but while you're up, bring me that copy of *The National Enquirer*. It's over there." Mrs. Callahan pointed to the desk. "I like to read about trashy people."

Carla obligingly lifted the tabloid off the pile of mail—then froze. The envelope to Mrs. Callahan's party invitation stared up at her. Carla made a bet with herself that when she turned it over, the back flap would be missing. She won!

"Mrs. Callahan, do you know who tore this envelope?"

"Of course, I know. He needed a piece of paper to write something so I told him to take it, but then he didn't write anything. Just threw it inside his damn briefcase and scooted out of here without so much as a goodbye."

"When was he last here?" Carla asked.

"I don't know. He just shows up. He has his own key, you know."

Mrs. Callahan's revelations stunned Carla. If her story was true and not the ramblings of a dipsomaniac, then Mrs. Callahan's friends were the cat burglar's victims. Carla didn't doubt that when the Malcombs' returned from their trip, they would discover that they had been robbed. It was obvious that the cat burglar broke into their apartment at the same time that he paid Kitty a visit.

Carla might know how the cat burglar selected his victims, but she had a long way to go to solve the case. She didn't know the identity of the cat burglar. She didn't know how he learned about Kitty's collection of jewelry. She didn't know if he timed the robberies to his visits to Mrs. Callahan or if it was the other way around. And finally, she didn't know why he left the jewels in her kitchen air vent instead of taking them directly to a fence.

She pressed on with her questions. "Does your visitor call before he visits you?"

"Never mind him. I want some gin. Give me a bottle. He always brings me a couple of bottles. Guess I finished the last one."

"Sorry, Mrs. Callahan, I don't have any gin." Carla kept a well-stocked bar, but was reluctant to contribute to her neighbor's decline into alcoholism, although her mystery visitor obviously didn't share her scruples.

"I didn't think you'd give me any even if you had some. Always thought you looked mean spirited, Missy."

"I am not." Carla bristled at the label Mrs. Callahan hung on her.

"And you know what?" Mrs. Callahan's eyes drooped again.

"I haven't the faintest idea."

"I've been meaning to talk to you about a problem. You may be from the suburbs where people don't give a hoot for their neighbors, but that is not the way we act in a respectable co-op apartment buildings." As Mrs. Callahan's fury mounted, her voice turned steady.

"I'm always considerate." Carla defended herself without knowing the charges.

Mrs. Callahan ignored her response to continue her tirade, "You left an ugly gray rug in the trash room pretty as you please. Did you expect everyone to climb over it, missy? I knew it had to be you, because until you moved in we had a very neat floor. Didn't want to tip one of the maintenance men to take it away, is that it?"

"You saw something gray?" Carla's insides felt as though they had nose-dived twenty feet onto a cement sidewalk.

"Of course, I saw it. I see everything that goes on here. Selfish little thing you are. No wonder your husband divorced you."

"Mrs. Callahan!"

"Too bad you don't like to hear the truth. I tried to find Timmy O'Grady to ask him to get rid of the rug, but as usual he was nowhere to be found. When I went back to check on it, it was gone. Didn't surprise me one bit. Miss Huntzinger in 20M probably took it. She's a damn pack rat. She decorates her apartment with all the junk that gets thrown out."

"I didn't throw out a rug, Mrs. Callahan. If you'll excuse me, I'm late for work."

Carla ran back through the secret door.

Chapter 37

Pins and needles raindrops, sharp as Mrs. Callahan's words, stung Carla when she stepped outside her apartment building. Across the street, a dark haired man half hidden under a canopy watched her juggle her umbrella and a satchel full of dirty clothing. He pushed his way onto the crosstown 57th Street bus with her. He stood close behind her when she stopped to admire a Ming vase displayed in the window of a Madison Avenue antique shop.

"Aldyn's body's been found!" Kitty's bracelets clanked in time to her wild hand waving that meant she wanted Carla to come into her office. "I nearly busted a gut when I read about her in the *Post* last night after Charlie and I got home from the Met. We saw *Aida*. It has lots of loud music and terrific costumes. Have you seen it?"

Without waiting for Carla's response, Kitty barreled along. ""I wanted to call you right away, but figured that you'd already gone to bed. I don't know if it will help, but I showed the story to Charlie and told him that now he has to tell you which of his clients knew Aldyn. The old coot said he'd think about it. But don't worry, I'll keep after him." Kitty gave her lopsided platinum up-do a self-satisfied pat.

"It would be wonderful if Charlie would bend his rules just a little bit, but I may be close to finding her killer on my own," Carla said, her voice full of newfound conviction. Early this morning she doubted that a middle aged, divorced Jewish woman from the suburbs could cut it as a detective. But her encounter with Mrs. Callahan changed all that. Her search was back on track.

"Wanna' let me in on how you plan to catch the killer?"

"I'd rather not say."

Kitty hadn't knocked around the country since she was eighteen years old or run a successful employment agency for more than twenty years not to be able to read between the lines and know that Carla didn't have a plan. And since Carla didn't have a plan, she felt free to offer advice. "I think it's time you ask Tony for help. He's smart. I bet he can pin down the murderer in two snaps."

"We'll see. By the way, Kitty, do you know a couple named Malcomb?"

"Marion and Ned? About my age? Travel a lot?"

"That's them."

"Sure, they live on my floor. Why are you asking about them?"

"No particular reason. Just curious. They're friends of my neighbor. She said they live in your building." Carla decided to end the conversation before she revealed too much. "Well, I better get to my desk and start on my calls. And bye bye, Tootie." Carla knelt down to pet the little Shih Tzu that sat patiently beside Kitty's desk waiting to be acknowledged. He came to the office nearly every day to be fondled and spoiled by Kitty, Carla, the apps and anyone else who visited Career Steps.

Carla's duties included introducing Career Steps' services to the personnel directors at major companies. She tried to make five "cold" calls a day, but today turned out to be one of those slow Fridays when everyone she wanted to speak was away, in a meeting or otherwise unavailable, making this a perfect day to catch up on paperwork and make a couple of personal phone calls, including one to Mimi.

Her friend sounded genuinely delighted to hear from her. "The Hamptons got hit hard by the storm last night. Mervin is on his way out there to see if anything happened to our place, but even if there's no damage, he'll stay the weekend." Mimi didn't sound at all anxious about their beach house.

"Why didn't you go with him?"

"Nothing doing. Mervin has his own nutty way of cleaning up after a storm. I used to help him but we always got into terrible fights, so now I let him do it himself." Her voice sounded gleeful at the prospect of her obsessively neat husband getting down and dirty with a mop and a pail.

Carla didn't believe that Mervin planned to clean up anything. He probably used the storm as an excuse to spend time with Nellie.

"How about coming for the weekend? We can go shopping and have dinner out," Mimi said hopefully.

"I'd love to, but I can't. I'm going to Hyde Park for Nancy's Renaissance Feast weekend" Besides being the birthplace of our thirty-second president, Franklin Delano Roosevelt, that picturesque town just sixty miles north of the city is home to the Culinary Institute of America, the world's premier culinary college.

"Tony promised to come, if he gets back from Washington in time. I'll let you know how Nancy's boar tastes."

"Nancy is cooking a what?" Mimi's voice rose a couple of decibels. By the degree of shock in her voice, Carla knew that she wouldn't welcome a doggie bag filled with leftovers from Nancy's *plat du jour*.

"It's all right. She'll brush its teeth and clean its ears before she cooks it. I'll explain everything when I get back. Goodbye."

Carla looked up from the phone to find Kitty standing beside her desk.

"Couldn't help but overhear you telling Mimi about the pig. Made me think about the pig roasts we had back in Sidewinder, North Dakota. First my daddy killed the…"

"Could we change the subject?"

"Sure, no problem. Matter of fact, I need to ask a favor of you."

"Anything you want." Carla smiled. Kitty did not ask for favors. She made requests that she didn't expect to be refused.

"I got a call from an important human resources director. Her company is looking to hire four assistants and she needs to see a batch of resumes this afternoon, but being that our fax machine is out of order, I said they'd be hand delivered this afternoon."

Carla flinched. The fax machine broke three days ago, yet Kitty continued to give it a periodic whack, flick it on and off and mutter, "Let's wait a little longer before we call the repairman." Carla gave up explaining that the problem did not resemble a cold that would go away without treatment. Now she wished she had been more insistent.

"Sure, Kitty, I'll be glad to go. Where is the office?"

"At Fortieth and Madison. You better leave now because the President arrives in town around five o'clock and Forty-Second Street will be closed until his motorcade passes. While you're in the neighborhood, swing over to Grand Central and pick me up a train schedule for Danbury. One of the gals from the Rockettes is throwing a reunion lunch next weekend up there for a group of us. Being that I don't drive too good, I'm taking the train."

As implausible as it might seem, more than fifty years ago the then svelte Kitty Larsen danced in nightclubs and ultimately made it to the famous chorus line. Sadly, her dancing career crashed to an abrupt end when she tripped over a loose banana on her Carmen Miranda costume and landed on a kettle drum in the orchestra pit. The drummer became the first of Kitty's four husbands.

Kitty's booming voice stopped Carla in the doorway. "Don't you dare give the resumes to anyone but the H.R. Director. The new jobs are real hush hush." She wiggled a finger to emphasize the secrecy of Carla's mission.

Carla felt as irritable as a panther with a toothache when she stormed out of the office of the architectural firm Zeller, Lapen & Harrington. It had been a wasted trip. The Human Resources Director left a half hour earlier to tend to an emergency at home. Although the rain had stopped and the sun had come out, rain puddles dotted the streets, and Carla's satchel full of dirty clothes felt ten pounds heavier than when she left home.

When she reached the corner of Forty-Second Street and Lexington Avenue, she found the area thick with crowds and cops. Vehicular traffic had been stopped, but pedestrians, including Carla, could still scurry across the street. She ducked into Grand Central Station seconds before a cop shouted into a bull horn, "That's it. Street's closed." A dark haired young man attempted to sneak under a barricade. Finding his path blocked by a burly cop, he slipped into a doorway to make a hurried cell phone call.

"The cleaning will be ready on Monday, but it'll take a week to shorten the four skirts. That okay?"

"Fine." Carla tossed her umbrella into her once bulging satchel, now as flat as a New Year's Eve balloon on January the twelfth. "Looks like the rain stopped, Henry."

"Appears that way, but you never can tell. At least we didn't get a hurricane." Henry DiAngelo, the neighborhood cleaner, flashed a quick smile. "I heard on NPR this morning that next week is the ninth anniversary of Hurricane Irene. Yep, it made landfall in the Florida Keys on the fifteenth of October, 1999. A real disaster; caused $800 million of damage. Did you know that hurricanes didn't get names until 1950? Anything wrong, Mrs. Miller?"

The color had drained from Carla's face. Although Irene occurred years ago and never struck New York, she couldn't ignore its ominous portent. Weather disasters of every kind signaled momentous events in her life. The temperature reached 106 degrees the day she was born; her wedding tent collapsed under eighty-mile an hour hurricane winds; Rob came into the world during a state-wide power failure. Not exactly a weather related disaster but close enough. While Larry the Louse sat warm and snug on a stalled train during a blizzard, Carla delivered Nancy unassisted at home. And her marriage ended last year during a Nor'easter.

"I said is anything wrong, Mrs. Miller." The cleaner repeated his question.

"I'm fine, Henry. I just got a sudden chill, as if someone walked on my grave." Carla laughed nervously.

At a video store on First Avenue, she selected *Casablanca* and *Notorious* for her evening's entertainment. Perhaps the romantic films paired with a little pesto pasta and a glass of wine would help her relax.

She arrived home shortly before six o'clock. She stepped into the foyer. Hazy sunlight filtered into the living room through the terrace doors and bathed the room in a warm welcoming glow.

The baby fuzz hairs on the back of her neck stood up at attention.

She sensed a presence near her.

She wanted to run.

But fear turned her legs to lead.

She opened her mouth to scream.

An arm grabbed her from behind.

A strong masculine hand clamped down hard over her mouth.

"Be quiet. Don't struggle. Do you promise not to scream if I take my hand away?"

"Mmph." She shook her head violently up and down.

The hand released its grip.

She turned to look up into her captor's face.

"No, not you!"

Chapter 38

"You're the cat burglar!"

All the doubts that had gnawed inside her for weeks exploded into a torrent of fury. Carla would destroy her attacker. Her hand locked around one of Bernadette Saxon's weights, and she smashed it hard against his head.

"Car…" he gasped as he crumpled to the floor.

Carla knelt beside his body. *How could he have deceived me like this? I trusted him. I hate him. I hope I didn't kill him. It wouldn't be fair if I go to jail for killing a rat like him.*

"Bravo, bravo!" A burst of applause shattered Carla's soliloquy. "You haven't killed Tony Vitale. You only temporarily knocked him. Divine inspiration to rap him on the head with an exercise weight."

"Who's that?" Carla turned toward the sound of another voice.

"It's me." Mervin Berk stood in the doorway.

"Thank goodness. But why are you here? You're supposed to be in the Hamptons."

Carla stood up. Her trembling arms reached to embrace her savior. He strode toward her. The back of her throat began to itch. Her nose tingled. *Beware of a man who is very close to you. He wears two faces. Do not trust him."* Charlie Blumenfaux's warning preceded her trio of sneezes.

"Ohhh, shh-iit," Carla gasped. "I've made a terrible mistake. You're the cat burglar, not Tony!"

"You're mad, Carla. I'm not the cat burglar or any other sort of criminal." Mervin stood directly in front of her, a tense cadaver-like smile stretched across his lips

"You are. You killed Aldyn. You killed Caitlin. You're Mrs. Callahan's visitor. You enter her friends' apartments while they're away. You steal their jewels."

Carla slapped her hand across her mouth to silence her stupid outburst. "I shouldn't have said that should I?"

"No, you shouldn't, but you did. You have a gift saying the wrong thing at the wrong time. I wondered how long it would take you to figure out the obvious." Quick as a cat, Mervin pulled her to her feet, grabbed her wrists in a tight grip, pushed her down onto to the couch, and sat down beside her.

"Wha…wha…what are you going to do?" she stuttered.

Mervin's eyes focused on a point beyond Carla's head. "Be quiet. Let me think, but first, tell how I gave myself away."

"You smell."

"I beg your pardon! I do not."

"You do. It's your cologne."

"Brigand? Love the name. It's so appropriate, don't you agree?"

"It suits you, but it makes me sneeze," Carla said defiantly. "That's how I knew whenever you were in the apartment."

Mervin's lower lip thrust forward into a childish pout. "I thought it so clever to wear a signature scent when I become the cat burglar. Had it blended exclusively for me years ago at a shop on Jermyn Street in…"

"...London." Carla filled in the missing word. "I remember. You went to England a few years ago to attend a law symposium. When you returned you and Mimi came to our house for a pizza dinner and you stood very close to me so I could get a good whiff of it. Then you pinched my bottom, you creep. I hated the smell then and I hate it now."

"Mimi doesn't like it much, either. Says it smells like dog breath. That's why I save it for special occasions," Mervin chortled. "Well, so much for my *dramatis personae*."

"And so much for your scent, but why did you wear it today?"

"I'm coming from a job." He patted his bulging pocket. "I stopped by to deposit my new loot and withdraw what I previously left. You might say that your apartment is my private bank." Mervin chuckled at his wit.

"Any further questions?"

"Only the obvious one—why are you a thief? You're a lawyer. You are supposed to uphold the law and..."

"...defend poor widows, fatherless children and on and on. It's so boring." Mervin stifled a yawn. "I don't know what would have happened to me if a damn clever medium hadn't showed me the way to escape from my dull life."

"Charlie Blumenfaux?"

Mervin cocked his head to one side like a curious crow. "But, of course. He was at your party. He usually mutters drivel about not stepping into a pool of danger or some such nonsense. Yet sometimes he makes perfect sense like the time he told me that if I want to dig myself out of the mire of my ennui, I must make dramatic changes in my life. That excellent piece of advice turned my life around. I immediately indulged myself in new adventures.

"You're crazy," Carla snapped.

"Crazy?" He mimicked her. "Maybe just a touch, but aren't we all? Robbery is exciting. It gets the juices flowing. You can't imagine the thrill I feel when I break into an empty apartment, open a safe filled with gems, scoop them up, then leave sleek as a cat—all the while knowing that I may get caught. It's like making love to your best friend's wife while he sleeps beside her." Mervin smacked his lips with pleasure.

"You did that, too?" Carla's amber eyes grew wide with surprise.

"What do you mean?"

"Nellie and you."

"You know that Nellie and I are…" He hesitated to search his mind for the appropriate word, "…involved."

"Yes, but I won't tell Mimi," Carla added quickly.

"I'm sure you won't." He shot her an icy, ominous look that belied his simple statement.

Carla eyes strayed from Mervin to Tony to the open door. She prayed someone would walk by and discover them. "How did you make the leap from having an affair with Nellie to robbing apartments?"

Mervin loosened his grip on Carla for just a second to twist into a more comfortable position, then quickly tightened his hold on her. "I began my dalliance with darling Nellie strictly for laughs. She reminded me of a little puppy eager to please. But I made the fatal mistake of falling in love with her, thus I had no recourse but to make plans for a fresh start somewhere else. The move requires a lot of money but I still have to provide for Mimi and the twins. I'm an honorable man."

"You became a thief because you're honorable?" Carla scoffed. "If you must have Nellie, why don't you divorce Mimi and split everything with her fifty/fifty. That's the advice you gave Larry and me. It worked for us."

"For you and Larry, yes, but that's not my style. No panache, no *joie de vivre.*" Mervin fluttered his hand. "The solution to my problem came to me one night as I watched a DVD of Hitchcock's marvelous film *To Catch a Thief.* You've seen it, of course?" He raised a pale eyebrow.

"Many times. I know the story from beginning to end. It takes place in Monte Carlo and everyone thinks Cary Grant is a jewel thief, a cat burglar."

Mervin nodded. "Exactly."

"But the cat burglar is actually a woman."

"The sex of the perpetrator is inconsequential. The story only provided me with a starting point. Naturally, I refashioned it to suit my needs. To answer the next question you are sure to ask, I only pretend to come in through the terrace like a true cat burglar—every apartment I rob has one, you know. Actually, I enter through the front door like a gentleman."

"I wondered about that. How do you open the doors and the safes?"

"As easy as unlocking my front door. My father owns a chain of hardware stores in Manhattan, two to be exact—one on the West Side, the other on the Lower East Side. They had a marvelously original name, 'Berk's Hardware & 24-Hour Locksmith'." Mervin laughed a humorless laugh. "Helping out on Saturdays and after school included a course in freshman locksmithing."

"Your father taught you to be a burglar?"

"Partially." Dear old dad's training was good, but a former client, a marvel of a safecracker, turned me into a pro. He also introduced me to a first rate South American fence. You wouldn't believe what a huge market there is for quality pieces south of the border. The only catch is that the jewels must be stored somewhere between his periodic visits to

New York, and, obviously, I dared not take them home."

"Obviously," Carla said sarcastically. "They would be difficult to explain.

"So you understand my predicament. I didn't know what to do until this apartment offered the perfect solution.

"You started leaving your loot here after I bought the apartment?"

"Sorry, Carla, but you're not the original unsuspecting custodian of the fruits of my labors. The former owner, Vic Reynolds, and I go way back. His tragic death was an accident, you know." A spark of sadness flickered in Mervin's gray eyes, then died. "Since he didn't cook, the kitchen made the ideal storage place. And as a bonus, I had free use of the place when he was in Florida."

While Mervin spoke, two things became very clear to Carla. He would never confess his life of crime if he planned to free her and Tony. And, since it didn't seem likely that Timmy O'Grady or the cavalry would come to their rescue, she had to save them. She only had to break free of Mervin, escape from the apartment, find a phone and call the police. No sweat, she could that, she assured herself. Now that she knew what had to be done, she turned her attention back to Mervin.

"I became furious when Mimi told me that you bought the apartment, but then I remembered that you rarely cook. Eureka! My jewels could remain in their snug haven."

"And Mrs. Callahan reported to you on my comings and goings so you could safely come into the apartment."

"Of course. That dipsomaniac bag of bones is a fountain of information. And what Mrs. Callahan didn't know about you, I got from Mimi, who unwittingly repeated her telephone conversations with you that outlined your every move"

"Me and my big mouth," Carla groaned.

"But a delicious one." Mervin laughed. A beam of sunlight struck his tie pin—a gold fox head with tiny diamond eyes

"Oh," Carla gasped. The tie pin was the "earring" that Aldyn found in her apartment.

Mervin's hooded eyes followed her gaze. "Too bad you noticed that the lost has been found. Aldyn found my tie pin the day of your party. Naturally, she recognized it. She never forgets anything, the bitch. Oh, yes, she held my interest for a short time. Her dirty little mind jumped to the wrong, but intriguing, conclusion that you and I were lovers, ergo she tried to add me to her list of blackmail victims."

Now Carla understood the initials "CM" in Aldyn's calendar. They meant "Call Mervin," not "Carla Miller." She wondered how many of the famous people recorded in Aldyn's Filofax also paid her to keep quiet about their indiscretions.

"But why did you kill Aldyn?"

Mervin's lips curled into a wicked smile. "I came to your apartment for my jewels, but I miscalculated the time of your arrival home. I also didn't know that she planned to visit you. A bit of bad timing that brought us face-to-face in the hall, where she stupidly threatened to expose me. As they say in spy movies, under the circumstances I had to terminate her with extreme prejudice—after which I retrieved my tie pin from her purse."

"Then I did see her body in the trash room, didn't I?"

"Correct."

"And when I left you took her body up to Caitlin Oliver's apartment, then you came back for it later and buried it in New Jersey." Carla's belated deductive powers amazed her.

"Right again, Detective Miller." Mervin sounded like a school teacher congratulating a student who had answered a difficult question.

"You left the threatening note in my bedroom."

"But, of course."

"And you were the man in the warm-up suit who pushed Caitlin into the path of the truck."

"And I heard you scream, but, out of friendship, I didn't harm you. It would have been a different story if you had seen my face and been able to identify me"

Carla turned pale at the realization that her failure to unmask the killer had saved her life—until now. "You were walking away from my apartment when you saw Caitlin," she said in a near normal voice.

"You are so smart."

"Her murder wasn't premeditated?"

"Like the others, no."

"But why?" Carla asked.

Mervin smiled. "When I saw the beautiful Caitlin and her jewels at a benefit party, I pretended to be interested in her and asked if I could call her. Imagine my delight when I learned that she lived in the same building as my 'bank.' After she discovered that the cat burglar had paid her a visit, she put two and two together and came up with me. Of course, she didn't know my real name. Be that as it may, I gave her cause to suspect me by admiring her pearls too profusely. Oh, yes, I wore Brigand that night." Mervin flashed a sneer-like smile.

Now Carla understood Caitlin's dying words. She recognized the scent of Brigand on the man who pushed her. There must have been too many conflicting smells at the accident scene to make Carla sneeze.

"I fought hard not to laugh when Aldyn babbled on like a fool at your charming party about Caitlin's jewels. I had already made off with them and had left them here in your apartment." Mervin chuckled at the irony of the situation.

"Carla," Tony feebly called her name as he struggled to get up. But before he could regain his equilibrium, Mervin lunged across the room and slammed the side of his hand at the exact spot where Carla had hit him. Tony fell back to the floor, limp as an unstrung puppet.

In his haste to take Tony out, Mervin released his grip on Carla. Free at last of her captor, she dashed across the room and flung herself across Tony's body. Her hand darted under his jacket for his gun. "Stay away. You stay away from me. If you come any closer, I'll use this." She waved the weapon wildly overhead.

Mervin strode toward her, oblivious to her threat. "Do you realize how ridiculous you are, Carla? Even if you knew how to use a gun, which I doubt, you can't shoot that one. The safety catch is on. Give it to me before you hurt yourself." Mervin wrenched the gun from her. "Now don't interrupt me again." He dragged her back to the couch. "I never did thank Mimi for inviting you to cat sit with her at Cousin Audrey's. That little sleep-over gave me the opportunity to get rid of Aldyn's body. All I had to do…"

More cautious this time, Carla kept her eyes riveted to Mervin's face as she inched to the edge of the couch. She waited until he became so enthralled with his own words that he didn't notice her movements, then she pushed down on her hands to propel herself off the couch.

"Stop!" he shouted.

Carla defied his command. She ran around the dining table to the door. Tony's body blocked her exit. She made a fast turn and sprinted down the hall to the bedroom. She was determined to get to her bedroom phone and dial 911 before he caught her.

Inches from her destination she stumbled forward against the mirror. It flew open. Carla flew down the dark hall to Mrs. Callahan's apartment. With Mervin in fast pursuit, she dashed through the apartment. Mrs. Callahan slept on the couch, a scavenged bottle of gin clutched to her breast. The old woman's apartment door and freedom beckoned. The brass chain was on. Carla's exit was barred. She reversed her course. She bumped into Mervin. She shoved him hard against a chair. She sped through the mirrored door back into her apartment.

"Stop, bitch," Mervin roared.

In a desperate effort to save herself, Carla ran onto the terrace.

"Now I have you." Mervin blocked the way back to the French doors.

Carla spun around. She was trapped. She re-experienced the terror she felt when the mugger grabbed her. Mervin reached her in one easy sprint. The gun slipped from his hand. He lifted her off the ground. He shook her hard like a dust mop. "You've spoiled my plans. I'll kill you." He half-carried, half-dragged her to the edge of the terrace.

"Let me go. Please let me go," Carla cried.

"Over the railing is where I'll let you go. Next I'll finish off your lover and tell the police that he was the cat burglar."

Carla's feet thrashed out like blades on a windmill. They swung wildly at Mervin's knees, his shins, any body part in striking distance.

"Damn you," Mervin bellowed loud as an impaled bull. Again Carla had kicked an attacker in groin. Excruciating pain seared through his body. He doubled over and dropped Carla beside her loving shrine to Bonkers. "I swear I'll kill you," he roared.

She grabbed her dog's leash. With her adrenaline pumping at double speed, she flung it at Mervin. He caught it. Still doubled over, he came toward Carla waving the metal chain overhead. He looked like a hunchback Argentinean gaucho swinging his bola around and around.

"Stay away from me. Stay away."

Carla ran from Mervin. This time she would escape. She didn't. She slipped and landed back in the living room.

Chapter 39

Crackle! Thud!

Carla cowered on the living room floor, those simultaneous sounds echoing in her ear. She wanted to run from Mervin, but she couldn't. Bolts of white hot pain shot up her ankle when she tried to stand.

If this was the end, she would meet her fate with dignity. Carla closed her eyes, bowed her head and extended her arms, imitating the pose she imagined Marie Antoinette assumed just before the guillotine gave her a royal pain in the neck. And there she waited for Mervin to reap his vengeance on her. She waited and waited.

When her arms grew too stiff to hold the position any longer, Carla opened her eyes. The fading sunshine shone on her potted plants, her white wrought iron furniture, her beloved chaise longues—and Mervin Berk lying still as death in the middle of a pool of water. Actually, he lay in the makeshift birdbath created by the clogged drain pipe. Pool or birdbath, it proved to be dangerous for Mervin just as Charlie Blumenfaux had warned.

The sight of Mervin in the water convinced Carla that she should have trusted the Seer to the Stars. His reading was correct; her interpretation was wrong. Mervin was the villain, not Tony, and Uncle Ben was never destined to save her. Her protector was dear, dead Bonkers, her short, white haired West Highland terrier. A vision of the ghost of him standing guard over her in her haunted apartment brought tears to Carla's eyes. She allowed herself just three mournful sniffles before she assessed her situation. She couldn't move. Tony looked as though he'd be out for a week. Mervin might come to at any time and finish them both off. On a scale of "not so bad" to "in deep trouble", she figured herself at "lousy" fast approaching "in deep trouble." She needed a flesh and blood guardian angel.

"Guess I'm too late."

Carla cautiously stretched her head up to look back to the foyer. A man with slicked back dark hair stood beside Tony's fallen body.

"You look familiar. Do I know you?" she asked

"Could be. I've been following you for a while. I'm Jack Marcelle. The Chief told me to take care of you."

"Take care of me? The Chief? Who is the Chief?"

An uneasy smile flickered on Carla's face. There were two unconscious men in the apartment. She knew the identity of the East Side Cat Burglar and she knew the identity of her lover. But which one was the Chief?

"Him." Jack looked back at Mervin, but he knelt down beside Tony.

"You okay, Chief?" he asked.

Tony moaned.

"Who knocked him out?"

"Me."

Jack shot Carla a quizzical look. "Take it easy, Chief. Everything is under control. Better stay down, though. You got one hell of a crack on your head."

I'm okay. I'm getting up." Tony poked at the egg-size lump on the side of his head that confirmed Jack's sound advice. He sat back down.

"Where's Carla? Is she all right?" His eyes scanned the room for her. "Carla, why are you on the floor?"

"Because I can't walk," she said. "I think I sprained my ankle. I tripped when Mervin chased me. He's on the terrace. He's the cat burglar. He tried to kill me." After one feeble attempt to stand up, Carla asked Jack to help her to the couch.

He gallantly picked her up, but instead of obliging her request, he put her gently down on the floor beside Tony. Tony's warm lips brushed her eyes, her cheeks, her open mouth.

"Don't try to sidetrack me." She pulled from his embrace. "It's your fault that all this happened."

"*Me*? You didn't give me a chance to explain before you clobbered me. And why are you here? You're supposed to be away for the weekend."

"I am?"

"Jack? What the hell happened here? Carla could have been killed. You told me that she went away for the weekend. Damn it. Did you sleep through all your training courses?" Tony's voice was weak but his words were sharp.

Jack shifted uneasily from one foot to another. His eyes strayed back to the terrace as he explained, "It's my fault. I caused the screw up, Chief. I followed Mrs. Miller this morning to her office. Then I hung out near the building all day and picked up my surveillance again when she left around four o'clock. I stayed right behind her when she came out of an office building at 40th and Lexington. At Forty-Second Street I got stopped by the president's motorcade. When I saw her go into Grand Central Station, I assumed that since she had a satchel, she planned to take a train. That's when I reported back to you that she would be gone at least over night. I goofed." Jack looked from Tony to Carla for forgiveness, but neither one accepted his lame apology. "If I had seen her return this evening, I would have warned you so we could have gotten her out of the apartment." Jack blushed at his blunder. "But I missed her. I stationed myself at the service door instead of the front entrance."

Carla directed her glare at Tony. "Why did you believe him? Didn't we have plans to go to Nancy's Renaissance Feast on Saturday?"

"I know, but I thought you were so angry with me that you went up there alone for the weekend and, under the circumstances, I was glad that you did."

"But what was Jack doing at the service entrance?"

"Waiting for the cat burglar," Tony said. "You and I were both looking for him, but I was one step ahead of you—I knew it was Mervin Berk."

"You were looking for the cat burglar? Why didn't you tell me? Why have you been lying to me?" Carla felt the foundation of their relationship crumbling away like an old sand castle. She remembered the small lies that Larry the Louse told her when he began his affair with Cybil, and, like Pinocchio's nose, they grew bigger and bigger as he became more involved with her.

"I'm sorry if I fed you information on a need to know basis. It must be my FBI training. Let's call a truce and put everything on the table."

"No!" She shook her head. Carla wanted to remain virtuously angry with Tony for his deceptions, but the ugly red welt on the side of his head forced her to change her mind. "Okay, but this time let's both be honest—you first."

Tony turned to Jack. "Examine Mervin, then call the one seven precinct."

He waited until his assistant went to the terrace before he admitted, "Victor Reynolds was my brother-in-law. Months before his 'accident',

Vic dropped hints that that something strange was going on in his apartment. Unfortunately, I was out of the country when he died and by the time I returned, you were the new owner of the apartment."

"Let me guess," Carla broke in. "You bribed my doorman to point me out and you arranged for us to get stuck in the elevator in my office building."

"How did you know that?"

"I'm smarter than you think. And your trips to Washington were phony. I should have caught on last night when you agreed that it was raining. The storm had already passed over Washington."

"I realized that after we hung up and hoped you didn't catch it."

"Don't interrupt. Your lies are despicable, Tony Vitale." Carla's amber eyes blazed with flames of indignation. "You dated me and pretended to care for me so you could snoop around my apartment."

"Come on Carla, when you put it that way it sounds worse than it is. After our first date, my original reason for meeting you didn't matter anymore. When you told me that you thought the apartment was haunted, I knew that whatever Vic suspected hadn't stopped with his death." Tony searched her emotionless face for a sign that she forgave him for not being one hundred percent truthful. "I was worried enough about your safety to assign Jack to guard you. I also called in a couple of favors at your police precinct to get a look at the crime reports in your neighborhood for the past few years. The cat burglar break-ins stuck out like a beacon. Every robbery took place within three blocks of your apartment."

"Big deal. I figured that out without any help from the police," Carla snapped.

The phone rang.

They froze. Then Carla stretched to reach it. "Hello," she said.

"Carla, this is Kitty."

"Hi." Her voice relaxed. "What's up?"

"You're never going to believe it, but Charlie finally broke down and told me that Mervin Berk is the other person at your party who is a client. He could be the cat burglar. Isn't that a gas?"

"Sure is. Listen, I'm sort of busy now. Could I call you back later?" Carla chuckled and replaced the received.

Tony looked at her quizzically, but Carla chose not to identify her caller. "Since you're so good at detective work, maybe we should become partners," he said softly.

Carla ignored his invitation. He continued, "When I met Mervin at your party, I remembered a story that Vic told me about a young lawyer at Melrose, Cavendish who exhibited the potential to become a criminal. After doing some digging, I discovered that Mervin was at the law firm during the same time frame that the possible criminal worked there. He is also the attorney for your neighbor Mrs. Callahan as well as for the famous safe cracker Buddy Alter. Did you know that his father was a locksmith?"

"I know, and I also know about Mrs. Callahan and the safe cracker."

"Well, you can't know that Mervin recently bought a small Caribbean island."

"Learned that days ago, and I know that he's having an affair with Nellie Cooper."

"I didn't know about Nellie." Carla's discoveries shook Tony's confidence. He continued in a subdued voice, "You brought everything to a head when you showed me the jewels in your air vent and told me that you were out to catch the cat burglar."

"So I'm to blame for what happened here?" Carla sputtered. If she hadn't injured her ankle, she would run far away from this nest of liars and murderers.

"That's not it at all. What I mean is you forced me to smoke him out faster than I originally intended. I encouraged to you to take your jewels to him and counted on you telling him about the cat burglar. I knew he'd come after his loot as soon as he thought you were away and I wanted to be here waiting for him. One of my men assigned to watch Mervin called me on my cell phone as soon as he left his office."

"How nice of you to set me up. You let me go to Mervin's office knowing full well that he's a criminal and possibly a killer. But with all your plans, in the end I, not you, took down the East Side Cat Burglar."

"Yes, you did." Tony reluctantly gave Carla credit for closing the East Side Cat Burglar caper. "But you know what I can't figure out?" Frustration made his voice thick. "Who is Mervin's informant? Who told him when it was safe to go into your apartment?"

Jack returned from the terrace before Carla could enlighten him. "What did you learn?" Tony asked.

"Mr. Berk received a minor electrical shock. I moved him out of the water. He's coming around now. He'll be okay. He must have hit the shorted out light fixture with the metal leash at the same time he stepped into the water. He booby trapped himself."

"Mervin didn't electrocute himself. Bonkers did it," Carla emphatically corrected Jack's theory. "He didn't like Mervin. It was his ankle that Bonkers nipped." Tony nodded, recalling their conversation about her dog. "His metal leash was Mervin's undoing. You understand, don't you?"

Tony shrugged his shoulders indicating that he didn't understand how

Carla's dead dog had a hand, or rather a paw, in subduing Mervin. And if he didn't understand that, then how would he react if she told him about Charlie's all too accurate reading? Carla decided that it would be her secret.

"But where did the water come from?" he asked. "The rain stopped hours ago. Was that another one of Bonkers' good deeds?"

"No. The drain clogs up whenever there is a heavy rainstorm."

Tony roared with laughter at her explanation. "Lucky you didn't fix the light or the drain, otherwise the stage wouldn't have been set for Mervin's near fatal shock."

"I could have killed him? That's terrible," Carla gasped. How quickly she forgot that if it she hadn't landed a well-placed kick, Mervin would have tossed her over the side of the terrace like a sack of potatoes.

"Yes, you could have, but you didn't. Why don't you tell me what else you know about Mervin."

"He's a mass killer."

"Who else did he kill besides Vic Reynolds?" he asked softly.

Carla flashed Tony a cat that swallowed the canary grin. "The model Caitlin Oliver and Aldyn Sheridan."

Her revelation had the desired effect on Tony. His mouth fell open. "Aldyn? You didn't tell me about her."

"I found her body in the trash room, but Mervin took it away before the police arrived. When they couldn't find her, they threatened to arrest me if I made any more false reports, which is why I couldn't tell them about the jewels and the cat burglar. And I didn't tell you about her, because I didn't think you would believe me."

Further explanations ceased when a high pitched voice shrieked, "What the hell is my lawyer doing on the terrace? Don't you know he's out there?" Mrs. Callahan staggered toward Carla but Jack rushed toward her and helped her into a chair.

"He's fine, Mrs. Callahan. He's just taking a nap. If Mervin is your lawyer, why didn't you speak to him at my party?" Carla asked.

"And what about that fellow on the floor, is he taking a nap, too? Why's his head bleeding?"

Mrs. Callahan looked from Tony to Carla for an explanation, then lost interest in her questions and answered Carla. "Mervin? The guy at your party, is that his name? Well, he, Mervin said I shouldn't let on that we know each other. I'm his accomplice, you know."

"You're his what?" Tony asked. He didn't see Carla's smug smile.

"Maybe that's the wrong damn word. I'm his snatch, his snitch, whatever. I tell him things, you know." Mrs. Callahan giggled a high tee hee laugh.

"When you moved in, missy, Mervin told me you were his client, too. Said your ex-husband is trying to kill you, or maybe it's this guy, your new lover. Say, now I know where I saw him before. He used to hang out here when Vic owned this place." She fixed a faded blue eye on Tony for a moment before she shifted her gaze back to Carla. "Whatshisname asked me to let him know when you left the apartment so he could have you followed."

"Shouldn't someone have followed the ex-husband instead of Mrs. Miller?" Jack asked.

"Not any of my damn business." Mrs. Callahan shrugged. "I just reported things to him, you know. Today I called him as soon as I saw you leave with your satchel. I thought you were going away for the weekend. But you didn't, did you, missy?" Mrs. Callahan snapped. Like any good spy, she didn't enjoy being out-maneuvered by her quarry. "You know there is one thing that always bothered me."

"That my ex-husband never showed up?" Carla asked.

"Hell, no. What I couldn't figure out is why any man would want to kill you. You're not pretty enough to drive anyone crazy. Must be wild in bed like me."

"Mrs. Callahan!" Carla gasped, Tony laughed, while Jack blushed at Mrs. Callahan's appraisal of her sex appeal.

"Shoot, where was I? Don't tell me," Mrs. Callahan hissed. "I remember. After Vic moved down to that middle of nowhere place Naples, Florida, Mervin sometimes went into the apartment through the secret door when he thought I was sleeping."

"What secret door?" Tony demanded.

"Didn't I tell you? I discovered it this morning." Carla had only a moment to gloat over her one-upmanship before she was interrupted a second time.

"Mrs. Miller?" Officer Murkowski stood in the doorway. "Looks like you've had some more trouble." Officer Ramirez stood in back of her, his notebook ready to take down Carla's statement.

Epilogue

"Everyone deserves a second chance." Rose Weinstein told Carla when she asked her mother to help her decide whether or not to resume her relationship with Tony. "That's what I did when your father got home. And his party was fab-u-lous, even though you forgot to ask. *Tut.*"

"But he betrayed me, Mother."

"No, he didn't. He tried to protect you. Think about it, dear."

Carla was still considering her mother's advice when the buzzer rang. She hobbled to the door, favoring her sprained ankle. Who's there?" she asked and without waiting for a response she flung open the door. There was Tony holding a dozen long stem white roses tied with a red satin ribbon. "Carla, I…" She placed a finger on his lips. "Hush, I forgive you," she whispered as a country and western song about love and forgiveness played softly on her disc player. Later that night Tony transported her to that magical land of rainbows and stars where the earth moved—several times.

Kitty and Tootie greeted Carla in the Career Steps reception room when she limped back to work one week after the "incident," which is the way she described Mervin's failed attempt to kill her. "Glad to see you, kiddo." Kitty flashed a broad welcoming grin and led her toward her cozy private office. "What a coincidence. A couple of months ago I nailed a killer, now you got yourself one. If we keep this up, we're gonna put the New York Police Department out of business."

"Yes, what a coincidence," Carla tried to sound enthusiastic. Apprehending one murderer was quite enough to last her a lifetime, thank you very much. Her long range and short range plans were to stay out of trouble, put her personal life in order and work hard at her job.

"Everything peaches and cream now that Mervin is in jail and you and Tony are back together?" Kitty's long furry lashes fluttered wildly in anticipation of hearing Carla's report on her newfound happiness.

Carla sadly shook her head. "Things haven't turned out the way I expected. Mimi and Nellie are sticking by Mervin. They blame me for his arrest."

Carla explained how shocked she was by her best friends' responses when she called them after Mervin was arraigned for three counts of murder and grand theft. Mimi told her in an icy voice that Carla had humiliated her and the twins, while Nellie sobbed that she had destroyed her only chance for happiness. Both friends ordered her never to call them again.

"Who said life is fair? They'll come around in time. But we have more important things to tackle." Kitty had no patience with petty problems, when big ones demanded her attention.

"While we were in here yakking about your problems, my problem walked in the office. That wacky Bernashmette is in the reception room. She's camped here for the past couple of days, and she's getting on my nerves. So I'm going to give you a break. If you get her out of my hair today, you go on full commission. You don't have to make the other placement. How's that for a deal?"

Carla smiled for the first time since her friends had abandoned her.

"What a coincidence. You won't believe it, but I thought about Bernadette all the while I was recuperating and I have the perfect a job in mind for her. But first I need to get the rules straight. All I have to do is find her a full time job. It doesn't matter who hires her, or where the job is. Right?"

"Right."

"Okay, you're on." Carla limped to her desk and smiled broadly at Bernadette. Today the app's ensemble included every imaginable shade of orange—from the pumpkin barrettes in her blonde hair to the Blazing Sun nail polish to the tangerine sandals on her feet.

Carla tapped in a telephone number. "Yes, I've found someone for you. "She's smart, she has sensational clothes sense and will accept any job that is connected with the fashion industry."

She paused to listen to the voice on the other end of the line. "Sure, I'll send her right over. She'll be there in three quarters of an hour. Her name is Saxon, Bernadette Saxon."

"Hold on a second, Harold," Carla told her brother.

"What's the problem Bernadette? Why are you waving at me like a crazy person?"

"My name isn't Bernadette anymore," she said in her wispy voice. "My numerologist told me that if I want to find love and good fortune, I must change my name to something with only five letters. So I did."

"Well, what's your new name?"

"Bunny!"

also available from publishamerica

LEFT TO DIE

by Roman Garreis

Josh lives a horrific life. Abused, beaten, and betrayed by those who were to love and protect him, he can no longer bear the misery and hits the streets in search of hope, only to find that life on the street offers no reason for hope at all. His only false refuge is to sink deep into one of his delusions, which takes place in an opulent mansion. Inside, a beautiful paradise awaits with seemingly angelic benefactors who supply his physical needs and desires and nurture his intellectual talents—only to find they have turned him into an unwitting instrument of evil and a powerful weapon that misleads others along the path of death and insanity. Captured in this delusion, his mind keeps him between what he was running from and what he ran to, and there amongst the abusers and users, he is left to die as the strain of his inevitable fate from the drugs, prostitution, abuse and decay takes its toll.

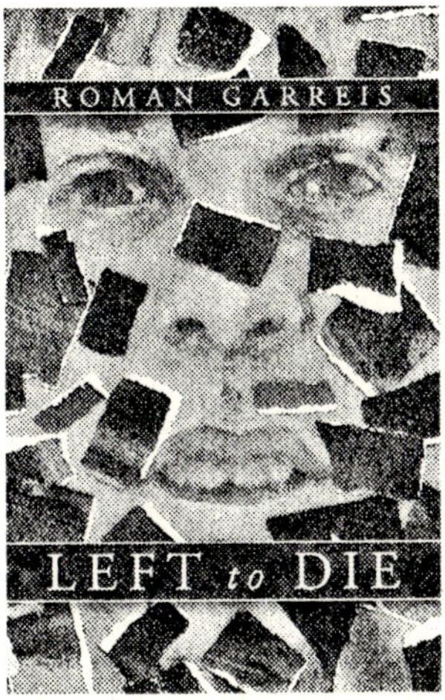

Paperback, 142 pages
5.5" x 8.5"
ISBN 1-4241-9301-X

About the author:

Roman Garreis was born in Philadelphia, Pennsylvania, in 1957 and grew up on the South Side. His parents were divorced when he was five years old. His mother had a habit of moving to different neighborhoods which, along with the divorce and the coldness of city street life, left him detached and beaten down. At eighteen years old, Roman left his troubled life behind, and he now spends his time helping others to do the same.

available to all bookstores nationwide.
www.publishamerica.com

Also available from PublishAmerica

THE UNALTERED CANVAS

by Vanessa Wheeler

In the yard of a man was a tragic murder. One that Jolie Summers had filmed like a true reporter. With her eyes firmly set on the throne of God she wiped her tears and began to embark on a life as an artist. But eyes spied her mad artist skills and took her life and turned it upside down. Could she gain her freedom? Or would she believe in their lives?

Paperback, 108 pages
5.5" x 8.5"
ISBN 1-60672-395-2

About the author:

The author, Vanessa Wheeler, was born in Fresno, California. She is currently working on her second novel. She loves her dogs, Christianity, art, politics, science, and psychology. She is a born-again Christian and hopes her characters reflect Christian imperfections to honor their bravery as believers.

Also available from PublishAmerica

SWIFT EAGLE'S ODYSSEY WITH THE BUFFALO

by Ken Eichler

Swift Eagle's Odyssey with the Buffalo is a sensitive story about a young Indian boy and a huge buffalo that saved the boy from a near drowning in a storm-swollen river and from some hungry wolves. The boy's parents sought help from the Great Spirit to save their boy from harm. Was it by chance that the buffalo was at the right place at the right time, or did the Great Spirit intervene to help the boy? While with the buffalo, Swift Eagle takes a sleep-induced magical journey to the domain of the Great Spirit. The buffalo in the story is from a herd of thousands that were near Swift Eagle's Cheyenne village. The boy's love for the buffalo is heartwarming as is his affection for his playmate Little Flower. You will feel you are at Swift Eagle's homecoming celebration.

Paperback, 59 pages
6″ x 9″
ISBN 1-60474-199-6

About the author:
After graduating from high school, I enlisted in the US Navy and served four years (1948-1952). After my discharge from the Navy, I enrolled in the University of Southern California and graduated from the School of Engineering in 1957. I was employed by North American Aviation, Inc. and later by McDonnell Douglas Company (MDC). My principal assignments were in contract administration. I retired from MDC in 1995.

Available to all bookstores nationwide.
www.publishamerica.com

Also available from PublishAmerica

COMING AROUND

by Ginger Williams

Iris Corrigan and William Pendleton embark on more than just a one-week Caribbean cruise in this exotic, erotic, sometimes funny, and almost disastrous, second-time-around, modern-day romance. Both having lost loved ones, under completely different circumstances, however, find themselves alone onboard the cruise ship *Whimsical*, but not for long. William, determined to get more than a tan on this trip, has a lot to offer Iris, which she soon finds out. And Iris has the one thing William has always desired, but never had—a family. News from back home in Tennessee, events onboard the *Whimsical*, three tropical ports of call, hot days and even hotter nights, all add up to one life-altering week. From heartbreak and devastation to love and passion beyond their wildest hopes and dreams, Iris and William are coming around...in more ways than one.

Paperback, 242 pages
6″ x 9″
ISBN 1-60441-821-4

About the author:
Ginger Williams lives in Franklin, Tennessee, with her husband Danny. Their three children and six perfect grandchildren live nearby. Whether it's riding their motorcycle on back country roads, dancing to the songs of their favorite rock 'n' roll band, or exploring their favorite Caribbean islands, they're always in motion.

Available to all bookstores nationwide.
www.publishamerica.com